CHRISTOPHER STANTON

Kings of the Earth

First edition

This book was professionally typeset on Reedsy.
Find out more at reedsy.com

For my family.

"That is what it is—a royal sport, for the natural kings of earth."

-Jack London

Contents

Acknowledgement

Thanks to Sara Kelly, Jon Paquette, Robin Samuels, Adam Meyer, Xaque Gruber and Tori Hartman for their invaluable editing help. I'm also grateful to James Alexander for his rad cover design and incredible support, and to Kirk Kjeldsen for the canasta and Kick. And thanks to Michael Grais, Mark Victor and John Carpenter for their inspiration during my teenage years of renting horror films from the video store on the corner.

1

Chapter One—JENNY

The morning sunlight cut a bright path across the floor to the bed where Jenny Bloomquist slept. It fell across her face and she opened her eyes gently, not yet willing to let go of her dream.

She remembered gliding through a celestial twilight toward a glimmering door of bright amber light. She remembered the sound—distant, but yet so close—of an orchestra tuning up, gathering itself before it plunged into a beautiful sonata. But most of all, Jenny remembered a tiny hand clutched in her own as they moved toward the door, down a path that was clear and true. A heartbeat; a chest rising and falling with each breath. A new soul next to her, with her.

Part of her.

Lance stood at the bedroom window, watching the woods that separated their house from the road and Lake Michigan beyond. He was already dressed.

It was the third weekend in November.

"Hi there," Jenny said.

Lance turned at the sound of her voice. "Good morning," he replied. "Didn't mean to wake you."

His body was lanky and muscled. His rumpled blond hair was tinged with gray. And he wore his indestructible wool shirt, cobalt blue and patched at the elbows. Jenny still couldn't believe that such an amazing man was actually her husband.

She pulled back the covers, then sat on the edge of the bed and yawned. "I had a beautiful dream," she said. "I was—"

Jenny paused carefully, not sure how to explain what she'd experienced. Although she had never understood the psychology of dreams, there was no denying the feeling she had just then.

"I think amazing things are in store for us," she finished.

Lance smiled fleetingly. He glanced out the window again, something clearly weighing on his mind.

"Want to go for a walk later?" Jenny asked. "Looks like it's not too gloomy out there."

"Well, the fog's gone," he said. "But this sun won't last long. The clouds are coming in from the north."

She heard the catch in his voice and her good mood began to dissipate. "What is it?"

"Nothing," he replied. "I promise. Just thinking about what an amazing time I had."

Lance had surprised the heck out of her with a romantic two-day trip down to Chicago and they'd gotten back into town the night before. Although she'd slept soundly during most of the drive home to Great Water, there was one thing Jenny couldn't forget: the enormous, deep red moon that sat low in the sky as they traveled through town and down the Cove Road that hugged the shoreline leading to their house. The wisps of fog that swirled around it made it look like some menacing alien planet on the cover of a 1970s sci-fi paperback.

"I'd love to stay with you," her husband said. "But I gotta get it in gear."

"Eric's waiting," Jenny finished. "Sorry, I almost forgot."

Every Saturday morning, Lance met a teenager from town to go surfing at Spivey Point. (Yes, Jenny told incredulous people all the time: their part of the Upper Peninsula offered some of the best surfing in all of the Great Lakes.) Lance was a mentor of sorts to Eric and a childhood friend of his father, who had left Great Water long ago. During their sessions, Eric did the surfing and Lance did the coaching from the rocky shore, because of his bad knee.

"I've got my lucky shirt," Lance said, noticing her concerned glance. "This thing is like wearing three sweaters at once. It's the kid who'll need a wetsuit."

He turned and scanned the woods again; it seemed like he was reluctant to leave.

Jenny leaned forward. "Tell me," she said.

"Nothing's wrong, Jennifer," he said. "I love you. That's all."

"Well then," she replied, "I love you more." And as Lance smiled, standing there at the window, the golden light of dawn outlined his body.

Then he was gone.

* * *

Jenny got out of bed and pulled back the curtains all the way, flooding the room with sunlight. Outside, a dense pine forest surrounded their property and a gravel driveway led through the trees to the road. A shallow brook snaked its way past the pergola and the rock garden and into the woods, eventually meeting up with Brisco Creek and emptying out in the lake.

Lance had planned it all—designed the house, the yard, everything. All for their amazing life together. Jenny still couldn't believe how drastically her life had changed in such a short amount of time.

She was twenty-five, a hometown girl who'd spent high school working nights and weekends at the Great Water Hotel—first as a maid, then, after she graduated, taking reservations at the front desk. She'd paid rent to her parents and slept in her childhood bedroom, with its peeling antique wallpaper and dead crickets cocooned in spider webs in the corners of the ceiling. She cooked countless dinners of macaroni and cheese for her father on the nights he worked late at the post office, her mother out at bridge club or drunk at the Bingo.

3

Then, one night at the hotel a little more than three years ago, everything changed. Lance Bloomquist—hometown boy, renowned architect with offices in Chicago and Toronto—checked in for an extended stay. He'd decided to move back to town permanently and build his dream house close to the lake.

Lance smelled of pine needles and spearmint. He was exactly twice her age. But it only took one look at his blue eyes, clear and sparkling, before her heart began to swell.

I love you. That's all.

Jenny turned from the window and went into the master bathroom to get cleaned up before she started her day. There was an enormous scalloped bathtub on one side of the room, a walk-in shower on the other. It seemed like it belonged in a photo spread in an upscale magazine she'd find in a hedge fund manager's waiting room.

Jenny had never even been off the U.P. before she met Lance, let alone applied for a passport or bought proper luggage. During their brief courtship, they shared everything from dinner conversations when he taught her about pitched roofs and uniformity of space and line, to impromptu flights to Vancouver and Stockholm for ski weekends and museum openings. Lance even assured her that it was perfectly okay to order the most expensive item on the menu, if for no other reason than because she deserved it. That was a concept that Jenny found it hard to get her head around, after a lifetime of Hamburger Helper and tuna noodle casserole.

Each moment together with Lance was thrilling and new, and he always took time to hear what Jenny had to say. He made sure she was an equal participant in every adventure they had together, from symphony concerts to white water rafting trips, even though Jenny constantly wondered if he would leave her one day because she was so unvarnished, like a castoff chair at a roadside flea market. But when he proposed—on the deck of a ferry boat on Puget Sound after the International Architecture Conference in Seattle, the stars scattered in the sky above them like glistening jacks—Jenny put all those doubts behind her. Even though they had only dated for two months and four days, she had never been surer of anything in her life.

The town whispered about their May-December romance; Jenny was sure of it. A former maid at the hotel had even sent her a lengthy email congratulating her on doing what every woman from the wrong side of the tracks should: marry a man with money. Jenny had been on courteous terms with Bernice Mitchell as a coworker, but she'd never considered her a friend, so the email felt completely unsolicited and out of the blue. Bernice even proposed throwing Jenny a wedding shower but Jenny, mired in embarrassment, never replied. The other woman loved to gossip and Jenny was positive that she had shared her opinion about her marriage everywhere she could, from the checkout line at the Price Slasher to the back pews of the Great Water Methodist Church.

Jenny eventually decided it was pointless to plug holes in a dyke that was destined to burst, so she never mounted a campaign in her own defense. She also figured that was one of the main reasons why she didn't have any close friends: people she'd tried to get to know socially since her wedding were either blatantly jealous or didn't believe that what she and Lance had was truly real.

Staring at her reflection in the bathroom mirror, she noticed her flat, shoulder-length hair, pale, sunken cheeks and bony shoulders that nearly poked through her pink nightgown. It had always been difficult for her to look into mirrors. All she could ever hear was her mother's voice, gravelly from years of chain-smoking cigarettes and complaining. Her constant barrage of criticism had grabbed hold of Jenny's self-esteem like the jaws of a fierce pit bull ever since she was a little girl.

But as she looked closer, Jenny saw something in her eyes. There was a spark there, bright and clear. It was then that she remembered her dream. She felt the tiny hand in hers, the golden light surrounding them. Jenny realized then that it wasn't just a dream. Something extraordinary had happened.

2

Chapter Two—MARTIN

Martin Van Lottom had been on duty at the Harborfront Stroll since midnight. The popular tourist spot was an outdoor shopping plaza that lay on a promontory on the lake. Now it was 7:36 in the morning and there was a potential incident occurring outside of Kristy's Kitchen.

"Come here and take a look at this," Arnold Jefferson said, staring at the flickering security camera monitors in their office.

Martin put down his magazine and glanced over. "What is it?" he asked. Arnold was his supervisor. He was originally from Texas and liked to gamble. The man had been working security since Jimmy Carter was president.

"Number One, who's that woman? And Number Two, what in tarnation is she doing?" Arnold asked. He had patchy white hair and jowls that wobbled when he spoke. The buttons on his gray uniform were in constant danger of popping.

Martin just wanted to go home and sleep, maybe stop for a pasty and orange juice at the diner on the way home. But he took his job as a security officer seriously, so he peered carefully at the bank of monitors. Camera #6 showed a woman in her mid-40s. She was beating on the windows of the cookware store that was located about halfway down the Stroll. The woman struck the windows again and again with her fists.

"Is she high on something?" Arnold asked. "I'll bet you anything she is."

Martin sighed. "Geez-o-pete," he said. "I'll be right back."

The Harborfront didn't officially open until nine on Saturdays, and the elderly couples who strolled it for morning exercise didn't usually arrive until eight. So Martin wasn't entirely sure what the woman was doing there so early.

He put on his cap and walked past Larry's Lobsters and Go Go Yogurt. He passed an overturned trash can, then a dead gull right in the middle of the cobblestone walkway. His pulse cranked up a few notches as he noticed the frightened expression frozen in the bird's glazed eyes. Martin knew right away that something was dreadfully wrong.

Rounding a corner, he spotted the woman right away. She was barefoot, dressed in sweatpants and a Maple Leafs t-shirt, and she stood right outside the cookware store, swaying back and forth like a broken pendulum.

"Excuse me," Martin said carefully. "Hi there."

She glanced up slowly, her matted blond hair covering her eyes. Martin recognized her then; she was the receptionist at his doctor's office. It was a huge shock to see this woman, always so perfectly made up and perky, looking completely traumatized.

"Hi," Martin said again. "It's Pearl, right? What are you doing here so early?"

"Did you see them?" Pearl whispered, shivering violently. Her cloudy blue eyes darted back and forth.

"See who?" Martin answered. "Why don't you come on along with me? We have some coffee in our office. That'll get you warmed up. How does that sound?"

Pearl shook her head. "They crossed over," she intoned slowly, as if she couldn't believe the words she was saying. "I saw them," she said. "I saw them all."

"You're not talking sense," Martin replied. "Who did you see?"

"They're all dead," she moaned. "They told me to follow them. They said the moon will show me the way."

Pearl dashed toward the store and threw herself against the window as hard as she could. The pane cracked. A display of Christmas plates on the other side of the glass teetered but didn't break. She stumbled back a few steps, completely dazed.

It took Martin a full ten seconds to process what he'd just seen.

"Stop," he yelled. "Please. You're gonna hurt yourself!"

Pearl punched the cracked window of Kristy's Kitchen with her bare hand. A section of glass about the size of a grapefruit caved in.

"What's the matter with you?" Martin cried.

Pearl raked the jagged glass edge of the hole across her wrist. Blood spurted across her t-shirt.

"I want to go," she pleaded. "I waited so long for this."

Martin dashed over to her. He grabbed her arm and tried to ease it out of the hole in the window. But the woman moaned again and fought him, hard. She sliced another deep gash along the base of her thumb.

"What're you doing?" Martin pleaded. "Come on, just come with me. You're bleeding, come on!"

He pulled her away from the glass and they collapsed in a heap on the cold cobblestones. Blood streamed steadily from her hand and wrist as Martin's mind raced.

Stop the bleeding then radio Arnold then call 911 then—

Pearl's eyes were bloodshot and filled with tears. Martin felt a surge of electricity pulse through his body, like her touch was a conduit for something desperate and powerful.

"I'll be happy on the other side," she whispered. "And you will, too."

* * *

The EMTs loaded Pearl into the ambulance. She was conscious but could only stare vacantly as the doors closed behind her.

"What do you think was wrong with her?" Martin asked Arnold. In more than two years working security, he'd never had to deal with anything so shocking. Shoplifting and littering were about the extent of it.

"I dunno. Meth, maybe?" Arnold replied. "You know how bad it's getting here in town."

"I know Pearl," Martin said. "She goes to yoga and only eats green leafy vegetables. There's no way."

Arnold sighed. "Why do you always think the best about people?" he asked.

"I guess that's the way I was raised," Martin replied.

"You'd shimmy up a telephone pole to rescue a stray cat if you could."

"I possess a certain naïve nobility," Martin said. "That's nothing to be ashamed of."

"Well, that'll change soon," Arnold said. "You're only twenty-eight, you barely seen any of the real world yet."

He glanced at the blood stains covering Martin's gray uniform shirt. "Your shift's over, hero," he scoffed. "Better get home and get yourself cleaned up before someone sees you like that and calls the cops."

* * *

Martin stopped at the Cozy Kitchen on the way home and got a breakfast pasty to go. The booths were filled with teenage surfers coming back from their morning sessions on the lake, at Moosejaw and Cherry Lagoon. They stared at his bloody shirt with genuine curiosity. One kid with one brown eye and one blue eye even asked him if he'd been in a fight.

Now he was back on the road and he couldn't get Pearl's face out of his mind. He'd never seen anyone with a look in their eyes like that, as if death were the only way out. Although he hadn't admitted it to Arnold, the incident had really frightened him.

He popped in his favorite Steve Miller Band cassette and turned up the volume. The muffler on his 1984 Cutlass Supreme rattled as he rounded a curve. The car was a hand-me-down from his grandfather and ran pretty well, all things considered.

"I went from Phoenix, Arizona all the way to Tacoma," Martin sang, somewhat off key. He took an enormous bite out of the pasty and tried to think happier thoughts. For one, he was definitely thankful that Patti, his current girlfriend, had given him a real spring in his step in the short time they'd been together. Martin bought her ice cream cones when he could, and their first date had been the buffet at Chang Wang, which was far out of his price range. He also—

THUMP! The Cutlass went right through a deep pothole. The cassette skipped to the next song, something about a jet airliner. Silverfish, the hardscrabble neighborhood where Martin lived, was dotted with empty warehouses and deserted office parks. Roads were constantly being torn up and repaved. It seemed like there was always construction happening that the town surely couldn't afford.

He looked ahead. The road ended in a sharp T. A concrete barrier separated it from the railroad tracks beyond.

His thoughts shifted back to the woman on the Stroll. What had brought her to that point? Martin figured it couldn't be drugs. Not Pearl. Had something snapped suddenly in her brain? Pearl had wanted death—that was clear. And that fact certainly scared Martin more than the broken glass or the spurting blood or anything else that had happened outside the store.

I'll be happy on the other side. And you will, too.

He suddenly realized with a start that he *had* seen that same look before—in his father's eyes, just before he died.

Martin shut his eyes, descending deeper into his rapidly shifting thoughts. He wondered if there was pain when you passed away? Or was there a release of everything all at once, like air escaping from a balloon? Was dying the only way to get rid of the thunderhead clouds that were constantly gathering in the back of his mind—the storm that he never admitted to anyone else was there?

Stop!

His eyes jerked open as the concrete wall rocketed toward him. Martin stomped on the brake pedal with a horrified yell—and the Cutlass skidded to a stop, just inches from impact.

He clutched the steering wheel, his heart racing. Sweat streamed from his temples. As Martin struggled to regain his composure, he realized that the voice of warning he'd heard right before he'd nearly hit the wall wasn't his own, but it was still very familiar. It belonged to his father.

3

Chapter Three—ERIC

Eric Calhoun was fourteen years old and liked two things: surfing and grilled cheese sandwiches. Nothing else came close.

He lived with his mother and her common-law husband on the second floor of a split-level at 244 Bearclaw Street in Great Water. It was the last building before the pine woods closed around the road as it disappeared up the hill.

The bottom apartment was empty. The tenants had been evicted long ago.

A narrow flower garden lay behind the building. Daisies and snap-dragons grew there in the summertime. But it was November now and the plants were brown and withered, the earth cracked with frost.

Beyond the garden was a large shack where Eric's dad used to shape surfboards, back when the three of them were a family. It was painted moss green and secured by a rusted metal lock. The key was in a drawer in the kitchen, buried underneath bent nails and expired coupons and dried up packages of Wet Wipes. Eric didn't go in the shack very often because it made his mother upset.

His father had taught him to surf the cold, shallow sets of Lake Michigan long ago. Eric remembered their walks down the hill toward the shore, the sun shedding hazy orange through the silent dawn. His father ambling next to him, a plastic travel mug of coffee in one hand, his longboard under his arm.

We're gonna hit some killer waves today, Ace. Just you watch.

Duane Calhoun had left in the middle of the night, six years ago. Eric had not heard from him since.

* * *

The heat kicked on just before 7:00. It grumbled through the vents and entered Eric's bedroom with an intrusive hiss, and he knew that was his signal to get moving. It was time to meet Lance Bloomquist for training.

Every Saturday morning, Eric walked two-and-a-half miles, past the Price Slasher and the summer cabins, shuttered for the season, to Spivey Point. It was undisputedly the best surfing spot on the north shore of the lake, but most locals avoided it. The woods nearby were supposedly haunted.

Lance was obviously unfazed by the rumors because he lived in an enormous, ultra-modern house in the pine forest right across the road. He was mega old, probably 50 at least. Lance and Eric had met by chance one day, in line at Rose's Surf Shop, and become friends. Their training sessions started soon after that.

Lance was an architect, but he had spent most of his life surfing at highly exotic places like Bondo Con Dios and Yak's Teeth. He was teaching Eric to be a Soul Surfer, which was a ridiculous thing to be in the rough-and-tumble, often violent surf scene in Great Water. It was not an identity that Eric had completely embraced, because it meant scorn and hazing among his fellow surfers. But Lance's vast experience and kind nature had convinced Eric to give him a shot. There was a Yoda-ness about him that Eric found comforting, like melted Swiss on sourdough.

The older man was well aware that Eric's all-time favorite movie was the 1987 surfing classic *North Shore*, which coincidentally featured the underdog hero, Rick Kane, getting coached on how to be a Soul

Surfer too. Eric owned a well-worn copy of the film on VHS that he had watched with Lance on more than one occasion. He'd even owned a hermit crab named R.K. who had died tragically the year before in a vacuum cleaner accident.

But Lance insisted that his teaching methodology was entirely unique and original. His sessions with Eric involved them talking a lot about the wind and glaciers and the paths that migrating geese took across the sky. Once he even brought his out-of-tune guitar and sang Eric a song he'd written about Lewis and Clark and how lonely and scared they must have been while exploring the American frontier. Lance didn't have a very melodious voice but he was definitely sincere.

Sometimes they actually surfed. Lance taught Eric the correct way to pop up and duck dive. He stressed the importance of paddling, and Eric's shoulders were huge from the practice. The sets on the lake typically weren't premium enough that Eric could catch any kind of real air, but that was fine. The fact that Lance cared enough to teach him crucial things about the waves made a difference, because Eric considered himself a surfer first and a high school freshman a distant second. When he heard news of classmates who had been suspended for various shenanigans, he was jealous to the point of distraction. He'd even formed the opinion that it would be much easier to do whatever he wanted—like surf all day—instead of what people expected him to do. Eric typically had more faith in animals (especially St. Bernards) than people.

Lance had proved to be the exception to that rule, and that's why Eric had let him into his life. At a time when his voice was dropping a half-octave practically every day and tiny blond hairs were appearing on spots in his body that defied all logic, he'd begrudgingly accepted that any role models would be crucial to his very survival, especially since his dad was long gone and probably wasn't coming back.

Eric opened his closet and browsed his small stash of vintage Ocean Pacific t-shirts and board shorts, but he thought better of it and chose an ensemble that was a little more appropriate for the season: a long underwear top and blue track pants. He would pull on his wetsuit later; thankfully, it was dry and clean and hanging in the shower.

Making his way down the dim hallway toward the kitchen, he stopped at his mother's bedroom and peeked through the half-open door. She was tangled up in the covers with Pete, pillow surfing. His thick arm was flung across her chest, his fingers resting on her chin as he snored like a rhinoceros with bronchitis.

Eric still couldn't believe his mother was living with another man. Pete had a scratchy black beard and one bad eye that he kept covered with a patch during the daytime. He was twelve years younger than her and was an Aspiring Actor, which meant that he did lots of theater at senior citizen centers in Grand Haven and once had a line of dialogue in a commercial for motor oil.

Pete had recently completed a starring role in a low-budget docudrama about Jack Spivey, the local fisherman who had gone insane in 1918. Spivey killed two people, including a little girl, before blowing his brains out in his cabin on Blackhawk Island. Eric's mother thought that was quite an important addition to Pete's resume. Eric was tired of hearing about it.

Pete tried hard, Eric had to admit. Every once in a while, they had Guys Movie Night, which meant that Pete ordered a pepperoni pizza with extra cheese and they split a six-pack of cream soda. Eric had to exercise extreme restraint because he could easily eat an entire extra-large pizza without a second thought or resulting stomachache, so learning to share with Pete was a good lesson that ultimately benefited their relationship. As for movies, Pete typically rented a black-and-white, old-timey Shakespeare movie that ended tragically. No one in them even spoke a language that sounded like English, but Eric pretended to enjoy them, even though he had no clue what was going on.

He did a quick surveillance of the available food in the kitchen and located a cherry pop in the fridge and a Cranberry-O Breakfast Bar in the cupboard, the last one in the box. Thankfully, Pete made his mother buy disgusting stuff that Eric never ate, like whole grain mushroom burgers and soy popcorn, which they purchased from a market run by hippies from a commune in Blaney Park. So there was usually plenty of regular food left for Eric to munch on. And if he got roped into eating one of Pete's health-kick dinners, he wasn't above smuggling bits of it into his napkin and into the trash when the adults weren't looking.

Eric tossed the empty breakfast bar box in the recycling bin in the corner. It was full of empty milk cartons and back issues of the Great Water Gazette, which Pete periodically scoured for odd job opportunities. Eric was glad the adults in the house had finally come around to taking small steps to save the Earth. He might not be academically motivated, but as a surfer, he definitely recognized the crisis facing the planet.

Before he left, he switched on the old color TV. All the news lately was about Gore and Bush fighting over the election results, and Eric had quickly learned to tune all of that out, just as he'd done with the Y2K hoopla months ago. Instead, he turned to the Weather Channel and listened to a smiling man in a striped bow tie give the local forecast for the weekend. No rain and no wind. Just temperatures in the thirties, and gathering clouds.

* * *

Eric met a kid named Myron on the road to Spivey Point. Myron wore a full black wetsuit and no shoes. He lived in one of the rougher trailer parks just outside town. He carried a dinged-up board, and a fresh cut on his eyebrow trickled blood down his cheek.

"What happened to you, brah?" Eric asked. He had adapted a hybrid California-Hawaii surf vernacular as his own, since the Great Lakes surf scene didn't have much of one. It annoyed his mother to no end.

"I was out at Moosejaw and some grungy carp started shit," Myron said.

"Who was it?"

"No clue. He was chugging cans of Schlitz and I think he lives in the woods across from Lighthouse Park."

"I know that dude," Eric said. "Webb Turner. My mom always told me to stay away from him. I thought he was a sealer."

"A dealer who surfs," Myron replied.

"Yeah. Full-on harmless, so long as you leave him alone."

"I thought the exact same thing. But he was talking shit about how he used to be some big shredder, him and the Three Kings. And something about how some woman was sending him messages on the TV. How she was waiting for him in the light."

"What's that supposed to mean?" Eric asked.

"He had this look in his eyes," Myron said. "Like a salmon just before you slit it open. Me and Ollie set him straight. We threw some rocks at him. Then he got back on his motorcycle and that was it."

"You got dinged pretty bad."

Myron wiped at his cheek absently. "Whatever," he said. "Just watch your back, Calhoun."

"Laters," Eric replied.

Myron started to walk the opposite way, back toward town. He stopped. "Hey."

Eric turned around. "What?"

"He was hollering about the moon," Myron said. "He was screaming about the blood red moon."

* * *

A few minutes later, Eric arrived at Spivey Point, his trusted powder blue, triple-fin board in hand. Here, enormous houses lay at the end of long gravel driveways, hidden by thick forests of pine and ferns. Eric had seen a dead badger in the middle of the road once, not half a mile from there. And on another occasion, he found a bullet casing on the beach. He kept it in an envelope in his underwear drawer, under the jock strap he had to buy for sixth grade gym class.

Eric made his way over a ditch and through some spiny bushes, then a couple of yards down a short sandy hill. The lake opened up in front of him, with a thin beach and a rocky outcropping that stretched far out into the water and curved a bit at the end, creating a natural barrier for the sets when the conditions were right.

The surface of the lake was absolutely still.

Lance wasn't on the beach. He wasn't waiting on the stump at the edge of the brush, or standing among the tangled driftwood on the lead-colored rocks.

Eric scanned the wet cement sky, spread in front of him like a heavy blanket, and wondered if somewhere, far across the lake, it was snowing. He weighed whether or not he should walk back up to the road and down the dark driveway to Lance's house in the woods.

The man was always on time. Always.

Eric decided that Lance would be impressed if he plunged right in and got things going on his own. He figured he could start with Dolphin Visualization, which involved wearing goggles and swimming along the bottom of the lake, noticing every minnow and pebble and bit of lake weed, just as a dolphin would. Or maybe he could practice paddling to the end of Spivey Point and back. He could pretend he was in the lineup at Yak's Teeth, waiting for the next twelve-footer to break in a perfect arc of blue.

But instead, he walked down to the beach to the driftwood patch where he and Lance often sat and ate scrambled egg sandwiches from paper plates and drank bottled sarsaparilla. He put his board down in the sand.

A gull flew low across the water. Eric followed its flight as it skimmed the surface, swept over the rocks and landed in a plum tree, a little ways down the beach. The tree grew on the edge of a grassy bank, where Brisco Creek rushed under a splintered wooden bridge and emptied into the lake.

The switchgrass around the plum tree was moving.

Eric wasn't sure what to make of this at first, because the rest of the world around him was completely still. The grass at the base of the tree was bent in the direction of the road, as if being blown from a strong wind coming off the lake. And the branches of the tree shifted and scratched the sky.

Lance had taught him enough about the patterns of the wind for Eric to know that something wasn't right.

He started walking across the sand, toward the bridge. Then he stopped and listened. He heard carnival music: the pipes of a rusty, antique organ. It grew in intensity, like the organ was being wheeled right past him. Then the sound faded.

Eric had not gone three more steps when a strong blast of warm air nearly knocked him onto the sand. Struggling to his feet, he glanced to the south, across the lake. It was like he was inside a wind tunnel, like a weatherman on assignment, reporting from the midst of a hurricane. There wasn't anything unusual on the lake; all he could see was the end of Spivey Point—a jumble of boulders jutting out of the water—and Blackhawk Island beyond, where the dockworker Jack Spivey had gone insane and shot himself in his cabin in 1918.

Eric lunged to his left. His thick blond hair settled back on his forehead. The air was calm again.

He saw a flash of color and looked toward the water.

A surfboard was washed up on the sand.

He ran down the beach to where the board lay. One of its fins was wedged in the sand, lake water washing across its deck. It was a nine-foot stick, triple-finned with plenty of rocker, and there was a design of butterfly on it. Its wings were spread wide and were splashed with bright streaks of psychedelic orange and purple.

Wrapped around one of the surfboard's fins was a long strand of blond hair.

4

Chapter Four—JENNY

The most challenging part of being married had been figuring out how to spend the times when she was alone. For most of her life, people had overlooked her like a dull pear on a grocery store produce display, and Jenny had grown used to that, even accepted it. But marrying someone who was so intelligent and cultured had led her to question what mark she wanted to make on the world.

After their wedding, she'd spent the ensuing two years volunteering around town: delivering meals to home-bound seniors and helping at-risk students plant community vegetable gardens in the poorest areas of Great Water. She'd even worked at an animal shelter that took in the most abused and vicious pets along the North Shore. Although people seemed to appreciate her efforts, Jenny wondered if she was trying to change how others saw her, but not how she saw herself. Looking inward was frightening and she was always afraid of what she might find.

So one summer afternoon more than a year ago, she took a bold leap and told Lance about her dream to open her own bed and breakfast. She even had the spot picked out, about three miles up the road, across from a meadow filled with daisies. The idea of a building and managing a tranquil place where people could escape their everyday problems felt like a way that she could be of service and show people who she really was. Jenny constantly watched cooking shows on PBS, read back issues of *Gourmet* at the library in Manistique, and even studied episodes of *Hotel* and *Newhart* that she'd taped off the TV as a teenager. She examined them closely to learn proper etiquette for hotel proprietors, as well as crisis management techniques.

Lance couldn't contain his pride after she'd showed him the spot she'd chosen for the building. Jenny, smiling shyly, was barely able to get the words out, her sentences full of stuttering apologies. She'd adapted this defense mechanism growing up with a mother whose modus operandi was blaming Jenny for her own mistakes.

"Sweetheart," Lance said, admiring the scenic spot. "It's perfect."

Gaining Lance's approval lifted an enormous psychological barrier. Soon after that, she started secretly writing in the notebooks.

Jenny had never been a role model student. She had done well enough to barely graduate from Great Water High, but only by cramming for tests the night before and learning the necessary facts and figures to pass. Retaining information was difficult for her if they weren't pasty recipes or hotel guest protocols. Her mother told her it was because she took after her father's side of the family, which was typical of the insults that the older woman cast about like strategically placed fishing nets.

Oprah Winfrey had a guest on her show one afternoon, a memory expert who had written three best-selling books. He told the audience that some people were visual learners and needed to see or read things—sometimes multiple times—to make them stick. Realizing that she fit that profile, Jenny bought a jumbo pack of pocket-sized spiral-bound notebooks at the Price Slasher in town, and she carried one with her at all times. Whenever she learned information that she thought might be important, she wrote it down as quickly and with as much detail as possible. This information could be anything from Frank Lloyd Wright's major accomplishments to facts about the trendiest new lakeside hotel in the Adirondacks.

During the countless social functions she attended with Lance, she did it discreetly, often slipping into an empty bedroom to jot down facts. Then each night, right after she brushed her teeth and gargled with extra strength Listerine, she read over that day's notebook entries. And incredibly, things were starting to stick. She could actually contribute to cocktail party conversations, instead of pretending to admire the rug or the curtains. And she was using the notebooks to flesh out her dream bed and breakfast, conceptualizing it, figuring out what would work. She kept them hidden in a locked drawer in a desk in her study, next to an unused vibrator that she'd received from a coworker as a Secret Santa gift.

Jenny and Lance had never talked about having a family, but that hadn't stopped him from being an absolute wolverine in the bedroom. Whether it was his vast experience, or the fact that Jenny had little, she soon learned that there were parts of her body that had been in hibernation for a very long time. Now everything was constantly tingling, from her fingertips to her nipples to her kneecaps. So after a bit of research in online chatrooms, she purchased a home pregnancy test at the Price Slasher when she'd stopped at the store recently to order their Thanksgiving turkey. Jenny was excellent at killing two birds with one stone.

Perplexed about which brand to buy, she chose a pregnancy test with a smiling black woman on the box. The cover model was svelte and wore attractive dark-rimmed glasses. A possible pregnancy didn't seem to alter her determination to remain stylish, and Jenny respected that.

So, on that Saturday morning on the third weekend of November, she opened the linen closet and removed the box from its hiding place behind a jumbo pack of extra-durable toilet paper. Jenny examined the label and read the directions with considerable trepidation. She had numerous unvirtuous high school classmates who'd gotten pregnant or had abortions before they'd graduated; Ingrid Lund had even given birth to twin girls at age 16 and left town in a cherry red Thunderbird driven by a much older man with a glass eye and an affinity for the music of recording superstar MC Hammer.

The process seemed straightforward enough, and Jenny settled down to start it. Before long, she was waiting. Wondering.

Then the second line appeared, and she knew the answer was yes.

Jenny sat on the edge of her bed and tried to smile, but she felt like a marionette, someone pulling the strings around the corners of her mouth to make her display something that was appropriate for the situation. She was used to giving everyone else what they wanted so they'd be pleased and satisfied. But what was she feeling right then?

I'm going to be a mom.

Instead of thinking it, she said it out loud, just to give the words a test drive:

"I'm going to be a mom."

She was alone in a changing room, trying on a new dress, with no one there to tell her if it fit.

Jenny reached for the cordless phone on the night table and dialed her parents' house.

Her mother picked up after the second ring. "Hello, who is this?" she asked, her voice as crisp as a Granny Smith apple. "It's barely 8:30 in the morning, do you realize that?"

Jenny swallowed hard. She knew instantly that calling home was a mistake.

"Mom—" she began.

"Jennifer? What is it? Why are you calling?"

"I'm sorry it's so early," Jenny said. "But I—"

Her mother would say she wasn't ready for a child. Or that she didn't deserve one.

"If you want to speak to your father, now isn't a good time. He didn't get much sleep last night. Kept shuffling around the house like a zombie. I didn't sleep a wink. I love the man dearly, but—"

Jenny desperately wanted to tell the one man she loved more than Lance her news, but she wasn't sure if he'd even understand. The unpredictability of his early-onset Alzheimer's invaded normal conversations persistently and made communication a challenge. He was operating as if nothing was wrong, but Jenny knew that this was only the beginning stages of a painful, steady decline.

She didn't have anyone else to tell, except for Lance.

"I was wondering if you could make your cranberry sauce for Thursday," Jenny said quickly. "The one with walnuts and shaved orange peel."

"You told me you had everything well in hand," her mother said. "But if you want me to help out—"

"Just bring it," Jenny said. "Please."

She hung up the phone quickly, blinking tears from her eyes, then pulled out the green spiral notebook from the pocket of her cardigan. Jenny turned to an empty page and wrote the date carefully at the top. Her pen hovered in the blank space below it, but she had no idea what to write.

5

Chapter Five—MARTIN

Martin decided to go see Patti immediately; he didn't want to go back to his gloomy apartment without talking to her first. She'd reassure him that he was just exhausted after working so many double shifts.

She worked at The Book Loft, which was in an artsy area of town several miles from the harbor and the crumbling stone buildings of downtown. The community college was there; it drew students from up and down the beach towns on the northern shore. Many visitors were surprised that Great Water even had a college, but the town was just large enough to have things like a dysfunctional City Council, spotty snowplow service and a lakefront fireworks display on the Fourth of July.

Patti was definitely the most special woman Martin had ever come across. She always laughed at his knock-knock jokes. She'd taught him how to make butterscotch chocolate chip cookies from scratch and introduced him to the world of Moroccan jazz. And when he'd revealed his dreams of one day visiting his brother Lars in Montreal, she had pressured him, gently but firmly, to sign up for an Introduction to French night class at the college.

Martin parked in a public lot and walked down a block of used record stores and sandwich shops. He passed The Rialto, whose marquee advertised a special premiere of *Jack Spivey: A Tragic Life, A New*

Beginning. The image on the poster, which hung inside a cracked glass panel just outside the ticket booth, was of Spivey (actually an unshaven actor who was his spitting image, down to the eye patch) aiming a shotgun toward a silhouette of a woman and a little girl. The rocky shore of Blackhawk Island lay shrouded by fog in the distance.

Martin shivered. He'd forgotten his jacket in the car, but the image of the child drew him closer.

Bridget O'Hara, the girl on the poster, clutched a wooden Pierre the Bear toy in one hand. Martin recognized the bear's oversized head and the wheels on its legs; it was the toy found in Jack Spivey's cabin—next to his dead body—after he'd murdered Bridget and her father, Benjamin, inside their home on Sunrise Avenue in 1918.

It was a toy Spivey had made by hand for the seven-year-old girl in a desperate attempt to win back her mother's love, after Lucy O'Hara had broken off their affair. Her husband had returned home from the war, even though everyone thought he'd been killed on the battlefield in Germany, so what had Spivey expected Lucy to do? He was a lowly dockworker and she was the wealthy wife of a brave soldier—and their ill-advised three-month romance was doomed from the start. Even Martin, who was moderately wise to the ways of women, could have told Spivey that.

The story hadn't ended on that frigid, bloody November night exactly eighty-two years ago. Lucy drowned herself in a shallow cow pond in 1922, after enduring four years of devastating grief that manifested itself in gruesome hallucinations of carnivorous Vikings stalking her through the upscale shops and quant lakefront restaurants of Great Water. There was even a song that longshoremen sang about how they found her corpse: lily pads wrapped around her neck like leeches; her checkered dress jaggedly torn, like she had taken out her overpowering madness on the garment before she waded into the water and let the darkness take her.

Every child in that part of the state had grown up playing with the Pierre toys. Generations of lumbermen cut down the trees to make them. Fathers and sons, mothers and daughters had worked at the Great Water Toy Company to craft them. Tourists traveled for hours to buy them from stores all over town. Deep down, Martin felt ashamed that Great Water was famous for something so horrible, but he'd grown to accept it, like people who had acne or who lived near earthquake faults. Tourism was the town's main source of income, after all—and because of the anniversary of the murders, that weekend would be packed with visitors.

"Hey, bro? 'Scuse us."

Case in point, Martin thought.

A young man and woman approached him down the sidewalk. They wore fashionably ripped denim jackets and flip flops, even though it was barely forty degrees out. Martin knew instantly that they were a couple; there was an air of comfort between them that spoke of intimate trust.

"Hello there," Martin said. "Good morning."

"We're looking for the statue of Rod Kalanchoe," the man said. He had rumpled blond hair and striking eyes like blue asters. "We've been driving around a ton searching for it. Do you know where it's at?"

Rod Kalanchoe was a devastatingly handsome local surfer who had drowned in the lake in 1982 while surfing Cherry Lagoon in a thunderstorm. The town had commissioned a monument to him because of the countless hours he'd volunteered giving surf clinics to at-risk children. He was a rare success story from Great Water.

Martin glanced up the street and saw a beat-up lime Chevy Caprice station wagon with dark brown paneling parked next to a fire hydrant. Several surfboards stuck out the rolled-down rear window.

"We asked at the grocery store but the dude wasn't much help," the woman added. She took a sip from a cardboard cup of coffee. Her auburn hair was up in a ponytail; Martin thought she resembled a young Cindy Crawford. They both sounded like characters from the cult classic *Valley Girl*, starring Deborah Foreman and Nicolas Cage.

"Sure, it's just down the road on the right," Martin said. "Look for the little park. Keep walking and you can't miss it."

"Righteous," the man said. "Kalanchoe was a badass."

"My name's Eden," the woman said. "He's Bryce. We're from Venice."

"Italy?" Martin asked. He winced as soon as he said it.

"Not exactly," Bryce replied, as if it were a common mistake. "Have you heard of Venice Beach? It's like Los Angeles, but way more mellow."

"Let me guess," Martin said. "You're here for the surfing."

"Absolutely," Bryce said. "We're driving cross country and nabbing all the best breaks. Of course we have to hit Moosejaw. I heard it's really popping off today."

"What's the deal with the people in this town?" Eden asked. "Everyone looks like their favorite puppy just died." She took another sip of her coffee and frowned quizzically.

"That's kind of a standard thing around here," Martin admitted. "Like suntanned people in San Diego or grumpy people in Boston. I work down at the Stroll and we get tourists from all parts of the United States. So that gives me a little bit of perspective."

Eden indicated the movie poster. "I know about the murders that happened here, but it's seriously warped to obsess over it," she said. "Seriously."

"I heard this town is cursed," Bryce added. "Unexplained disappearances and such, over the years. We even saw three different signs for ghost tours. They all stop at this place called Blackhawk Island. That sounds like the perfect name for an Indian burial ground to me."

"Is this town actually haunted?" Eden asked. "I mean, for real?"

"It's mainly a tourism thing," Martin said. His voice sounded rehearsed and impartial. "Like that mountain town in California where they supposedly spotted Bigfoot," he continued. "There's Bigfoot gas stations and Bigfoot hamburgers. People here play up the stories. Otherwise there's no real reason to come to Great Water."

Eden regarded him with a look of barely concealed pity, as if he were a man trapped in a fishbowl who was convinced that there was no world outside his own. "That's why we won't be staying long," she said. "I want to hit those waves and then get the heck out of here."

* * *

There was a new employee putting up a display in the front window of The Book Loft. Martin had never seen him before. The kid had a shaved head and was missing an eyebrow. The display was all books about true crime and illicit affairs gone terribly wrong.

The store manager stood nearby, gesturing emphatically as the kid arranged a cardboard cutout of Jack Spivey in the window. The sleeves of the manager's plaid shirt were rolled up, above the elbows.

"Hello," Martin said. "I'm looking for Patricia, is she in?"

The kid regarded him. His name tag was on upside down. "Are you a cop?" he asked.

"I'm a security officer," he proclaimed, trying to inject some pride into his voice.

The manager frowned when he saw the blood on Martin's shirt. "Upstairs," he said to Martin. "More to the left," he told the kid. "Geez-o-pete."

Martin made his way through Fiction and Literary Criticism to the spiral staircase that led up to the second floor. He found Patti in Travel, doing inventory. She was pale and wore jeans and a heavy wool sweater. Her lavender hair was damp and fell into her eyes like exotic seaweed.

She looked up at him in surprise as he approached. "What're you doing here, Martin?"

"I wanted to see you," he answered, surprised at the edge in her voice. He stepped closer to touch her on the cheek, but she turned away.

Patti put her clipboard down on a cart full of books. "What happened to your shirt?" she asked.

"A woman tried to kill herself at the Stroll," Martin explained. "She

29

slashed her wrists. I'm still a little shaken up about it."

"Listen to me," she said, barely looking at him. "I don't want to see you anymore."

The fluorescent lights overhead blurred into bright streaks of red and orange as Martin struggled to focus. "What're you talking about?" he said. "I thought we were having such a good time together."

"Just forget about me and move on," Patti replied. "And don't ever come in here again looking like that, okay? You're gonna get me fired."

She pushed past him and vanished into the shelves. Martin desperately wanted to follow her, but he'd seen *Fatal Attraction* three times in the theater as a teenager and figured that for now, that was a line he probably shouldn't cross.

6

Chapter Six—JENNY

Jenny set the table with the good blue earthenware dishes. The Jamaican Blend coffee was brewing in her brand new coffee maker, the French toast was nearly ready and the sausages were sizzling away on a pan on the stovetop. She had even arranged a delicate centerpiece of dried harebell and tickseed in an antique vase.

She opened the massive refrigerator and noticed the uncooked turkey on the bottom shelf, squatting there like an uninvited house guest. Even though Thanksgiving was less than a week away and she typically wrapped herself in days of planning and cooking like a comfortable quilt, the holiday seemed of miniscule importance in the grand scheme of things.

"Everything will work out for the best," she told the turkey. "It has to."

Glancing at the clock, she realized that Lance would be back in less than ten minutes; he was always remarkably punctual. She tried to imagine his face when she told him the news. At least someone would be happy for her, and that one person was all she needed for now.

There was a sudden smell in the air like smoldering wires.

Jenny stiffened and glanced around the room. Working in the hospitality industry had sharpened her radar to detect potential maintenance problems immediately, and implement solutions. Maybe there was a blown fuse?

ZZATT! All the lights in the kitchen buzzed menacingly, then went off.

"Come on," she implored. "Not now."

The overhead light switched on, then off again, as if adding insult to injury. Jenny went to the wall and flicked a switch several times. The room remained dim, but morning light shimmied through the side window curtains, bathing the room in an uncomfortable haze.

ZZATT!

The small TV on the counter flickered on suddenly and a blurry image came into focus, from a long-ago variety show. Karen Carpenter sat on a plastic porch swing surrounded by pots of red and white lilies. She looked like a gossamer vision from a Vietnam-era daydream.

We've only just begun...

Jenny watched in a daze as the late singer rocked back and forth, gently caressing her microphone, the image frazzled by static as she sang:

A kiss for luck and we're on our way...

Jenny turned off the TV with a shaking hand, feeling like she'd entered some kind of time warp. She hurried to the window and drew open the curtains all the way, letting in the sunlight. The fuse box was located in the cellar, but going down there alone was the absolute last thing she wanted to do right then. Something told her that this electrical mayhem was more serious than just a faulty circuit.

A huge black hound was right outside the window, watching her.

Jenny stepped closer to the window pane to get a better look at the side yard. A patch of strawberries grew untamed in the summer, but now the space was withered and bare—except for an enormous dog that crouched in the dirt. The creature had mottled black fur and powerful haunches, and its paws were scabbed with pus. It stared directly at her with eyes that burned crimson with pure hatred.

The dog didn't look like a pet that belonged to any of her neighbors along the lake; Jenny was certain of that. It looked like something straight out of *The Hound of the Baskervilles* or *The Omen*. Something that foretold of horrible things to come.

She rapped hard on the window. The dog didn't move.

Jenny knocked harder. "Get the fuck out of here!" she hollered.

The beast bared its teeth. They were jagged and bloody, as if it had just finished devouring a litter of kittens.

"I'm not scared of you!" she yelled through the window. "Got it?"

The dog let loose a terrifying howl that filled her mind with the most horrible things she could ever imagine. It was the scream of a starving prisoner shackled deep in a dungeon; the lament of an elderly woman at her husband's bedside as he took his final breath. It was the shriek of a man trying desperately to escape a burning car and the cry of a woman drowning in a churning sea.

Jenny shut her eyes and gritted her teeth. She decided to take charge of the situation, like any worthy bed and breakfast owner would. This creature was an invader and it needed to go.

The most important lesson that she'd learned while working at the animal shelter was that all these dogs needed was someone who would show them who the boss was. Jenny figured that maxim had to apply to Hounds of Hell, too. Looking around for something to scare it off with, she grabbed a huge jar of pasta sauce from the counter and marched through the kitchen and out the front door. Lance insisted on having no guns in the house, so an ordinary grocery item would have to do the trick.

Without a moment's hesitation, she stomped down the slate walkway and around the corner of the house, ready to confront it with her heavy projectile. She shielded her eyes from the glare coming off the metal chairs on the patio.

The hound was gone. Jenny blinked twice, then scanned the yard. She checked the bare strawberry patch where she'd seen it crouched. There were no paw prints in the dirt.

* * *

The electricity was back to behaving as it should, so Jenny decided to proceed as normal; the breakfast was too important to abandon. She tended to her sausages and made the final preparations on the French toast. All she needed to do was go down the hall to see if she'd remembered to buy maple syrup from Pete Miller at the little general store over by the lumber mill.

The pantry was the first door in a long corridor that led away from the kitchen, under a skylight, toward the rear of the house. Lance's study was located at the end, just before the glass doors that opened up on the back terrace.

Jenny left the kitchen and stepped inside the dark little room, with its high shelves stocked with canned goods. A bag of russet potatoes and a plastic sack of onions lay on the floor.

The light bulb flickered on above her. Jenny closed the pantry door to take a look at the shelf that was just behind it, where she kept items like syrup and flour.

Then she heard it.

It was quite faint at first. But then she heard it again, clear as day and getting closer by the second: the hollow call of a horn. It didn't sound like a brass instrument from a marching band, but something carved out of ancient, gnarled wood — or bone.

Jenny reached for the door handle. Just as her fingers grasped the metal, the horses came.

Horses thundered down the hall on the other side of the door. Heavy hooves stomped and pounded; men yelled to each other in a guttural foreign language. The shelves of the pantry jostled violently. A jar tumbled off the top shelf and sent nails skittering across the floor in a jumble. And as Jenny watched in horrified fascination, the pieces of steel hopped across the floor and were sucked through the crack under the door.

Jenny stopped breathing. The ground swayed beneath her feet and she felt a pulling in her chest, as if by invisible hands, drawing her against the door. The pull grew more intense, and she was flattened

34

against it, bits of sugar and spilled flour swirling around her like a twister, cans toppling and spilling on the floor beneath her.

The sounds grew fainter, then abruptly stopped. Then the suction released her, all at once. Jenny stood there for a few seconds, trying to catch her breath.

She opened the door and peeked out cautiously.

The hallway was empty.

A warm gust of wind knocked her backwards onto the floor. Jenny cried out in pain as her head smacked against the wall. The stench of sulfur and decayed flesh filled her nostrils. Screaming her husband's name, Jenny scrambled to her feet and ran back down the hallway and into the kitchen, slamming the door behind her.

* * *

Jenny spent the next few minutes in the downstairs bathroom, shivering and sobbing, her heart beating twenty times a second in her chest. She felt nauseous for a bit, but then the feeling passed.

The back of her head still hurt where it had struck the wall. She felt it gingerly; a bump was already forming there. Realizing it was pointless and even a little embarrassing to be hiding in the bathroom of her own house, she splashed her face with cold water and then took two Tylenol.

She opened the door carefully and peeked out. The coast was clear.

Jenny tried to examine the situation logically. She had no history of mental calamities or haphazardly confusing fantasy with reality. As far as she knew, all her senses were functioning normally. So there was no question she hadn't imagined what she'd heard—and felt—in the pantry. There was a huge welt on her head to prove it.

She didn't know enough about pregnancy to determine if hearing horses stampeding down the hallway or seeing Hounds of Hell in the yard were typical side effects of the condition, but she figured now, after serious consideration, that that wasn't the case. Jenny didn't remember writing that in any of her notebooks.

Ghosts? She put them in the same box as aliens. Jenny never rented horror movies—she preferred stories about women who undertook missions at great personal risk, like *Not Without My Daughter*, starring Sally Field.

She decided her next step was to go down to the lake and find Lance. Her big announcement would have to wait.

Jenny took the sausage pan off the burner and then untied her apron. Instead of going to the closet for her coat, she stopped at the end of the hallway that led to the rear of the house. A framed Le Corbusier print hung crookedly on the wall, and there were streaks of fresh mud on the floor outside the pantry. She took a couple of steps down the hallway. Faintly—ever so faintly—she heard a strange sound, drifting toward her like a memory. It was the lilting strains of a carnival pipe organ: a calliope.

The doorbell rang. Jenny ran to the front door, brushing back a few stray strands of hair, and opened it. Eric Calhoun stood on the front step. He wore a black wetsuit with light blue stripes on the arms. His summer tan had not yet faded and his wavy, dark blond hair hid his doe-like eyes.

"Hi, Mrs. Bloomquist," he said in a small voice, as if he was afraid of interrupting something. "I was wondering if Lance was here."

"No," Jenny said, her heart beating faster. "I thought he was with you."

"He didn't show up," Eric said, and nudged the doormat with his foot. "It's not like him," he added. "Lance is the most responsible adult I know."

Jenny thought of Lance glancing out their bedroom window earlier, as if he wanted to tell her something.

"Maybe he just—went for a walk," she said. "Maybe he just needed some time to himself."

"But don't you think he would've told someone?"

Jenny forced a reassuring smile. "Come on in," she said. "I can try his cell phone and see where he is."

"No, ma'am, I should probably get home. My mom's expecting me for something. We have to go into town. I just wanted to check about Lance."

It was then that she saw a surfboard resting on the step behind him. It had a psychedelic butterfly painted on it. Jenny had never seen anything like it before.

"I found it down on the beach," Eric said, off her gaze. "It's not Lance's, is it?"

"No," Jenny said. "At least, I don't think so. He keeps all his boards in his study, or in the garage."

Eric pushed his hair out of his eyes. He seemed disappointed, like he'd been expecting a different answer. "Maybe someone left it there," he said. "One of the old timers from town. That's the only answer I can think of."

Jenny had a sudden mental picture of Lance, lying face down on the rocky beach at the edge of the water, gulls pecking at his hair. She clutched her sweater around her chest. "Eric," she said. "Did you see anything different down at the lake this morning?"

"Different?"

"Like, strange. Different than normal."

"No, ma'am."

"Are you sure?"

"It was just mega windy," Eric said, finally. "Right where the creek empties out. I'd never seen it like that before. Blowing straight off the water and under the bridge."

Jenny remembered the warm wind that had knocked her down in the hallway.

"Mrs. Bloomquist? Did you guys have a fight? You and Lance?"

Jenny thought about Lance standing over her that morning, the love in his eyes, the light of dawn outlining his body.

"Of course not," she said. "Everything's fine, why would you think that?"

"Sometimes people leave after they have fights," Eric said. "And sometimes they don't come back."

* * *

Jenny gave Eric some sausages and apple slices, wrapped in a napkin. She watched him head down the gravel driveway and vanish through the trees.

The phone in Lance's study rang. Her heart pounding, Jenny raced down the hallway, under the skylight and into the room that her husband kept so private. It was dim and low-ceilinged and smelled of freshly cut cherry wood. A crack snaked jaggedly across the window that overlooked the back yard. Tiny pieces of pane glass lay scattered on the rug.

A huge cabinet stood to the right of the window; it contained three ancient surfboards, standing side by side. They were the boards of The Three Kings: Lance and his two best friends from high school, Duane Calhoun and Webb Turner. Each board was airbrushed with a different animal: a badger, an eagle and a wolf. Lance had not yet told her the story behind them and she had never met either of the men.

The phone was on his desk. A jar of pencils and protractors lay tipped on its side, as if someone had already been there before her, knocking about, looking for something.

Jenny picked up the handset of the peculiar push-button phone. She noticed a library book—*Vikings in America*—sitting next to it.

"Hello?"

"Is this Lance?" a garbled man's voice on the other end asked. He sounded like an Appalachian moonshiner.

"Who is this?"

"This is Pike," the voice replied. "Is this Jenny? Did he go through with it?"

"Through with what?" Jenny asked. She sat down in his swivel chair, gripping the phone tightly.

More garbled static spat in her ear. It sounded like the person was on the highway, passing an eighteen-wheeler. Windshield wipers scraped. A car horn blared.

"He did, didn't he? I warned him."

"I don't know who you are, but you're scaring me. How do you know Lance?"

"I shouldn't have let him go," Pike said. "Just stay out of the woods and keep off the path. Do you understand?"

"What're you talking about?" Jenny pleaded. "What path? Where is my husband?"

The line went dead. Her mind racing, she scanned the desk and saw Lance's Rolodex. Silently thanking him for being so old-fashioned, she skipped to the P section and found cards for Philadelphia City Planning and Pete's Motors and someone named Paul Gullafsen, but no Pike. Then she realized his filing system.

The card for Lucas Pike had two numbers scratched out in red pen. She dialed the third number that was scribbled in pencil. It had an Ohio area code. The phone rang five times before it went to an answering machine.

This is Lucas Pike, Traveling Paranormal Investigator. I'm out battling demons at the moment, so leave a message at the beep and I'll get back to you once I've crossed back into the physical plane.

She yelled into the phone after the beep.

"This is Jenny Bloomquist! Get up to Great Water right away. I need to know what the hell is going on!"

She slammed the receiver down in the cradle. Not missing a beat, she dialed Lance's cell phone. It went straight to voicemail. She contemplated leaving him a message, but Jenny was starting to wonder if her husband even wanted to be found.

7

Chapter Seven—ERIC

E ric trudged up Bearclaw Street, carrying the butterfly surfboard. His mother was at the mailbox, sorting through the mail. She had her hair up and wore a pretty blue dress with stars on it.

One envelope caught her attention, and she frowned. She held the envelope up to the sun, as if trying to see through it. Then she shook it.

"Hey, Mom," Eric said. "Howzit?"

His mother quickly inserted the envelope in the middle of the stack of bills and advertisements in her hand. "Hi, sweetheart," she said. "Did you have breakfast? Your hair's not even wet."

"Lance bailed on me. I got shined."

"What're you talking about? Speak English."

"He never showed up. I think him and Jenny had a mondo fight."

His mother noticed the butterfly board and her expression changed to barely concealed surprise. "What's that?" she asked. "What do you have there?"

"I found it by Spivey Point," Eric said. "It's rad, isn't it? Psychedelic. And it's super light, too. I don't think they make boards like this anymore."

"What do you mean, you found it?"

"It was just up on the beach, by where Lance and I usually meet.

Why?"

A whistle sounded then, mournful and faint. Eric knew it was from the lumber yard on the other side of the hill, signifying the end of the graveyard shift.

"Mom. What's going on?"

His mother squeezed his shoulder and forced a smile. "You need to go get ready for the premiere," she said finally. "We don't want to spoil Pete's day."

"But—"

"Leave the board out on the porch," she said. "All right?"

* * *

Eric put on his only pair of dress pants, which were pleated khakis. Pleats were completely against everything that he believed in, but he figured he could make that sacrifice for Pete. Then he picked out a thin tie that had black and white piano keys on it; he'd bought it at a Boys and Girls Club downtown, across the street from the free clinic. Eric had worn it to Yink Bradley's eighth grade graduation party, and had made out with two separate girls that night, against his better judgment—and only after they'd confessed they both had raging crushes on him. Kissing girls might be something he was expected to do as a fourteen-year-old on the cusp of manhood, but it truly frightened Eric; each time he did it, it was like hurtling down a steep, rickety staircase in the dark, with no flashlight. It was even hard for him to give his mother a simple kiss on the cheek without feeling like something horrible was about to happen.

Eric was about to knock on his mother's bedroom door to ask for Pete's help in tying the tie properly, when he overheard them talking in low voices.

"It can't be the same board," Pete said.

"They never found it," his mother said.

"Diane—"

41

"It's just too strange. First the letter and now this. You know Eric sees Rose all the time. What if—"

There was an abrupt silence. Then the door creaked open and there was Pete. He wore a tuxedo shirt with ruffles and scuffed cowboy boots. His mother stood behind him, holding a tube of lipstick. She wiped her eyes and smiled at Eric.

"Hey, Little Chief," Pete said. "Ready to go?"

* * *

Eric had trouble sitting still during the premiere of Pete's movie at the Rialto. He was too busy thinking about Lance and the surfboard and the bare branches of the plum tree blowing in the strange warm wind, wondering how it all fit together.

The movie was half-documentary, half-regular, and he was glad it was only fifty-three minutes long, including credits. Everyone seemed to think that it was the biggest thing to happen to Great Water since pretty much forever, even though it was a story that school kids learned in third grade, if not sooner. All the people connected with the movie were there, including the director and seventeen local actors who starred as the dead German soldiers and old-time townspeople in the film. It told the Jack Spivey saga, tracing his life as an ornery dockworker who lost his left eye during a barroom brawl with a Merchant Marine, to his first chance meeting with Lucy O'Hara in a movie theater showing the latest Mary Pickford film, to the tragic tale that everyone knew.

It was surreal for Eric to see Pete, a guy whom he had seen in his boxer shorts on more than one occasion, up on the screen, playing Spivey in the reenactments of actual and imagined events. He figured Pete had gotten the part because both he and Spivey wore eye patches, but one night that summer when his mom was working late, Pete had confessed to Eric over a late dinner of takeout Chinese food that there was one element of Spivey's story that he especially identified with.

42

Jack had scrawled in his diary on the night before his death in 1918 that he actually felt like he was disappearing; that he was half in the physical world and half in a world of slithering darkness, and there was no way to ever be complete again. He also wrote several entries about the blood red moon and how it was communicating violent commands to him. Pete told Eric that even though he was an ordinary guy on the surface, like Spivey, he also wrestled with metaphysical conundrums that ran deeper than the Mariana Trench. But thankfully none of them involved thoughts of violence.

The only rad part of the whole hullabaloo was that they got to sit clear up at the front of the theater in the VIP section, which was blocked off by masking tape so that random people couldn't just sit there. Pete had told him on the drive over that movie critics would be in the audience, and possibly agents from Chicago or even New York. Eric had no idea what agents were.

The lights dimmed just before the movie started. The director, who wore a homemade poncho and was from Finland, stood up and gave a rambling and mostly incoherent speech about the historical and pseudo-cultural importance of the film. She invited them for a brunch reception afterward at the Cozy Kitchen. Then everyone clapped and Eric's mother, who wore perfume that smelled like fresh lemons, gave Pete a huge kiss that seemed to last forever.

After the lights came up, the audience streamed out of the theater into the popcorn-strewn lobby, which had recently been restored to mimic the theater's Depression-era glory years, with debatable success. Eric trailed quite a bit behind his mother and Pete as they tramped up the carpeted aisle, stopping to shake hands and accept congratulations from friends and strangers.

Suddenly, Eric heard a buzzing in the air, like static electricity. He stopped, then glanced around. The seats and theater walls rippled ever so slightly, like the surface of a pond as a water strider skims across it.

"Hey, Mom," Eric said. "Did you see that?"

Diane and Pete moved farther up the aisle, not hearing him. Eric sniffed the air and smelled something strongly metallic and burnt. "I—" he said nervously. "I think—"

There was a horrifying scream from the balcony. A man teetered right on the narrow plaster ledge that separated it from the twenty-foot drop to the seats below. He had bright red hair and wore a checkered blazer and it seemed like he was about to jump.

"No!" the man shrieked. "Make it stop! Please make it stop!"

The balcony behind him was empty of patrons, but there were still a few scattered guests in the theater below, including Eric and his mother and Pete. They all gaped at the man in alarm.

"Hey!" Pete yelled. "Get down from there!"

"That's Walter Rock," his mother said suddenly, like she'd spotted someone in a police lineup. "He works at the Price Slasher," she added.

"Walter!" Pete called. "You're going to fall! Back up now!"

Walter Rock jumped off the balcony like he was escaping a raging fire. In the split-second it took him to reach the floor, Eric's brain took a freeze-frame picture of the man's arms and legs flailing, checkered blazer tails lifted up like a windblown awning, one loafer kicked off and tumbling separately to the floor like a chunk from a wayward asteroid.

Eric's mother screamed as Walter landed on top of several seats with a sickening CRACK, his limbs folded around like a macabre game of Twister.

"Somebody call 9-1-1!" Pete yelled. A woman at the other side of the theater dashed up the aisle and into the lobby.

Eric's mother stood frozen in the aisle, her face paralyzed with shock. Eric pushed past her and ran over to Walter. Blood streamed down the man's cheek from a deep cut in his scalp. A bone jutted horribly through a jagged rupture in his slacks, just above the knee. Eric didn't see his missing shoe.

"Get back!" Pete said. "Don't touch him!"

But something about the man drew Eric closer. He was whispering something over and over again, too far gone to even feel pain.

"What is it?" Eric asked, his voice trembling as he bent down. "What

44

did you see?"

Walter Rock grabbed Eric's wrist. "They're eating each other," he whispered. "I saw one of them up there."

"Who?"

"He had blood all over him," Walter said, his face a mask of pure horror. "I saw one of them and he grinned at me—*like I was next.*"

* * *

They were sitting in a window booth in the Cozy Kitchen. Pete came back from the buffet table then; his plate was piled high with cornbread and fried chicken legs and runny scrambled eggs. He stood there for a few seconds, waiting for Eric's mother to scootch over in the booth so that he could slide in next to her.

"Everyone's talking about what happened to Walter," Pete said, as he began to eat. "Are you guys still shook up?"

"A little," Eric said. "It's not something you see every day."

"That's for daggone sure," Pete said. "I bet he was high on something."

"The paramedics told me he's gonna make it," Eric said.

"Actually, we were just talking about Lance," Eric's mother interjected. Her earrings, which had little jade angels hanging from them, caught the light. "He didn't show up for Eric's training session this morning," she added.

Pete paused, a forkful of eggs halfway to his mouth. "Oh," he said. "Hmm. Well, when am I gonna get to meet this Lance cat?"

"He's always busy," Eric said. "He's an architect and he travels and he surfs all over the world."

Pete exchanged a meaningful glance with Eric's mother. "I could surf," he said. "I'm a quick learner. Actors are constantly learning new skills. I know jiu jitsu. I competed in the Lumberjack Olympics two years in a row. Plus I can cook crepes."

"Surfing takes a lot of practice," Eric said. "You have to be in excellent physical shape."

"Your mother would tell you that I'm quite an outstanding physical specimen," Pete said. He pinched Eric's mother's hip.

"Hush now," she said and smiled.

"Lance teaches me the spiritual side of it, too," Eric said.

"What do you mean by spiritual?" his mother asked.

"It's personal," Eric said. "I don't expect you to understand. You guys are kooks."

"Will you listen to this ornery kid," Pete said. He wiped his mouth with the back of his hand. "Holy smokes," he said.

"Eric," his mother said. "I think it's pretty great that Pete wants to surf with you."

"I really want to," Pete added. "I don't care if it's cold. Or if it's snowing, even. I'll find a wetsuit that fits my bulging muscles."

It was silent then, except for the clatter of dishes and the low chatter of the people in the restaurant.

"Eric," his mother said pointedly.

"I don't want to surf with anyone else except Lance," Eric said. "I'm sorry, that's just the way I feel."

Pete took a gulp of coffee. "What's so great about Lance, anyways?" he asked.

"He's teaching me to be a Soul Surfer," Eric replied. "And I don't understand why you aren't more upset that he's gone."

"I'm sure Lance is fine," Eric's mother said. "Sometimes married couples have—"

Her voice trailed off. She pulled at one of her earrings.

"Maybe an abrupt change of subject would be appropriate right about now," Pete said.

"No," Eric insisted. "I'm tired of having to keep my mouth shut about Dad. I want to know what happened. What'd you do to make him leave?"

"You can't talk to your mother like that, Little Chief," Pete said.

"Did you guys stop having sex?" Eric asked. "Isn't that why couples split up?"

Pete spit out his scrambled eggs. "That's enough," he warned.

"Or maybe he got too kinky for you," Eric said. "Was that it?"

"That's enough, goddammit," Pete said. "We don't talk about things like that here."

"Scrub it, kook," Eric said.

His mother gave Pete a slight, placating smile, then turned to Eric. "Sweetheart," she began. "I know you're upset right now. What happened at the theater scared me, too."

"I'm not talking about that. I want to know why you never went after Dad."

"I'm not sure I wanted to," she replied.

"How can you say that? He bailed on us out of the blue and that's what you think?"

Eric's mother took something out of her purse then. It was an envelope, hand-addressed.

"I don't want to hide this from you any longer," she said softly.

"Diane," Pete countered. "I don't think—"

"No," she insisted. "It's addressed to Eric, so he should read it."

She pushed the letter toward him, across the table. The postmark was SAN DIEGO, CA and the stamp was an upside-down puffer fish.

It was from his father.

Eric stared at the letter. It didn't seem real.

"You opened it," he said. "Why did you open it?"

"Just read it," his mother said. "Please."

Eric opened the letter. It was written on pink stationery. It had an image of a kitten, hanging by its front paws from a tree branch. HANG IN THERE! was written below it in thick black letters. There was a ten dollar bill and two fives along with it.

Dear Ace,

How are you? It has been a long time, I know. I'm sorry about that.

47

I live south of San Diego. Beach town, palm trees, one stoplight in the middle of the main drag. Pelicans. Nobody ever wears shoes, but I got used to that real quick. There's even an oil derrick across the street from me in this old parking lot.

I'm married now, Ace. Her name is Misty. We opened a surf school called Ace's Surf School. Is it OK that I used your name? Misty handles the business part. Snacko Thompson stopped by once, when he was in Diego for a meet. I had him sign a board for you.

Maybe when I get enough dough saved up and if some of my horses come in, I can buy you a plane ticket out here. We've got a spare bedroom in our cottage and I want to fix it up for you. I miss you. I love you.

-Dad

P.S. Here's some money for school supplies or board wax or what-ever you need.

8

Chapter Eight—MARTIN

Martin stood inside a phone booth on Pullman Street, two blocks from The Book Loft. The sliding glass door only closed partway; sparrow feathers drifted across the floor. His nausea had subsided a bit, so he was grateful for that. He was breathing normally and starting to think clearly again.

She's just confused. She's upset and confused and she just needs a little alone time.

He wasn't sure why he had gone in the phone booth. Who was he going to call? He couldn't ask his brother for advice. Lars was probably out on assignment for the television station in downtown Montreal, or spending an intimate Saturday morning with his stunning girlfriend Delphine, eating croissants and French sausages in a waterfront café. Or maybe he was taking her shopping for expensive lingerie and furry high-heeled shoes.

Martin pushed that thought from his head. It was hard not to think about Delphine in a sexual way.

Speaking of intimacy, his sex life with Patti was quite lively, and that was contributing to his confusion. None of his previous girlfriends had ever complimented his performance in bed except for her. Martin's endowment was slightly more than eight and one-fourth inches long, but he'd always felt embarrassed by it, instead of empowered. Patti encouraged his efforts to pleasure her—especially by oral means—so

Martin had gathered a bit of confidence. But even though he was twenty-eight, he was still a bit frightened of the jars full of pink jelly and battery-operated gadgets that she kept in a drawer in her nightstand. Now he was worried that he would never find out exactly what they were used for.

A truck rumbled past, hitting a deep pothole.

THUMP.

The walls of the phone booth shook.

He checked his voicemail. There was a message from Wiley, one of the other security guards, asking him to take his shift that night. That was a no-brainer.

Then there was a message from his landlord, Mr. Polk. Martin was two months late on his rent and Mr. Polk had initiated eviction proceedings. Although he'd expected it, Martin started to get nauseous again. He had very little money; barely any savings except for $183 in an IRA, which he had rolled over from his last job, working as a stockroom assistant for a company that sold pet chew toys.

Finally, there was this:

BEEP

"I need my money by midnight on Sunday, you fucker. Or else I'm sending my boys after you!"

BEEP

Martin had quickly discovered that Webb Turner was the wrong person to borrow money from. And he was even more shocked that an unassuming, well-meaning person like himself would so easily get mixed up with the shadiest person in Great Water. Having a mutual acquaintance with Webb—a busboy at Larry's Lobsters who sold meth on the side—was all it took for Martin to be more than one thousand dollars in the hole. He certainly didn't want to end up like "Snails" McPherson, the local TV repairman who'd lost everything in a messy divorce and borrowed heavily from Webb to keep his shop from going under. The police had found Snails' severed feet in a fountain at the community college, but the rest of him was still unaccounted for.

Since he wanted to live until Thanksgiving at least, Martin knew he had to do something quickly. The only option he had was to ask his mother for help.

* * *

Martin's father had died six months before.

His mother still lived in the ivy-suffocated brick house that Martin and Lars had grown up in, at the bottom of a hill in Goosebeak, the wealthy section of town. Much farther up the hill, past several sharp bends in the road, lived the most well-heeled residents of Great Water: families who had made money in the lumber trade and who owned private boats and had performing arts centers named in their honor.

It was hard for him to visit the house without thinking of his father; Martin had never loved anyone more. George Van Lottom had been a great bear of a man, with an untamed red beard and wispy hair. He constantly knocked into things, breaking china cups and vases as he gestured wildly during his stories of the sunrise he had seen that morning, or the latest blunders of the local politicians. He loved the music of Arlo Guthrie and could play three of his songs on the harmonica, blindfolded.

A month before he died, George Van Lottom had stopped eating. He tried to hide it from Martin and his family at first. But as he became weaker, the skin receded from his cheeks and his eyes became sunken, like two dull lake stones. They had taken him to the hospital and hooked him up to feeding tubes, but it hadn't done any good. His body rejected the nourishment. George Van Lottom simply gave up living.

Martin knew it was because of what had happened almost a year ago, when his father had been accused of exposing himself to two thirteen-year-old girls in Lighthouse Park on a Saturday morning in December. It hadn't been true, of course, but there were stories in the newspapers and testimonies from the girls, who were raccoon-eyed, tube-top wearing vixens from the trailer parks outside of town and seemed like the type who would make up stories, just for the attention. People around town seemed unwilling to let the story disappear and slowly but surely, it wreaked havoc on Martin and his family, like rust devouring a perfect pewter cup.

He had never cried—not once—since his father's funeral, which had been on an uncomfortably cold and rainy May morning when the weather fit the mood of everyone huddled under black umbrellas in the cemetery on Blackhawk Island. Lars gave a brief tribute and his mother thanked everyone for coming, and then his father was in the ground and gone. Afterwards, his mother baked gingersnaps and cherry chocolate bread and had guests over in the parlor, and to Martin, it felt like a Sunday morning after church type of day, not the end of his father's life.

Martin pulled in the driveway. The garage door was closed, and the shades on the second floor windows were still drawn, even though it was nearly ten o'clock. The leaves had been raked and the oak trees stood barren against the slate sky. He knew that the back gardens, which he planted every year, were already frosted over and in hibernation for the winter.

Before he got out of the car, Martin made sure to remove his blood-stained uniform shirt, which left him in a white undershirt. Then he made his way up the three short stone steps to the back door. A late autumn wreath made of dried berries and wheatgrass hung on a nail, just above the knocker. He pushed open the door and stepped inside, stopping to wipe his muddy work boots on the doormat. The smell of baking swept over him: a mix of chocolate and brown sugar that made him lose himself, just for a moment, in the memory of home.

His mother poked her head out from the kitchen. "Martin," she said. "How are you, dear?"

Nora Van Lottom was slim and elegant and had close-cropped gray hair. She wore a cream-colored turtleneck, tan slacks and a checkered apron. Martin extended his cheek for her to kiss.

"Hello, mother."

"You're just in time to help me take the cookies to the O'Hara house. Where's your jacket?"

The kitchen was bright. Baroque classical music played low on the radio. Ingredients and cooking utensils were spread out on the counter in a jumble: a glass jar of flour and a plastic bag filled with chocolate chips; mixing bowls and measuring spoons.

"I'm running late," his mother said. "Help me get this food together."

"Food?"

"The premiere of that film was this morning and then they're having a reception at the house for everyone," she said. "And reenactments of course. You promised that you'd help me set up."

"I forgot all about that," Martin admitted.

She glanced at him with a familiar look. He was sure she could tell that something was wrong; his eyes were bloodshot and his voice sounded shaky and frail.

"Have you been getting enough sleep?"

"Definitely not," Martin said, and laughed unconvincingly.

"Are they working you too hard at the mall?"

"As usual," he said. "But I'm earning my money. A woman tried to kill herself this morning. I had to call 9-1-1. The cops interviewed me for twenty minutes."

His mother didn't seem to be listening. He felt like he was speaking a foreign language, like Swahili.

"It's been kind of a rough morning," he added. "But I'm tough, I'll get through it."

His mother sighed. "You never told me what happened with Lance Bloomquist," she said. "I thought he was going to write you a letter of recommendation after that project you helped him with. The outdoor garden at that building in Toronto."

"That hasn't exactly happened yet," Martin said.

She touched his cheek. "You aren't eating properly," she said. "Could you tell Dr. Fong that when you see him?"

"See him when?"

"Your checkup," she said, and frowned. "I called to remind you, didn't you get my message? You have an appointment at eleven thirty this morning."

"No," Martin said. "I forgot. That's what happens when you call and make appointments for me."

"You aren't taking good care of yourself, Martin. You worry about everyone else too much."

"I'm taking those multi-vitamins you gave me," he said. "And I just bought a set of free weights. I've designed my own exercise program to target each of the major muscle groups."

He decided not to tell her about the $49.95 ab roller that had arrived on his doorstep two days before. Martin was easily swayed by persuasive TV commercials but then often forgot that he had even ordered the item in the first place.

His mother stared at him. It was the same probing look that he had seen dozens of times.

"Do me a favor and get my good blue coat from the front closet," she finally said. "And I'm sure you've left an extra jacket here that you can wear."

The front of the house was dark and silent, save for the ticking of the ancient grandfather clock at the foot of the stairs. Martin passed the parlor, where his father had spent the last days of his life, sleeping fitfully on the sofa bed and drinking brandy and watching old Packers games that he'd recorded on VHS, sometimes calling Martin in to witness instant replays that he deemed particularly spectacular.

The ghost of his father still hovered there. Martin could still see his pale, gnarled feet, sticking out of his pajama bottoms, the last days before he died. He remembered his father's touch on his shoulder, once firm and loving, then frail and distant, as Martin lifted him off the couch and into his wheelchair.

"Dad," he whispered. "Dad, can you hear me? Why did you have to go? Why did you have to leave me here?"

Martin stood there in the front hallway, listening. He heard the ticking of the grandfather clock, and the classical music coming from the radio in the kitchen. He felt the tears welling up, but he willed them away.

Suddenly, he sensed someone behind him, standing in the corner. There was an electrical pulse in the air, like agitated lightning bugs swarming around his head.

Martin swallowed hard. A single bead of sweat formed on his forehead. He waited for what seemed like forever, petrified to even move.

"Mom?" he whispered.

"We have to go now," she replied, as she entered the hallway and went to the coat closet. "I don't want to be late."

His heart beating faster, Martin turned around slowly and checked behind him.

There was no one there.

* * *

The O'Hara house was on Sunrise Avenue, which meandered across the hill and sloped down toward town and the lake beyond. Jack Spivey had murdered Benjamin O'Hara in a jealous rage in the upstairs master bedroom, and shot O'Hara's daughter Bridget on the front lawn, in the middle of a patch of withered dandelions. Historians insisted that he didn't mean to kill her, but Martin had his doubts.

Martin's mother became head docent of the O'Hara house shortly after his father died. Nora Van Lottom had always been fascinated by local history and quickly became a favorite at the house because of her sweet, attentive manner, and her willingness to discuss gruesome subjects. Nora had taught Martin the longshoremen's ghoulish song about Lucy O'Hara when he was six years old.

His mother parked in one of the reserved spaces in an adjacent lot. A man walked past them in a German World War I Army outfit, drinking a cup of coffee and eating a cornbread muffin. He had apparently been shot in the eye.

"It looks like the cast of the movie is here," Martin's mother said excitedly. He followed her out of the car and waited as she opened the rear door of her S.U.V. "Hattie Templeton told me we're expecting at least two hundred townies for the reception," she said. "Plenty of trunk slammers, too." She handed Martin several Tupperware containers. "Take these cookies and follow me into the kitchen," she said.

Martin stood there, staring at the bare maple trees, thinking how much he missed Patti's touch, her soft breath on his neck when they held each other.

"Mom," he said. "There's something I need to ask you."

"I had a feeling," she replied.

"I need to borrow some money."

"What is it? What's wrong?"

A person in a giant Pierre the Bear costume waddled past, nearly tripping over one of the railroad ties in the parking lot.

"You're making commitments to phone solicitors again, aren't you? They're the bane of my existence. I told you to just hang up. Then the pledge card comes in the mail and you feel guilty! I thought I talked to you about this."

Martin swallowed hard. "It's my car," he said.

His mother blinked. She closed the rear door of the SUV. "Well, haven't you been getting the oil changed?"

"I ran over a plastic tarp a couple of weeks ago," Martin said. "It melted a bit and now the undercarriage is entirely corroded. And the muffler needs to be replaced."

He was surprised at how easily the lies were coming. At least the muffler part was true.

"That sounds serious. How much is that going to cost?"

"One thousand, three hundred dollars," Martin said, pulling the figure out of the air. "I took it to that shop on Pinewood, where Chris

Burgess used to work. That's where I got the estimate."

"Well, Martin," his mother said. "That's a significant amount of money."

"I'm supposed to be getting a promotion," Martin said. "Off the night shift and maybe become a supervisor."

Another lie.

"That's something positive," his mother replied.

"And then I can start paying you back. Giving you part of my paycheck each month. With interest, if you want."

"Martin."

"We can even draw up some kind of contract if you want."

"Martin," his mother said again. "Tell me what's really going on."

"I told you," he said. A breeze blew his curly brown hair in his eyes. Every joint in his body ached with the need for sleep.

"No. What do you really need the money for?"

Martin looked at her. "Mom," he said. "I don't want to—"

"I want so much for you to be happy," she said. "I want you to be settled like your brother is. But it just seems like you always have these, these hardships."

"Hardships? What do you mean by that?"

"You get mixed up with these women who don't treat you with respect. They're no good for you. Like that carnival worker, and the woman who was an ex-convict."

"She was a prison guard," Martin said. "She used to be a prison guard. Part time."

"I want you to find a nice woman. And now this purple hair girl, well, I have my doubts."

"I love Patti," Martin interrupted.

"That's what you always tell me. That's what you say, each time you bring them to the house for Sunday dinner. But then you end up going your separate ways."

"I care deeply for Patti," Martin said again. "You just don't know her yet."

His mother smiled. "I sure hope that's the case," she said. "I hope you're right. And if you need thirteen hundred dollars for your car, that's fine. You're my son and you need reliable transportation. But if it's for something else, and you're not telling me the truth, then you're going to have to deal with that yourself."

9

Chapter Nine—JENNY

No one was at the beach at Spivey Point; her only companions were the shadowy water and the jagged rocks and the dead beach grass. The buzz of the disconnected phone line still echoed in Jenny's mind, its unanswered questions swarming like angry hornets. She'd checked the garage—his Jeep was still there. And there was no note from him under a magnet on the refrigerator or left on the table in the foyer. No messages on her voicemail, either.

Somehow, some way, her husband's disappearance had to connect to everything that had happened—the electricity going haywire, the satanic hound in her garden and the stampede of horses through her back hall. But Jenny was unwilling to scribble it her spiral notebook yet. She prided herself on being practical, even in a town like Great Water where people profited off the unusual and macabre, and she wanted to try every path before she turned down the one that was most unfamiliar.

Turning from the water, she made her way up the short sandy hill to the road. Jenny paused there for a second, a thick wall of fir trees and moss in front of her, broken only by a dark space where their driveway met the asphalt.

She decided to walk down the road in the opposite direction, toward the bridge. It spanned Brisco Creek as it spewed into the lake in a tumble of churning rapids. Dragonflies darted there in the summer, and men in wide-brimmed hats cast fishing lines for sunnies and small-mouthed bass. The water there was deep, twenty feet at least.

Maybe Lance had fallen, or been hit by a car and lay by the side of the road, unable to move or call. Having a mother like Jenny's had equipped her with the ability to easily imagine the worst.

She stopped in the middle of the bridge and looked down. The creek would be frozen in another few weeks with the onset of the long winter. Oak leaves floated in the water, spinning in circles in the current.

Suddenly she heard a noise—a metallic humming—coming from the top of the creek bank.

Jenny glanced to her right, to the edge of the woods. She saw someone—a blond little girl—disappear into the pines.

"Hello?" Jenny called after her. "Wait a second!"

She ran to where the girl had stood just moments before. The tall grass at the edge of the bridge abutment lay trampled down in a path that led away from the road. It almost appeared like a narrow plow had veered off the road and into the woods.

Jenny bent down to take a closer look. The dry weeds and switchgrass were straightening ever so slightly, returning to their normal position, but the trail was unmistakable. So was the hoof print in the soft dirt.

"Hello?" she called into the forest, her voice wavering. She stepped off the bridge and followed the trampled path as it sloped away from the road. It ran alongside the creek, over flat granite slabs and under crooked pine trees with peeling bark. Jenny had never explored this part of the woods before, but she knew that the creek would eventually lead back to their yard and the rock garden and the pergola.

"Is anyone there?" Jenny yelled. She stopped and listened expec-tantly. Leaves drifted down and landed on the ground; a squirrel scampered into the underbrush. But no one answered.

Jenny knew very few of her neighbors along the Cove Road; most houses were the summer residences of wealthy lawyers and corporate executives from places far away. She'd never spotted any small children on the beach or playing by the creek. She was beginning to wonder if the girl she'd seen was real.

"Daddy?"

Jenny glanced around, her pulse quickening. She couldn't tell what direction the small voice had come from. "Who's there?" she yelled.

"Mommy's gone!"

"Tell me where you are! Tell me where you are and I'll come find you!"

It was clearly a little girl's voice, one she'd never heard before. But the acoustics in the forest were skewed; she couldn't determine if she was ten feet away, or a hundred. There was definite fear in the girl's cry for help. It seared right through Jenny's heart and brought out a fierce protective instinct she'd never felt until that moment.

"Can you hear me?" Jenny yelled, spinning around, desperately searching for any sign of the child she'd seen. The only reply was the rushing of the creek as it tumbled toward the lake.

There was a sudden flash of red in the feeble morning sun and she spotted a child's plastic pail at the edge of the water. Puzzled, Jenny leaned down to pick it up; it was the kind children took to the beach to make sand castles with.

As she examined the pail, an enormous black beetle crawled onto the handle, mere inches from her fingers. It looked like a carnivorous beast straight out of the Amazon jungle.

The beetle hissed at her and clicked its pincers. Then it lunged at her thumb and Jenny let go of the pail with a yelp. It fell into the creek and floated away.

The clicking noise intensified. Jenny turned back to the path and saw an undulating carpet of beetles, more than twenty insects across, streaming toward her. She leapt up on a dead tree stump with a shout as the insects massed around its base, gnashing their pincers. They glared at her with bright red eyes. A stench of sulfur filled her nostrils.

Some of the beetles climbed up the bark. Jenny kicked at them, smashing their shells with her tennis shoes. She imagined their pincers digging into her flesh, tearing ragged chunks from her fingers, and she kicked harder, more desperately. After what seemed like an eternity, the clicking became a collective hum. The beetles moved en masse in the direction that Jenny had come from.

She stepped off the stump and tried to catch her breath. The path veered sharply off to the right and as Jenny moved forward cautiously, she found herself in a dirt clearing scattered with pine needles. And standing not twenty feet ahead, in a clump of dead weeds at the edge of the water, stood the little girl.

"Hey," Jenny called. "Why'd you run away?"

The girl was at least seven years old. She wore a plaid taffeta blouse and matching skirt. Her knee socks were black and a wide-brimmed straw hat shielded her face. She stared at a spot in the clearing.

"Where are your parents?" Jenny asked. "Are you lost?"

The girl swayed side to side like a metronome. She seemed blurry, like she was made of television static. Something about her was familiar.

"Have you seen a man with blond hair around here?" Jenny asked, her pulse quickening again. "A man with blond hair and a gray beard? Have you seen anyone like that?"

The girl was humming—a low, guttural sound like a band of thunder—and rocking back and forth.

She held a Pierre the Bear toy in one hand.

Jenny knew then that things were deeply, deeply wrong. But she couldn't move.

"What are you doing back here, all by yourself?" she asked the girl. "I just want to talk. Why won't you speak to me?"

The girl turned to face her then. Jenny felt her heart sink.

It was Bridget O'Hara.

No.

"Hsssh," Bridget rasped, and raised her arm. She pointed a bone-white finger at Jenny. "Hsssh," she whispered. "Hsssh."

There was a gaping hole in the little girl's cheek. The flesh was torn like a gunshot wound just below her left eye, and there was bright white bone and gristle underneath. A beetle crawled out of it and clung to her chin.

Jenny screamed.

Bridget took a step toward her.

"HSSSH..."

The little girl's rasping hum grew louder as she stumbled across the clearing toward Jenny, lurching, dragging her shiny black shoes in the dirt.

Jenny felt paralyzed. She wasn't sure if what she was seeing was real.

The hollow blare of a horn echoed in her ears.

The air in the clearing parted for a split second, and Bridget was gone. The Pierre toy fell in the weeds where she had stood just a few seconds before.

Jenny's heart pounded as she picked up the wooden bear with shaking hands, then searched frantically for the path—any path—that would lead her out of the dark woods. She spotted trampled ground on the other side of the creek and dashed across the shallow water, her tennis shoes instantly soaked.

Climbing up the bank on the other side, she ran down the path of flattened pine needles, past rotted tree stumps, branches ripping at her clothes. Bridget's whisper rattled in her ears and she screamed, pleading for it to stop. The pine trees thinned then and her back yard came into view, followed by the corner of her house, and Jenny realized that the trampled ground led right through the rock garden to her husband's study and the pantry and everything that had happened that morning.

10

Chapter Ten—ERIC

Eric was still at the restaurant. Thoughts pounded through his brain like the surf at Pipeline; they rushed past too fast for him to grab. His father was married now and living in California and he was okay. He wanted Eric to come out to see him. He was surfing every day. There were pelicans and palm trees there. He was okay and he still loved him.

He still loved him.

"Eric," his mother said. "Listen to me. I don't want you anywhere near him."

"Mom," Eric said. "Just bag it, okay?"

"You watch your mouth, young man," his mother replied. "Watch your mouth and listen to me."

The film director came over to their table. She still wore a poncho, even though they were indoors. It was crocheted and had lightning bolts and black thunderclouds all over it.

She leaned down and kissed Pete on the cheek. She touched his lips with her index finger. "My star," she said. "You're my big Marlon Brando, my big John Wayne." She sounded like she had a mouthful of marbles.

"Um," Eric's mother said. "Excuse me."

"We're in the middle of a family discussion, Silke," Pete said to the film director. "Thank you, though. Thanks for that enthusiasm."

"I'm glad the film was so well received," Eric's mother said, glaring at Pete, but speaking to the film director. "You really did well by our town."

Eric pushed his plate aside and got up from the table.

"Where do you think you're going?" his mother asked.

"Home," Eric said. He made his way across the restaurant, past the counter where people sat eating cheeseburgers and pasties and sipping blue mugs of coffee.

Pete grabbed his arm then. He grabbed Eric's arm and turned him a bit, so they were face to face as they stood near the hostess stand, right near the door. Eric didn't realize Pete had followed him.

"C'mon, Little Chief," Pete said, wiping his mouth with the back of his hand. He always called Eric that. "Why don't you come back and sit down so we can discuss this?"

"Why, what's the point?" Eric said. "She won't listen to me. None of you will listen."

"That's not true. You tell me now. Tell me what you've got to say."

Eric looked Pete in his good eye. He could tell by the way Pete stood there expectantly, waiting for Eric's next words, that he really wanted to help.

"This is family stuff, Pete," Eric said, his voice softening a bit. "You haven't been around long enough to understand it."

Pete blinked twice, and took his hand from Eric's arm. "What's this really about?" he asked. "You can tell me. I'm actually a highly sensitive person."

There are the nights I lie in bed, wondering when Dad will come home, wondering if I'll always feel so alone. Wondering what I did to make him leave.

"It's about people keeping secrets from me," Eric replied. "It's always been that way, as long as I can remember."

"Do you mean your mom?" Pete asked. "I really don't think that's a fair accusation."

"Why don't people trust me? Why can't they tell me the truth?"

"Look," Pete said. "I'm real sorry I grabbed you. Please come back and sit with us. Finish your meal. We can talk about it."

Pete was speaking to him, but Eric couldn't hear any words. He only heard the fluttering of pelicans, and the metallic grind of an oil derrick, pumping away in the dark. He had never heard those sounds before, but he was able to imagine them, at that moment.

"Tell my mom I said goodbye," Eric said. He ran past the hostess stand and out the door, into the cold morning.

* * *

It was only a twenty-two minute jog back home, according to Eric's waterproof watch, and he wanted to keep moving. His brain functioned better when he was in motion.

The streets were empty, even though it was almost noon. He passed the post office and the Christmas tree lot. Potholes buckled the cement and the sewer gratings overflowed with dead leaves. A faint damp breeze blew up from the lake. Far off on the horizon, beyond Blackhawk Island and the bay, hard gray clouds gathered in a strong line, like soldiers readying for battle.

Eric didn't want to be anywhere else but with his dad. That was clear to him now. The memories of their time together, of his dad cheering from the shore as Eric caught his first wave, were still too strong to forget. And since Lance was gone, maybe even for good, then Eric figured that it was finally time to start making decisions for himself, deciding what was right instead of leaving that up to his mother and Pete and adults who didn't have a clue what they were talking about.

Since his father had a spare room in his cottage by the beach, maybe Eric could live there and learn to shape surfboards properly. Maybe he could even help his father give lessons at Ace's Surf School. Eric didn't know the official rules in California, but maybe he wouldn't have to go to school if his dad taught him at home.

I love you.

66

Eric couldn't remember the last time someone had told him that. Since his father left, Eric had felt like a balloon floating up into the sky, lonely and small as it disappeared into the gray beyond. He spent much of his time alone, except for at school, where packs of girls in discount designer jeans followed him around the hallways at Great Water High, whispering to each other about how cute he was. Girls were bolts of dangerous energy that he strove to avoid at all costs, along with Mr. Mudd, his Algebra teacher, who constantly called on him in class with questions that he could barely understand, let alone answer.

Surfing was the only time he ever felt truly safe and at peace. It was the only time when no one could touch him.

Eric stopped at the bottom of the steps that led up to his apartment, and he knew then that he shouldn't have lingered there, for the cold black thing rushed back to him in a flash, the memory that was always in the back of his mind:

Eric, I need you to shovel off the steps. It's icy there and someone's gonna slip—

Then: his mother lying at the foot of the icy steps in the snow, clutching her rounded middle, screaming.

Eric!

It had been only that past February and his mother had fallen all the way down the steps, scraping her forehead and her knees and then, in the hospital room with the heavy curtains drawn shut, she had lost the baby. The baby that she and Pete had created together, Eric's little brother or maybe a sister, was gone.

Of course Eric's mother told him that losing the baby had nothing to do with him, that she could have slipped anywhere, it was just an accident, but Eric never believed it. He had forgotten to shovel the steps, but maybe he didn't want his mother to have the baby at all. The thought of his mother creating a new family with Pete and without his dad and without all the things he remembered from his childhood, like the Pizza Hut on Saturday nights or his father letting his mother win at Monopoly, made his stomach ache. Sometimes he even felt like crying.

* * *

According to the United States map that hung on the wall above his bed, right next to the poster of Snacko Thompson shredding Yak's Teeth, San Diego was only three-and-a-half hand widths away from Lake Michigan. Eric wasn't sure how long it would take to get there, but he wondered if Tuesday was being too optimistic. He had a fourth period Algebra test and preferred to be on the other side of the country by then. He could even get there in time to watch the Macy's parade on TV with his dad on Thursday morning. Eric wondered if they ate turkey for Thanksgiving in California, or maybe something healthier, like tofu.

He took a look around his room, trying to shift his racing mind into packing mode. There were several precariously piled stacks of library books on his desk. Eric always checked out more books than any normal human being would be able to read, but he never regretted it. He liked learning random facts and snippets about a wide range of subjects. And paying overdue fees helped support Great Water's struggling public library, which was about the size of a three-car garage.

Managing money had never been one of his strong points, especially since he never had much of it. He had sixteen dollars in his wallet, and another eight rolled up in a tube sock in his underwear drawer, for emergencies. Eric removed the money from the sock and added it to his traveling fund, along with the twenty dollars from his father. He located two pairs of clean underwear in the drawer as well, and a pair of black dress socks, which he normally only wore for special occasions, like when the eighth grade choir performed at the Ice Sculpture Festival. Eric figured it would be best to wear handsome socks when he met his father's new wife, Misty, in order to make a positive impression.

His favorite board shorts were light blue with dolphins on them, and he added them to the pile, along with a woolen ski cap, in the event of snow. He didn't have a suitcase, or even a duffel bag, because he had never traveled anywhere before. He decided to use his backpack to carry his important belongings. It had an extra zippered compartment inside, in which he placed two jars of board wax and his green toothbrush. He put his clothes in the backpack and his University of Michigan hockey puck that his best friend Taco Wallace had brought him back from a trip to the Lower Peninsula that summer.

Eric decided that he wouldn't take a razor with him. He figured that if he grew a beard during the trip, it would make him look older, and that could only be beneficial to him in the long run.

Hey kid, what're you doing back there, in the back of the bus? Hey kid—oh, excuse me, sir, I thought you were a fourteen-year-old kid who might be running away from home.

The only problem with that theory was that he had not yet grown any real facial hair yet, save for a vague speckling above his lips. The hair he was managing to grow was appearing in unusual places that were invisible to the naked eye. Eric wasn't sure how to speed up the process; whether there was a food he could eat—like spinach or oatmeal—that might help. He knew from history class that the Vikings were blonder than him and had thick beards and mustaches. Eric didn't see why he should be any different.

Money was potentially a problem. Forty-four dollars might not be enough cash to get him to California. Eric figured that he could work along the way, like in the Sally Field movie he had watched with his mother about a blind gardener who went from house to house during the Great Depression, begging for work in exchange for leftover stew and a bed for the night.

* * *

Before he left for good, Eric went out back, to the shack where his father used to shape surfboards. There was something he had remembered, something very important that he needed to check.

He rarely went to the shack because it made him miss his father too much. Whenever he entered the stuffy room, he could still imagine the smell of sawdust and fiberglass, and the fact that his father had left all of that behind made him angry and confused.

As Eric unlocked the door and stepped inside, he thought he heard his father's gruff voice.

You keep sweeping up, Ace. One day I'm gonna teach you how to shape your own boards.

But there was no one there, only the cold quiet room with a metal platform in the center and a single window, rimmed with cobwebs. A pair of safety goggles lay on a workbench. A yellowed poster of Gerry Lopez hung crookedly on one wall, its edges thick with mildew.

An old Polaroid was taped underneath the poster. Eric had never really paid it much attention, but overhearing his mother talk about the board had made him remember it.

In the photo, his father stood next to a woman with long blond hair on a rocky beach. His father had shaggy hair, also blond, and wore cut-off shorts and a beaded necklace. He appeared to be about twenty years old, and held a board with a badger painted on it.

The woman was smiling; it was the content look of a woman in love. She had one hand on a surfboard. It was the same butterfly surfboard that was sitting on Eric's front porch.

11

Chapter Eleven—JENNY

I t was past lunchtime when Jenny arrived at the police station in downtown Great Water. The building was across the street from a public park, where gulls swooped around an elderly woman feeding them bread crumbs from a plastic bag.

Jenny's mother was waiting for her near the front entrance of the building, smoking a cigarette. She wore a faux rabbit fur coat and bright red slacks. "What the hell happened?" she asked, stubbing out her cigarette in a potted pine tree.

"I told you on the phone, mother," Jenny said. "Lance is gone."

"Well where is he? Where could Mr. Superstar Architect be?"

"He didn't come back from the lake this morning," Jenny said. "His car's still in the driveway. I called all of his closest friends and no one has heard from him."

Jenny's mother sniffed, then wiped her nose with the back of her hand. Her short strawberry-blond hair was thinning at the temples. Jenny had never noticed that before.

"Jennifer," her mother said, her breath hovering in the air. "Why would he just run off like that?"

"I don't know. He kissed me goodbye this morning and told me he loved me and now he's gone."

"Did he drown? Did he run off with some other floozy who was after him for his money?"

71

Jenny felt her heart twist, but she decided to let the insult pass. "I don't know," she said. "I was hoping the police could help me. Why are you wearing your fur?"

"I wanted to look nice," her mother replied, as if it were an absurd question. "Why are you carrying that toy? Haven't you showered this morning? You look like a concentration camp victim."

Jenny felt tears start to well up; she blinked them away. "Where's Dad? Why didn't you bring him?"

"I didn't tell your father because I didn't want to worry him," her mother replied. "You know how ill he is."

"I need him here," Jenny said.

Her mother leaned over and kissed her on her cheek. Her breath was sour and damp.

"You're going to have to make do with me," she said. "Now, let's go inside and get this over with."

* * *

Jenny and her mother took a seat at the desk of a young police officer. His neck was bright pink.

"We ordered burritos for lunch from Poncho's and mine had bell pepper in it," he explained to them. "I'm pretty allergic."

"Poncho's burritos usually have peppers in them, genius," an older policewoman said from across the room. The phone at her desk was ringing off the hook, but she ignored it. Other officers rushed about, taking statements from numerous town residents who all seemed upset or frightened or some combination of the two. The station was in crisis mode, but the officer talking to Jenny was completely relaxed.

"Sometimes my eyes swell shut," the young officer continued, as he took a sip from his massive plastic soda cup. "When you're allergic to different foods, the symptoms can be real diverse. Chris Slater, this guy I work with, says that—"

"Maybe you'd like to know what happened this morning," Jenny interrupted. "I'm very concerned that something has happened to my husband."

"Well, first off, I was curious why you brought me a Pierre toy," the officer said. He picked up the wooden toy that Jenny had taken from the creek bed.

"The little girl left it behind," Jenny said.

"Little girl?"

"The one I saw by the creek near my house."

"Who was she?"

Jenny looked from the police officer to her mother. "I'm not positive," Jenny said. "But I think it was Bridget O'Hara."

"Jennifer," her mother said. She smiled embarrassedly at the officer.

He put down his soda cup. Tiny black hairs curled around the edge of his nostrils; his necktie had a sailboat pattern on it. "That little girl has been dead since 1918," he began.

"I know how insane it sounds," Jenny replied. "But I'm telling you what I saw. Something strange is happening around Spivey Point."

"Did you say Spivey Point?" the older policewoman interjected.

Jenny nodded. "I saw her," she insisted. "Bridget was there and she spoke to me. Then she disappeared and left that toy behind. It was right there by the creek in the woods."

"That's a new one," the policeman said, stifling a chuckle.

The older policewoman got up from her chair and walked over to them. "Roger," she said, "are you listening to what she's saying?"

The policeman seemed not to hear. "You're saying this is the original toy?" he asked.

"Yes," Jenny said, her face reddening. "The one they found in Jack Spivey's cabin after he killed himself."

He leaned across the desk. The end of his tie dipped in a mound of salsa he had dumped on a piece of aluminum foil. "Really," he said.

"I'm not making this up," Jenny insisted.

"I'm not a historian," the officer said. "Nora Van Lottom at the O'Hara house, she's the lady who would know all about it."

KINGS OF THE EARTH

"She's Martin's mother," Jenny's mother said. "Didn't you go to school with him? Tall boy with messy hair?"

"Roger," the older policewoman said again. "Do you know about the Graham woman?"

"Who's that?" Jenny asked.

The woman handed her a piece of paper. *MISSING*, it said across the top in large block letters, colored in with red and green magic markers. A blurred photo of a young woman was Xeroxed onto the page. She had feathered hair and wore a turtleneck sweater. One of her eyes was set higher than the other, like a crooked jigsaw puzzle.

MISSING: Bernadette "Bernie" Graham, the paper read. It listed her height and weight and date of birth. *Last seen near Brisco Creek Bridge on Saturday, November 20.*

Jenny took in a breath. *This morning.*

Please contact her husband Michael at this phone number, the paper read at the bottom. *Thank you for reading this.*

"He was here about an hour ago," the policewoman said. "Wanted to file a missing person report. Told us some ridiculous story about horses taking his wife away. It sounded to me like he'd been hitting the Rolling Rock again."

"You knew the crazies would come out of the woodwork this weekend," the policeman told his coworker. "Like that woman who slit her wrists at the Stroll this morning. All that blood red moon hooey. People saying they had dreams about this and that."

"What?" Jenny exclaimed. "What are you talking about?"

"Bunch of *Blair Witch Project* mumbo jumbo," he answered. "Some folks have seen too many scary movies."

"Well, I think people choose to believe in these stories to help them make sense of their personal psychological turmoil," the policewoman said.

"I'm sure that's true in my daughter's case," Jenny's mother said. "Wouldn't you agree, Jennifer?"

* * *

Jenny splashed cold water on her face from a drinking fountain in the lobby. Her mother stood nearby.

"Listen," the older woman said. "It's one thing if Lance drowned in the lake or got hit by a car or ran off with some hussy. But you can't expect the police to help you if you make up stories about ghosts and horses in your hallway. And think about how it reflects on your father and me. It's just not appropriate."

Jenny picked up the Pierre toy. "What do you think this is?" she asked. "Do you think I bought it at a souvenir shop in town?"

Her mother didn't blink. "You used to make up some really fantastic stories when you were a little girl. They were obvious cries for attention. I watch Oprah, you know. I understand the psychology."

"I don't know why I expected you to be even the least bit sympathetic," Jenny said. She had already decided that she wasn't going to tell her mother she was pregnant. Not anytime soon, at least.

"Well, I'm a realist. Take it or leave it. Now I recommend that you go back in that room and apologize to that officer for wasting his time. If Lance has been murdered or abducted by a cult, there's not much you can do about it, is there?"

"I don't have to apologize for a thing."

There was a long silence.

"Well," her mother said. "Always doing things your own way. Far be it from me to try to help."

She turned and strode out the sliding glass doors, into the chilly afternoon.

Jenny stood there, too upset to cry. She wanted desperately to go see her father, who spent most days in bed or sitting on the front porch, wrapped in an old bathrobe and reading paperback Westerns. He had recently taken to going for walks on his own, without telling his mother or Grace, the nurse who took care of him. Jenny just needed him to tell her that everything was going to be okay.

12

Chapter Twelve—MARTIN

G oosebeak Medical Center was the largest hospital within thirty miles, so it attracted patients from up and down the shore. Martin dreaded going there because it reminded him of the countless hours he'd spent at his father's bedside.

He walked across the spotless lobby and stepped inside an empty elevator. A Carpenters song played intrusively from hidden speakers.

A kiss for luck and we're on our way...

Martin pushed the "eight" button and kept his eyes on the tiled floor. He realized with dismay as the doors closed that his work boots were still caked with mud.

THUMP.

He glanced up, startled. It sounded like someone had dropped a bowling ball on the ceiling above him, which of course made no logical sense whatsoever. It definitely wasn't a noise that any reasonable person would associate with a properly working elevator.

The walls around him shuddered and groaned, as if straining to support an enormous weight. Martin jabbed the button again, willing the elevator to move. He glanced up. Was the ceiling bulging downward, right in the center? Or was it just—

Just what?

He checked the floor indicator. The "L" lit up and then went dark, like it had gained a mind of its own. The elevator began to descend.

Wait a second!

Martin turned around and gestured frantically to the security camera perched above him as the elevator continued to go down. "Hey!" he hollered. "Hey! Is anyone there?"

THUMP.

There's someone—or something—above me.

He pushed the red emergency button like his life depended on it. The elevator stopped with a jolt and everything went pitch black.

"Hello?" he called, a feeble waver in his voice. An unassailable chill invaded the compartment; the frigid air in the elevator shaft had finally found its way in.

THUMP.

It's right above me.

Martin's training for the security guard position at Harborfront Stroll had instilled in him a refusal to panic under any circumstances, but something told him what was happening wasn't at all normal. He pawed the control panel in the darkness, pressing buttons randomly as the music sputtered to life again—

Sharing horizons that are new to us—

Karen Carpenter's voice was like a thick needle jabbing his spinal cord. "Hey!" he yelled at the top of his lungs, in the slim chance that someone could hear him in the blackness. "Help! I'm in here!"

We've only just begun—

THUMP.

I'm gonna die in here, Martin realized desperately, his eyes stinging with icy tears. *I'm going to freeze to death in a pitch dark hospital elevator. Or a monster is gonna rip its way in here and claw me to bloody shreds. And I don't think anyone's even gonna miss me.*

Then, like the opening curtain at a macabre play, the doors rumbled open. Martin took a deep, shuddering breath and realized that the elevator had never left the lobby.

* * *

He got off on the eighth floor and made a right. Immediately, he spotted two policemen standing in the hallway outside of Dr. Fong's office.

Martin nodded at them as he approached. The taller of the two had a shaved head and a biker moustache and looked like he could pile drive Martin into the carpet like The Ultimate Warrior.

"You're Martin van Lottom," the cop said, like he was reading Martin his rights. His name plate said SLATER.

"That's correct," Martin said, surprised. "Yes, I am."

"Can I ask what're you doing here?"

"I have an appointment with Dr. Fong," Martin replied.

"Is that right," the cop said. He was blocking the door to the office. His neck was steroid-thick and his shoulders were boulders underneath his dark blue shirt. He had one hand on his baton, which was strapped to his belt.

Martin wondered if the cop knew about his Webb Turner situation. He didn't think asking would be a good idea; he was still perspiring heavily in the aftermath of the elevator incident.

"It's for a checkup," Martin said, his voice catching. "It's for my regular yearly checkup."

The cop regarded him for a long moment. Martin wondered if he had time to run.

"Funny coincidence," the cop finally said. "I heard what happened this morning at the Stroll. Good thing you were there to stop that woman from doing herself in."

Martin let out his breath all at once. "I did what I could," he said.

"Her coworkers are taking it hard," the cop said. "But it looks like she's gonna be okay."

The cop took a step to his right and Martin squeezed past him into the office.

Another cop was interviewing the front desk clerk, so a nurse checked Martin in on the computer and gave him some forms to fill out. There was an upside-down Thanksgiving pilgrim taped to the back of the monitor.

"How is Pearl doing?" Martin asked.

"Thankfully her cuts weren't as deep as they first thought," the nurse said. She wiped her nose. It looked like she'd been crying.

"Well, that's a relief," Martin said. He knew that Pearl had worked there for ten years at least, maybe more.

"They stitched her up, but now she's in Psych."

"Psych?"

"Getting evaluated," the nurse said. "Pearl said she saw a Viking riding a horse, right across the middle of the lake."

* * *

Dr. Joshua Fong was in incredible shape for a fifty-one-year-old man. He had all his original teeth, enormous biceps and no gray hairs. He practiced medicine on Saturdays because every Monday he took a thirty-seven-mile bike ride across the Upper Peninsula, regardless of the weather.

Dr. Fong sat in a chair across from Martin in the examining room. He had finished taking Martin's blood pressure, as well as poking and prodding him in every conceivable way.

"How are you doing, Martin?" Dr. Fong asked. "I mean, really?"

"Well, I'm still a little shook up," Martin said. "I'd never seen someone try to commit suicide before."

"Of course not," Dr. Fong replied. "We all love Pearl. And if in the next few days, you have trouble sleeping or functioning, because of what you saw, I want you to give me a call."

"Okay," Martin replied. "I'm sure I'll be fine, though."

"As for your exam, I have plenty of concerns. Your blood pressure is too high. And something tells me that you haven't changed your diet at all, even though your cholesterol was well into the red zone at your last checkup."

"It's challenging to make those lifestyle changes," Martin said. "I work all the time."

"I'd like you to cut back on the caffeine and get on a regular exercise program," Dr. Fong said. "This doesn't mean mowing the lawn once a week. I need you to get your heart rate up for thirty, forty minutes. Three times a week at the least."

"Okay. Is that all?"

"You haven't told me how you've been feeling. Emotional well-being is equally as important as physical health."

"Most of the time, I feel swell," Martin said. "Like I said, I'm always working, so that doesn't give me a chance to think about other stuff."

"Martin," Dr. Fong said, and smiled widely. His teeth were perfectly white. "Please. You can trust me."

Martin sighed. There was a poster next to the blood pressure machine of a pit bull licking a rabbit. HAPPINESS IS INFECTIOUS, it said.

"I have headaches," he finally admitted. "Not just once in a while, but all the time. It feels like my brain is trying to break out of my skull."

Dr. Fong scribbled something on his clipboard. "Go on."

"Also, I'll be just sitting at home, watching TV maybe, and I feel my heartbeat speed up. For no apparent reason."

"Why didn't you tell me about this sooner?"

"I figured there's nothing anyone can do about it. Besides, I'm used to dealing with things on my own."

"I want to help you," Dr. Fong said. "These symptoms you're describing, they could be signs of something more serious."

"Like what?"

"I'm not the right person to make a judgment on that. But it's clear to me that you're not eating right, you're not exercising and you're sleep-deprived. This could open the floodgates to a whole family of problems down the road."

Martin imagined the Hoover Dam being destroyed by a torrential, apocalyptic flood. He took a deep breath.

"I have another doctor that I want you to see," Dr. Fong said. "Her name is Carolyn Szymanski. She's here at Goosebeak, on the fifth floor."

"What kind of doctor?"

"A psychiatrist."

"What?" Martin exclaimed. "Absolutely not. I'm not crazy."

"Martin," Dr. Fong said. "Your mother told me, in confidence, that you have problems distinguishing fantasy from reality. She says you actually admitted that to her once."

"I never said that."

"Oh no? Well, what did she mean?"

"I guess sometimes I daydream," Martin said. "But that's all. Who doesn't?"

"Seeing Dr. Szymanski is a necessity," Dr. Fong said. "I'll give you a card with her number, and I want you to call her on Monday for an appointment. Now is there anything else you want to tell me?"

Martin tried to breathe evenly. It was hard to always pretend like there was nothing wrong. He'd gotten pretty decent at it over the years, but in the doctor's office, under the harsh florescent lights, it was difficult to hide.

He cleared his throat.

"I feel—"

"Yes?"

"I always feel like I'm fighting something much bigger than myself," Martin said. "It's invisible and it's extremely strong."

He felt his eyes fill with tears. He blinked them back.

"I don't know how to beat it."

* * *

Martin lived in an apartment complex across the street from a lumber yard. The building was called The Tropicalia. It was painted orange and shaped like a U. In the middle of the courtyard was a fenced-in swimming pool that was drained of water, even in the summertime. A dead squirrel lay inside the pool, in the deep end. One of its eyes was missing.

Martin had lived in the same apartment since graduating from high school because he wanted to prove to his parents that he could survive on his own and put down roots, so to speak. But that was often difficult because he felt like people were always comparing him to his brother.

Lars had majored in journalism and business at Traverse City College. He had anchored the newscasts at the campus television station and played on the hockey team and even had done some modeling print work—suits and ties, mostly—for Lumleys, a local department store in Traverse City. Lars moved to Montreal after graduation and found work at a television station there, as the youngest-ever host of the early morning news and entertainment program, *Bonjour.*

Martin loved his brother. He loved him, but there was something else underneath; a dark jealousy that made him deeply ashamed. If people ever accused him of it, Martin knew he would fight like a raccoon cornered in a sewer, scratching and clawing, before he'd ever admit it was true.

He found his usual spot in the parking lot, between a battered VW Bug with Nebraska license plates and a Dodge pickup with an "I Love The Lord And The Lord Loves Me Too" bumper sticker. Behind the apartment complex, buckled railroad tracks zigzagged across a field of weeds. The sun seemed to have disappeared for good now, replaced by a line of hard gray clouds gathering far off to the south.

Martin took another pull from his Jumbo Fizzy Blast soda, then finished it all in one gulp and tossed the bottle on the floor of the Cutlass. The veins in his neck throbbed; the four No-Sleep pills were already starting to kick in. He didn't care what Dr. Fong said. He needed more caffeine if he was going to make it through the rest of the day.

* * *

Traces of Patti were all over Martin's apartment. There was the framed watercolor of a moose that she had bought for him at the Fruitport Arts Festival. Her Ace of Base CD was in the boom box on the counter. And all around was the faint scent of her, the lingering quiet of her smile.

And there were plants everywhere. Even though it was November, there were ferns and succulents and ivy in containers in every corner and on every bookshelf. From the time he was a child, Martin had been interested in plants and gardens, and had excelled at taking care of them and helping them thrive. He figured that plants had simple needs, and if he just gave them water and sun, he'd never disappoint them.

That developed into learning about gardens and green spaces in urban areas, and he'd been lucky to work with Lance Bloomquist, a famous local architect, in designing a garden in a plaza in downtown Toronto. Lance had taught him more in a few months than four years of college ever could. They'd completed the project that summer, but Martin hadn't seen Lance since then. Thankfully the architect had scheduled a brunch date for them for Sunday morning.

Martin picked up his clunky cordless phone and dialed the number at The Book Loft. Patti didn't have a cell phone. No one did in Great Water, except for the drug dealers.

"Hello," a voice said disinterestedly. Martin recognized it as the kid with the shaved head and missing eyebrow from that morning.

"Hello, may I please speak to Patricia, please."

"I think she had to leave. I think she had to go do something."

"What?"

"I don't think she's here. She went to go see somebody. A guy or something."

Who?

"Well, can you have her call Martin, please?"

"Whatever," the kid said, and hung up.

Martin dropped his keys in the wicker basket on the bookshelf and went to the refrigerator in the kitchenette. Inside, wrapped in a wet paper towel, were three Bonsai trees seeds that he would plant on Monday. He had already purchased a tiny pot and filled it with moist peat, and even picked out a spot near the window that received sun for the majority of the day.

But now, as he contemplated the wet paper towel, next to an open box of baking soda and a carton of skim milk that he would never drink, he realized what a foolish idea it was. What made him think that the seeds would sprout or even grow tall enough to become a tree that he could prune with a tiny pair of scissors?

These thoughts crashed down suddenly, like a collapsing chandelier, and Martin stood there, his head pounding, feeling like he was going to burst out sobbing.

Please, no, not now. Not now, when I need things to be clear.

It was a constant up-and-down; that's how his life had always been. Feeling supremely confident about himself, that the people in his life really cared about him, that he was working toward something positive. Looking in the mirror and thinking that his massively curly brown hair and high cheekbones were actually handsome, like a rock star from the 1970s who was famous for overdosing on heroin at the age of twenty-seven. Then, days later, wondering what the point of it all was. Not bothering to take a shower in the morning or do his dishes. Clocking in and out of work without listening to anything or anyone. Why did it all matter?

There was a Styrofoam container in the fridge as well. It was from Larry's Lobsters: fettuccine with scallops. Patti had ordered it Wednesday afternoon at lunchtime but hadn't been able to finish the entire meal.

Martin dumped the food down the sink and ran the garbage disposal. But he kept the light blue napkin that had been tucked inside the container. He knew Patti had touched it and it reassured him to have something that she had felt, too.

He smelled the napkin and then placed it carefully on a bookshelf, next to two treasured possessions: his six-inch stuffed Snuffleupagus and his snow globe from the Pictured Rocks National Lakeshore.

Then Martin turned on the TV and fixed himself a sandwich: salami with three Kraft American Singles. He was out of mustard but substituted pickle relish instead. He had several hours before he had to head back to work, so he figured he should try his best to push the bad thoughts out of his head and relax.

Martin had a collection of Christmas specials that he kept in two shoeboxes underneath the TV stand. He'd found some in the bargain bins at video stores; others he'd taped straight off the television. Most guys he knew had a stash of porn videos; Martin had *Ziggy's Gift* and *The Little Drummer Boy: Book II.* He watched Christmas specials throughout the year, even in the dead of summer, but he would never admit that to anyone, least of all Dr. Carolyn whatever-her-name-was.

He felt safe when he watched them, and he needed that now. They made him remember being curled up on the couch next to his father, their enormous white pine Christmas tree casting a warm glow across their living room. Lars deemed Christmas specials too babyish, and his mother thought television destroyed brain cells, so it was something just Martin and his father shared every holiday season, even into his high school years. George van Lottom even seemed to enjoy them more than his son did.

Martin decided on *Tis the Season to Be Smurfy.* He took a bite out of his sandwich, then retrieved the video and inserted it into the VCR. Then he settled back on the couch, pulling his favorite green Afghan, which his mother had knitted for him, over his legs.

Martin particularly enjoyed *Tis* because of how hard the snow fell in thick, steady flakes throughout it. He also liked how cozy the Smurf village appeared as the creatures decorated it for Christmas. Martin was a Smurfs purist and never grew attached to later additions to the cast, like the Smurflings, but he was willing to forgive their role in the special because of its intense festiveness.

The falling snow relaxed him and soon he wasn't even listening to what the Smurfs were singing about.

THUMP.

Martin opened his eyes with a jolt. There was a buzzing in the air, like an electrical charge. He lifted his head off the pillow. The TV was off. Someone was watching him in the dim room; he could feel it.

"Who's there?" Martin whispered, glancing around. He knew he'd locked the apartment door behind him.

The TV flickered back on. Snowy static tumbled across the screen.

Martin felt his pulse jump. The refrigerator clicked and rumbled. The faucet dripped once, then twice.

He heard a rustle over by the window, where a tall bookshelf sat. It was mostly filled with plants, set in small pots he'd scavenged from thrift stores around town.

A tendril of ivy reached across the room toward him.

Martin's breath caught in his throat. As he watched in shock, two more tendrils stretched out of a blue clay pot and grew one foot, then two, as they extended toward the couch.

He sat up quickly and drew his legs close. Something slithered across his wrist. Martin looked down and saw a thick band of ivy encircling it. He tried to slide his hand out of the loop, but it tightened like a vice.

Help!

Ivy strands poured out of the pots on the bookshelf and crisscrossed the living room like a spider web. They stretched across Martin's body in every conceivable direction. He struggled to break free but they pinned him down mercilessly.

Help me help me please help—

He opened his mouth to scream and the ivy entered it, moving down his throat and suffocating him with its leaves that felt like thick velvet.

The walls and furniture dissolved into nothingness. The room grew pitch black. A frigid numbness spread across his body as Martin thrashed around, panicking, trying to breathe. A door appeared, far up ahead in the darkness. It swung open slowly and bright orange and red lights shot out of it like comets.

Martin shut his eyes; it was like staring into the sun. But he could sense a figure standing next to the door. Martin couldn't see his face because the light was so bright, but he knew the man was waiting for him.

* * *

A truck horn blared from across the street.

Martin opened his eyes. He blinked once, then twice. The ending credits for *Tis the Season to Be Smurfy* crawled across the TV screen.

He glanced around the room, drinking in its comforting familiarity. Everything seemed normal; the plants sat quietly by the window.

I'm okay. For now, I'm okay.

The tears came again. Martin wasn't sure if he was crying because he was so frightened, or because he was happy to be alive. But this time, he decided to let go. His whole body shook as he sat on the couch, sobbing, with no one there to hear him.

After a while, he stopped. A draft found its way through a crack in the window, and he shivered and got up from the couch. He was about to pull the drapes shut when he spotted someone outside, standing next to his car in the parking lot.

Martin went outside in his shirt sleeves. He didn't bring a weapon because he figured if the man had a gun, there wasn't much he could do to defend himself. Webb Turner's men were brutally efficient. Martin figured he should be brave and hear what the hooligan had to say.

He crossed the parking lot. It had gotten much colder; his breath hovered in front of him like a whisper of frost.

The man was gone.

Martin went over to his car. The windows were covered with condensation; a fresh crack snaked across the windshield. Written in the moisture, in bold capital letters, was a word he couldn't read.

13

Chapter Thirteen—ERIC

It grew significantly colder as Eric walked along the Cove Road toward Spivey Point. He often had to stop to shift his grip on the butterfly surfboard in the stiff lake breeze. He wished he had remembered his favorite pair of wool gloves that had the fingers torn off, like the kind Sylvester Stallone wore in *Rocky*.

The Polaroid photograph was in the pocket of his sweatshirt, along with the letter, written on the pink stationery with the kitten on it. It felt like his father was with him, and that made Eric believe that everything was going to be okay. He also had a stash of several letters in his backpack that he'd written to his dad over the years, but never sent.

Jenny and Lance had had a fight. That was the only answer that Eric could come up with, and it felt right, for now. Regardless of how bodacious Lance was, everyone had their moments when they needed to just leave and be alone. Lance was off in the woods by himself, maybe playing his harmonica and meditating or writing a new song about Pocahontas. He was a grown man who had made his own decision to change things up, and it felt pretty radical to Eric to finally make his own choice, too—a decision to leave.

He was stoked he had snagged a shortcut so he would avoid his mother and Pete on their way back from the Cozy Kitchen. The route had taken him through a crowded trailer park at the bottom of a hill. A dog with bristly red fur and a bandaged leg had chased him for half a block, howling and stumbling on the gravel, before it gave up.

Beyond Spivey Point lay the road that led through the woods to the highway. One direction sped north to Canada, the other the opposite way, toward Mackinaw Island and the bridge that led to the Lower Peninsula and California. There was a truck stop there right near the highway entrance, and he was bound to find a friendly person who could give him a ride.

* * *

Rose's Surf Shop had stood stoically in the middle of a gravel lot surrounded by ragged pine trees for as long as Eric could remember. The shop sold other things, like tackle and night crawlers for bait, and huge containers of propane. But Rose, who ran the place, was from Hawaii and had grown up surfing the North Shore with her six brothers. So her main offering was top-quality surf gear, and Eric remembered his father taking him to the shop as a very young child and Rose slipping him packets of corn nuts and Hawaiian chocolate, for free.

Eric pushed open the front door. There were surfing posters all over the walls: Snacko Thompson and Gus Parsnip and numerous other dudes who shredded. There were aisles of corn chips and a Frogger machine that still worked, and a glass cabinet with expensive fishing reels and hunting knives. And near the back of the store, past rows of boards that were stacked up like glorious colored dominoes, was Rose.

She sat on a stool behind the counter, reading a hunting magazine. She was well past fifty, and her long black hair, tinged with strands of gray, reached halfway down her back. Her ripped black t-shirt had a punk band's name on it. Eric had a few of their CDs.

"Howzit, big shredder," Rose said. An opening in the wall behind her led to her office; two green swinging shutter doors, like in an Old West saloon, hid it from view. Eric knew that she slept back there because she had nowhere else to go.

"Hi, Rose," Eric said. Hawaiian slack key guitar music played from a boom box on a shelf. Eric had never known that type of music before he came to Rose's. It made him think of sitting on a screen porch on a cool June night.

"I bet you come for the money," Rose said. "And I want to apologize to you right quick for that. You probably heard about that thing with the police."

Eric had been victorious in a surf contest that past August, co-sponsored by Rose's and The Crystal Palace, an adult entertainment venue out by the lumber mill. The contest referred to The Crystal Palace in that way, but Eric knew it was a nudie bar where women with big breasts danced to Aerosmith songs. Apparently the place was under investigation by the police, so that's why the delay had happened with his prize money, which was seventy-five dollars. Rick Kane, the hero of *North Shore*, also won a surfing contest—in a wave pool in Arizona—and headed to Hawaii with his winnings.

"It's okay, I heard about what happened," Eric said. "But I came here to talk to you about—"

He stopped when he saw Rose's expression.

"Little man," she said, her voice thin. "Where did you get that board?"

"I found it by Spivey Point. Why?"

Rose seemed to be at a loss for words, so Eric placed the Polaroid photograph on the counter. "Did it belong to her?" he asked.

Rose contemplated the photograph and rubbed her eyes. She seemed significantly older then, like a woman who'd seen far too much and couldn't forget any of it.

"Listen to me good," she said. "You can't be walking around town with that stick."

"Why?"

Rose came out from behind the counter. She took the board from Eric and ran her hand across the deck. Her arms were tanned and

90

crisscrossed with scars.

"Rose. Please tell me."

Her eyes grew cloudy and green, like the sky just before a tornado strikes. She smiled at him sadly. "How would you feel?" she asked. "How would you feel if out of nowhere, someone brought you a missing piece of your heart?"

The front door jangled as someone entered the store. "Rosey," a deep voice called. "Are you here?"

"Get down," Rose hissed.

"What—"

"Hide," she whispered. She pushed Eric down on the floor and pointed to the room with the green shutters. Eric found himself crawling on the dusty floor, past the counter and under the shutters to a small office with scratchy brown carpet. There was a desk covered by scratches and a black-and-white TV on a nightstand. A half-sized refrigerator sputtered in the corner, a map of Hawaii hanging above it. Framed surfing photos lined the walls.

"Webb Turner," he heard Rose say. "What brings you here?"

"I came to say goodbye," the man named Webb said.

Eric rose to a sitting position and tried to peek around the wall and underneath the shutters. He could see Rose's legs, and the cubes of board wax inside the glass counter.

"Well where you going?" Rose asked. She sounded nervous, more so than Eric had ever heard her before.

A man with shaggy gray hair came into view. He wore dirty blue jeans and a ripped flannel shirt and was more than fifty years old.

"Ada's been talking to me," he said.

"What you going on about?" Rose asked.

"I watch Channel 11 and I hear her," Webb replied. "Real late at night, before the infomercials come on. She told me she's waiting for me, so I'm leaving for good. I'm gonna be with her again."

"Ada is long gone," Rose said. "You talking crazy."

Webb saw the butterfly surfboard then.

"What the fuck is this?" He reached for the board and turned it up on one end. "How'd you get this?" he asked, his voice growing louder.

"Someone brought it here," Rose said.

"Who?"

Just then, Webb glanced back toward the shutters, and Eric quickly moved out of sight, his heart beating faster. To him, Webb Turner sounded like a man who would shoot a stray dog just to hear it howl.

"I don't know," Rose told him.

"You're a lying bitch. I came in here all polite and I find you with this board?"

"You mind your business," she said. "You mind your business like you've always done."

"How can I do that when you show me her board? The last thing she was touching before she left me?"

Eric took another peek around the corner of the wall. Webb stood very close to the opening in the counter that led to the back office. And Rose was the only thing standing in his way.

"You go back to your house in the woods," Rose said. "Go back to your beer and forget about it, like Lance did."

"What do I have to go back to? Johnny is fucking around with another man, I know it. All I hear at night are the troops marching to battle in my head. And the fog came in last night, with the blood red moon. You know as well as I do what the fog means, Rose."

"It's just fog," Rose said.

"Bullshit," Webb said. "It brought back this board, didn't it? It's the curse of this fucking town. I'll never leave this place unless I put a bullet in my skull. Or I follow Ada out on the lake. Paddle out just like she did and wait for the fog to take me."

Rose took the board from him. "This don't belong to you," she said. "Ada was a good girl, that's why I took her in. I took her in after every fight she had with you."

"We never even argued," Webb said. "I loved her more than I did myself."

"Ada loved Duane," Rose answered. "You're fooling yourself if you think different."

"Duane Calhoun skipped town and forgot about all the people he hurt real easy, didn't he? And I have to see his kid around town, the spitting image of him, and I'm supposed to forget it? I'm still here. I'm still here, rotting from the inside out."

"Ada never loved you," Rose said.

Webb struck her with a heavy punch in the jaw. It sent her crashing against the wall behind the counter. Papers flew everywhere as she slumped on the floor, not moving.

"Don't tell me what belongs to me," Webb said. He picked up the board and held it in one hand.

Eric sat there, a few feet away, paralyzed with fear.

"Get out of my store," Rose whispered.

"If you see Eric Calhoun, tell him to come see me," Webb said. "I got a few lessons to teach him before I leave."

14

Chapter Fourteen—JENNY

Michael Graham insisted that they meet immediately. The man from the flyer at the police station lived at the other end of town, where the Cove Road carved a precarious path between steep, bare hills and the rocky shore.

Jenny followed a gravel drive up the hill to the cottage, shuttered and simple and protected by a strong bare oak tree alongside it. A pickup truck sat parked on a rutted section of the lawn where no grass grew.

A slim man with an unkempt brown beard met Jenny at the door. He wore a buttoned-down flannel shirt and heavy work pants. He stepped from the doorway onto the narrow front stoop to shake her hand.

"I'm Michael Graham," he said. His hands were calloused. Black circles rimmed his bloodshot eyes.

"Hello. Thank you for seeing me, Mr. Graham."

"Call me Mike."

He ushered her into the living room, which was dim and dusty. Stacks of unopened mail lay on a coffee table, stained by faded white circles. An ancient Zenith color TV was tuned to a football pre-game show. A greasy, heavy wrench sat on top of a stack of newspapers in the corner, along with two empty beer cans.

"Please sit down," he said. "I can make some coffee if you want. Or beer or tomato juice."

"I'm fine," Jenny said. "Thank you." She sank down into the sofa, which was orange and brown checkered and smelled like Febreeze. A broken cuckoo clock hung above the television set.

"The tomato juice was my wife's. Bernadette loved that stuff." He switched off the TV and stared at the floor with a despondent look.

"Would you like to tell me what happened?"

"She's been gone since early this morning. The police haven't done jack shit to help because they think she ran off with some other guy. I told them Bernie wouldn't never do that. I just don't know what to do." A shaft of light found its way around the blinds and crossed his bright green eyes. "I'm sorry," he said. "I'm just in a state of shock right now."

Jenny noticed another empty beer can on top of the mantel. "You said on the phone that your wife disappeared by Brisco Creek Bridge," she prompted.

"That's right."

"My husband and I live in the house nearby."

"I know. I went and knocked on your door this morning, but nobody answered."

"That's because Lance has also been missing since this morning," Jenny said. "And I think—"

She paused, taken by the confused, anguished expression on the man's face. He stood there in the dim, cold room, waiting, clearly wondering what had become of his wife, the woman with the crooked eyes and feathered hair. The woman who had probably sat in that very spot on the couch dozens of times before, perhaps sipping tomato juice, or eating a piece of toast. Or knitting. Or—

A yell pierced the silence. Jenny glanced at him in alarm. She hadn't realized there was anyone else in the house.

"That's Katie," he said. His left eye twitched.

Jenny could only stare back at him.

"My girl," he added.

Michael Graham moved past her and walked unsteadily down a short hallway that led to the rear of the house. He knocked twice on a door and then went inside.

Jenny sat there as a minute passed, then another. The wind blew down the hill and rattled the windows. The furnace switched on. A dog barked outside. Finally, she got up and knocked on the door that she had seen him enter.

"Mr. Graham? Mike? Is everything okay?"

Jenny opened the door.

Michael Graham lay on a twin-sized bed, on top of a comforter emblazoned with bright blue whales and cinnamon-colored lobsters. He had his arm around a pale girl around seven years old, with limp, dark hair. She wore pajamas and was sitting up in bed, drawing on a sketchpad, which she had propped up on her knees. There were magic markers spread out around her like Pickup Stix.

They both glanced up at Jenny. "Sorry," Michael Graham said. "I didn't mean to leave you out there like that." He brushed the little girl's hair away from her forehead and smiled. "Katie was just showing me what she saw in her dream," he said.

"It was real," Katie said. Her lips were thin and gray.

"Of course it was," he replied. "My mistake. This is Jenny, sweetheart. She's just here for a visit."

The curtains were drawn; the room was lit by a single lamp on the nightstand. And all around them, pieces of sketchbook paper were taped to the walls. Most of the pictures were drawn with magic marker—sets of eight basic colors that were always on sale in the school supply aisle in the Price Slasher. But there were a few pencil drawings, too, and a picture of a horse that had been carefully ripped from a library book.

The drawings were similar: all were alive with brilliant flashes of color; reds and oranges and bolts of blue that shot across the page and led toward a door, far up ahead. Amorphous figures stood guard in some of the pictures—dark blobs with white flashes for eyes, surrounded by deep green halos of light. They hovered around each door, or just beyond them, blending into each other, indistinguishable but somehow familiar.

"She hasn't stopped drawing since this morning," Michael Graham said. "It makes her feel better. So I just let her."

Jenny stared at each drawing. The images felt so alive. "What did you mean, Katie?" she asked. "What did you mean when you said it was real?"

"I saw those lights when my mom went away."

"Listen, sweetheart," Michael Graham said, frowning, "why don't you try to sleep for a while? I can fix you some pancakes with chocolate chips when you wake up."

"I don't want to sleep anymore. I don't like my dreams."

He debated this, then finally kissed her on her forehead. "All right, angel," he said.

"Can you tell me what happened to your mom?" Jenny asked.

Katie was about to speak when her father took her hand. "Hold on a second, sweetheart. Remember how the policeman laughed at what you told him?"

"He just didn't believe me, Dad."

"The police around here never care one speck about people like us. That's why."

"I want to believe," Jenny said, sitting down in a chair. "Please."

Michael Graham regarded his daughter with concern. He smoothed the hair back from her face. "I don't want to upset Katie," he said to Jenny in a low voice. "She's been through so much today."

"We need to figure out what happened to your wife. And maybe my husband, too. Any details will help."

"Bernadette is alive," he said, his voice rising.

"I believe Lance is too. So we don't have anything to lose, do we?"

He locked eyes with Jenny; his hands shook. Jenny smelled beer on his breath. Finally, he gave a deep sigh.

"My wife took her out to the creek real early to look for crayfish," he began. "Katie likes crayfish and squid and all kinds of marine creatures. We told her that she wouldn't find any because it was so cold, but she

97

still likes to look."

"I found your pail," Jenny said. "Right by the side of the creek."

Katie nodded solemnly. "Mommy helped me build a dam made out of sticks," she said.

"I guess they were deep in the woods. Bernie was up on the creek bank, picking berries."

"Go on."

"Then Katie heard horses. "

Jenny's heart leapt. "Horses?"

"Dad, there was a horn first."

"That's right, you did say that. There was the sound of a horn and then horses came through the woods and Bernie was—"

Michael Graham stopped to wipe the tears from his eyes. He had the look of a man who was struggling to hold on to the last piece of driftwood before the currents pulled him under.

"My wife was sucked away through the trees, just like that. Katie heard her scream, so she ran up the bank. Then she felt something pulling her, too. Like when she's pedaling down a steep hill on her bicycle and closes her eyes, just for a second. That pulling, in your chest. Isn't that what you said, sweetheart?"

"Mom called my name," Katie said. "I ran through the woods after her and it was pulling me, too. But I hung on to a tree real tight and I didn't let go. There were men on horses riding past me but they didn't see me."

"What kind of men?" Jenny asked. Her pulse was pounding, but she tried to make her voice even and calm.

"Scary men with beards and helmets with horns. Riding through the woods and along the creek. They were hollering at each other. After the pulling stopped, I ran after them and I saw the lights up ahead."

"The lights that she keeps drawing," Michael Graham said. "The lights that she sees in her dreams."

"They were going towards a hiccup," Katie said.

"What do you mean?"

98

"There was a hiccup in the air. Like when you throw a stone in a pond and it makes a ripple."

"So the men on horses were riding toward this ripple in the air. And there were lights?"

Katie nodded. "Different colors. They were really bright. The men rode right into them. Then the hiccup got smooth and the lights went out and it was just the woods again."

Jenny took a deep breath. "Katie," she said. "What do you think happened to your mom?"

"I don't think she's dead. I know that for sure."

Michael Graham took his daughter's hand again.

"I think she's just... waiting," Katie said.

"Waiting for what?"

Katie focused on her then, and Jenny saw in her eyes all the colors of her drawings, bright reds and oranges, all at once and beautiful.

"Waiting for someone to cross over," Katie said. "Cross over and bring her back."

* * *

Jenny stood with Michael Graham out in the hallway. They watched Katie sleep through the half-open door.

"My daughter isn't crazy," he said.

"I believe you," Jenny replied.

Michael Graham looked at the carpet. Cobwebs hung low around the baseboard. "I'm glad somebody does," he said. "I don't even believe in God, let alone heaven or a spiritual world or alternate dimensions or whatever *X-Files* thing this is. At least, I didn't think I did. How in the hell are we going to get them back?"

The dark possibility that she would never see her husband again flickered past Jenny's eyes like the shadows of passing tree branches. She knew that grief would be too much for her to bear.

"I—"

99

For a few seconds, the world around them was completely silent.

"I don't know," she said. "But I'm not giving up."

He nodded. "Hold on a minute. I need to show you something."

Jenny waited as he stepped into a room across the hall. He returned with a catcher's mitt, holding it as if it were an antique vase.

"I found this in the woods, near the creek," he said. "When I went back to look for her. I didn't show it to nobody. I just didn't know what to make of it."

Jenny took the mitt from him. The leather was so worn that it felt almost soft, like moss. The black stitching was threadbare. And written in faded pen on the outside was: *Jimmy Greenjaw, Great Water High, 1933.*

15

Chapter Fifteen—ERIC

"I can't afford no ambulance," Rose said. She had managed to get up from the floor and lie down on the mattress in the back room where she slept. Eric had given her a cold compress full of ice cubes for her jaw.

"Please," he said. "You could really be hurt."

Rose smiled at him ruefully. "I been through rougher stuff than this," she said. "I have six brothers, don't forget."

"You stood up for me. I was too much of a squid to do anything."

"He took that board. I didn't do so good after all, did I?"

Eric sat down in an unvarnished chair with rickety legs. He rubbed at the scratchy brown carpet with the tips of his Nikes. "Rose," he said. "Why won't anyone tell me what this is all about?"

"You're just a boy. You go to school, you surf. Lance teaches you. What more do you need?"

"I found that board this morning and everyone starts freaking out," Eric said. "Who did it belong to? Where'd it come from?"

Rose sat up. She put a pillow behind her back as she re-wrapped the compress full of ice. "That stick belonged to a girl who disappeared a long time ago," she said.

"Disappeared?"

"She went out surfing on the lake and then she was gone."

"Did she die?"

"Nobody knows," Rose said. "But Webb knew her. Webb loved her."

Eric sat there, listening to the faint strains of Hawaiian slack key guitar music from the boom box in the store. "My mom always told me that Webb Turner was just some carp who lived in the woods," he said.

"She's right. Your mom, she's trying to do right by you. Make sure your mind is clear. Of course she ain't gonna tell you about all this mess in the past."

"Well, it's too late for that now, isn't it?" Eric asked. "I brought that board back home this morning and she acted like it was Kryptonite."

He wondered if he should tell Rose about the letter from his father. Less than an hour ago, he was positive that leaving was the right thing for him to do. Now, Eric wanted to stay and find out why his mother had been keeping so many secrets from him. Secrets that surrounded the butterfly board and the woman who owned it.

"Promise me you'll stay away from Webb," Rose said.

"Negatory," Eric said. "I can't do that. Da Hui stole Rick Kane's board and he had to stand tough and prove himself to get it back. It's time for me to do the same."

"This ain't a movie," Rose said. "This ain't *North Shore*. This is real."

"I'm not a man if I run," Eric replied.

"Listen, little grommet," Rose said, her expression grave. "You see what Webb did to me. Who's to say he ain't gonna do worse to you?"

* * *

Eric decided to keep off the main roads so that no one would spot him. He also needed to make arrangements for that night, so he called his best friend Taco Wallace from a phone booth outside a boarded-up gas station at the edge of the forest. They had known each other since kindergarten and Taco was one of the few people whom Eric truly trusted.

"I need to spend the night tonight," Eric said. "Is your mom working the graveyard shift?"

"Maybe," Taco replied. "What trouble are you in now, Calhoun?"

"I'll explain later," Eric said. He could hear someone playing *PaRappa the Rappa* on the Playstation in the background.

"You always say that. I want to be Hannibal on *The A-Team* for once. Why can't I be the man with the plan?"

"Because I need your help. Can someone pick me up at Harborfront Stroll after midnight?"

"By someone, you mean me, right? So now I'm your personal chauffeur. Well, I think it's time you start riding your bike here like a normal person, surfer boy."

"You have a single fin mentality," Eric replied.

Taco sighed, but Eric could tell he was smiling on the other end of the line. "You owe me one, Calhoun," he said. "Again."

"*Gracias*," Eric said. "Most excellent. Don't tell my mom or Pete you talked to me. I'll scope you tonight."

Eric hung up the phone and stepped out of the booth. There was a hum in the air, like telephone wires on an August night.

Hello there.

A man stood at the edge of the forest, less than ten feet away from him. He was around forty and had thick blond hair that was soaking wet and drooped over his eyes. He wore only a pair of pink board shorts that seemed out of a different era.

Startled, Eric's breath caught in his throat. "Hi," he said, finally. "What were you doing back there?"

Waiting for you, the man replied—but his mouth didn't move. *Why aren't you out on the waves?*

"Do I know you?" Eric asked. Something about the way the man's eyes were hidden by his wet hair made his pulse quicken. The stranger was barefoot and muscular and radiated power.

Maybe. I'm just looking for a surf bud.

The man took a step toward him, but his feet made no sound on the

103

loose gravel.

"I—I don't have my board," Eric stuttered.

No problem, compadre. Just take my hand and we'll swim out to the break together.

Eric backed up against the phone booth. There were no people around, no cars coming down the road. No one would hear him if he screamed.

"I really have to go," Eric said. "I have to meet someone."

The man reached up and wiped his hair away from his eyes, which were nothing but hollow sockets. A black beetle crawled across his cheek and down his neck.

Eric tried to take a step, but he felt glued to the gravel. Then he realized who the man was.

"You're Rod Kalanchoe. You drowned in the lake. There's a statue of you downtown."

I came back just to see you, pal. I want to show you something, way down below. It's dark down there, and you can finally have sweet dreams.

"Stay away from me," Eric whispered. Summoning every bit of strength he possessed, he lunged away from the phone booth and took off running, his backpack clumping against his back as he beat a path down the road.

* * *

It was about a mile from the gas station to The Crystal Palace. Eric stopped running long enough to lean again a tree and think. After careful consideration, he decided to explain the appearance of the strange man in the woods as a side effect of him not getting enough sleep. Eric had been plagued by insomnia ever since his father left, and he figured the ghost of Rod Kalanchoe was just an instance of his exhausted mind working overtime. Maybe he'd even imagined the man jumping from the theater balcony, too. The alternative was too upsetting to consider.

The Crystal Palace was tucked away in the woods like a pioneer outpost. The huge sign in the parking lot displayed an intimidating neon Viking sitting on a throne, as if daring people to come inside. Its owner was named Randolph Brown, but everyone called him Bates, for reasons unknown. He had been a close friend of Eric's father, and Eric had hazy memories of Bates babysitting, taking him out to Pizza Hut and the go-cart track when both his parents were working.

Diane Calhoun barely tolerated Bates back then. She spoke of him in the same way that one would of a rabid raccoon, and Eric remembered quite a few loud disagreements between his parents about him. He didn't know what the guy had done to make them fight.

There had only been one Bates sighting in the six years since his father had left, which was pretty remarkable for a town as small as Great Water. Eric and his mother were shopping at the Price Slasher and he caught Bates watching them from behind a display of detergent. At that time, the Crystal Palace was recently up and running and extremely successful, despite occasional intrusions from local lawmen.

Eric was torn at that point, because he wondered then if Bates was still in touch with his father, and he had a dozen questions to ask. But he also knew talking to the man would make his mother angry. Concerns for her feelings had won out that day at the grocery store because he hated to see her upset. Now he had a second chance.

He walked across the lot and approached the building. Bates' 1967 light blue Chevelle was parked near the door, still looking like it had rolled straight off the factory assembly line. Eric remembered taking rides in the car in the summertime, up and down the northern shore. Bates would never let him take ice cream cones inside it.

I just like nice things, Eric. There's nothing wrong with that, is there?

A sign at the entrance said the club opened at two o'clock on Saturdays, and that was more than an hour from now. The thought of knocking first crossed his mind, but instead, he pushed on the heavy wooden door and was surprised to find it open.

It was very dim inside, and as his eyes got used to the lack of light, he was intrigued to find that there were mirrors everywhere, in almost every direction he looked. Eric thought the place looked like the climax of *Enter the Dragon,* except with red sofas and a floor that felt suspiciously sticky. And there was a stage—a kind of elevated walkway—zigzagging throughout the room, like an adult version of the Yellow Brick Road.

A banner strung across one part of the stage read: WELCOME SPIVEY FANATICS.

Eric knew that most of the local businesses were running events or special deals related to the Jack Spivey story, because of all the tourists converging on the town that weekend. Would there be strippers dressed in World War I army uniforms? A "hot" Lucy O'Hara lookalike contest? He could only begin to imagine the possibilities. Taco's older brother had been to The Crystal Palace more than a few times, and he once told Eric that Bates would try anything once, if it meant more customers.

"What're you doing here, Eric?"

Bates sat at the end of the bar, going over a stack of receipts with a calculator. He was a very thin man in his early fifties. He was nearly bald, and wore tortoiseshell glasses and an expensive-looking mock turtleneck.

"Hi," Eric said. He didn't know if he should stand still or sit down at the bar or just leave.

"I thought I locked that door," Bates said. "Your mother would kill me if she knew I let you in here." He took a drink of something from a very short glass.

Eric peered at him in the shadowy light. The man seemed to bear no resemblance to the fun-loving guy who took him to three consecutive showings of *The Lion King,* just because Eric was obsessed with warthogs. That was still undeniably one of the best days of Eric's life.

"Did you hear what I said? You have to leave."

106

"But I need to talk to you."

"I'm sorry about your prize money from the contest, if that's why you're here. I have it in the register. I can get it for you after I finish this."

"That's not why I came," Eric replied. He decided to sit down at the bar, two seats down from Bates. He felt like a cowboy at a saloon.

Bates scanned him from top to bottom. His expression changed; a sly smile crossed his face. Eric smelled the alcohol on his breath.

"Sit closer, champ," he said. "I ain't gonna bite."

"No thank you," Eric replied. "I'm good."

"Come on. You used to sit on my lap all the time when you were little."

"I'm a little too old for that, don't you think?"

"If you say so," Bates said. "I think you're growing up real nice. Starting to look like a man."

"Thank you," Eric said. "I guess."

"What do you have in that bag? Are you running away or something?"

"I actually am," Eric replied.

"Yeah, right. You know as well as I do that nobody ever gets out of this town."

"Some people have."

Bates took another swig of his drink. "You better get to the point," he said. "My girls start getting here in twenty minutes."

"Do you know anything about a woman who disappeared on the lake? Back when my dad was around nineteen?"

"Who told you about that?"

"I found her surfboard on the lake this morning. And I'm sure it's the same one she was riding when she vanished."

"Bullshit."

"Webb Turner stole the board from me. And I'm gonna get it back. But first I need to know why no one wants to talk about it."

"Stay the hell away from that homo drug dealer."

"I'm not afraid of anyone."

Bates laughed. The sound reverberated through the room like an echo in a well.

"Little Eric Calhoun's not a kook anymore, I see."

"I never was," Eric replied. "My dad made sure of that."

"You need to leave. Or else I'm gonna call your mom and tell her to come pick you up. I have a feeling she won't like that."

Eric swallowed hard. That was the last thing he wanted to have happen. "Tell me what happened on the lake," he said.

Bates shrugged. "Your dad never talked to me about it. It shook him up too much. So I knew never to ask any more questions."

"Why does he have a photo of that woman and her board hanging in our shaping shack?"

"Because he was in love with her."

Eric took a breath. "In love?"

"That's not hard to understand, is it? On second thought, what are you, fourteen? Maybe it's too soon for you to know what that's like."

Eric began to seethe. This man hadn't talked to him in more than six years. What gave him the right to make judgments about his life?

"What about my mom? Didn't he love her?"

"You'll have to ask him that yourself," Bates replied.

"Why did he leave us?" Eric asked. "Why hasn't he sent me a letter until today?"

Bates raised his eyebrows at this. It seemed like he wanted to reply, but instead he finished his drink and turned off the calculator. Then he sighed.

"Your dad was never prepared for you, Eric. He knew he was never cut out to be a father, and that's why he bailed."

It took a few moments for these words to sink in. But even after Eric thought about them, they still seemed wrong. All the awesome memories he had of his father were proof of that.

"My dad was nothing but good to me," Eric said. "Good to us."

"Your mom might have a different viewpoint on that."

Eric picked up his backpack and started toward the door. It was time for him to deal with things on his own, not listen to people who didn't know what the hell they were talking about.

"Wait a second," Bates called. "What about the seventy-five bucks I owe you?"

"Keep it," Eric said. He had his hand on the door when he heard Bates get up off his seat. Eric glanced back. There was a flicker in the man's eyes, a hint of worry underneath the pavement-tough exterior.

"Just stay away from Spivey Point," he said. "Don't go near it, especially tonight. Understand?"

"Why?"

"Because if you do, we'll never see you again," Bates replied. For a moment, he looked like the man Eric remembered.

* * *

Eric found his way to the Great Water Public Library and sat down at a study carrel in a secluded corner where all the dusty reference books were kept. He was glad to get out of the cold and have a place to figure out his next move. As he sorted through his bag to assess his food situation, he found the stash of letters to his father.

* * *

Dear Dad,

I'm writing this because Mr. Grewall says it might help. He's the guidance counselor and he's old, so I guess that means he knows what he's talking about. Since I don't know where you are or if you're even alive, this feels entirely weird.

This is what happened. A few days ago, the bell rang and I got my books and went down the hall to my fourth period class, which was French. I went past the front door and I saw it was real sunny outside. There were dandelions already out in the lawn. And the

grass was so perfect. It looked like someone had colored it with a green crayon. Straight from the box.

I had this urge to go outside and walk. Forget about French and go down the steps and across the lawn and walk through the dandelions and just keep going. I didn't think anyone would miss me, so that's what I did. I went past the principal's office and the secretary glanced up for a second through that big window and then she went back to her paperwork. Like I said, nobody would miss me.

Then I was outside. The sun felt mondo warm. I took my sweat-shirt off and tied it around my waist. I decided to just pick a direction and walk. I stopped thinking about everything that was tumbling around in my head. I just concentrated on the rhythm of my legs moving back and forth. My feet pushing off the sidewalk. It felt like I do when I surf. Connected.

That's the last thing I remember.

It was 9:35 at night when the police found me. They told Mom that I was sitting in the middle of this vacant lot behind the concrete factory by the railroad tracks. My shoes were missing and my backpack was gone and I was crying. I had walked more than seven miles that day but I don't remember any of it. But that's what they told me, so I guess that means it's true.

Eric

16

Chapter Sixteen—MARTIN

Martin heard his phone ringing. He raced down the second-floor hall, unlocked his apartment door and rushed inside. Then he hustled across the kitchen and grabbed the receiver, right before it went to voicemail.

"Hello?" he said. "Patti?"

"Do I sound like a goddamn chick to you?"

Martin let out a breath. The man on the other end of the line sounded like he wore brass knuckles and kicked puppies in the head, just for the sheer amusement of it.

"No, sir," he said. "You definitely don't."

"Do you have Webb's money or not?

"Yes, I do," Martin replied. "What's the best way to get it to him?"

"Well you ain't putting it in a pretty envelope and decorating it with scratch-n-sniff stickers, if that's what you're thinking, you pansy."

Martin knew that now wasn't the time to take the man to task for his derogatory language.

"I don't think I've met you before," he said. "Do you work with Mr. Turner?"

"No, I mortally injure people who don't pay what they owe him," the man replied. "And you're next on my list if you don't drive that rust bucket of a car of yours to The North Shore by three o'clock. We'll be waiting for you."

* * *

The North Shore was a burger shop on the main drag near Moosejaw. It was a haven for surfers who stopped there for food after their morning sessions. There were a few bars nearby, along with a check-cashing place and a video store called Colpire Video that specialized in obscure surf films from before Martin was born, along with Italian horror films from the 1970s and 80s, for some strange reason. The parking lot was always empty.

Martin thought things over during his drive across town. The money he owed was in an envelope in his jacket pocket, and he decided he would pay Webb as quickly as possible, no questions asked. Martin didn't own a gun and he figured that even if he did, Webb was too experienced a nefarious criminal for Martin to even think about gaining the upper hand in any confrontation. He was just ready for this whole business to be settled. He was embarrassed that he'd sunk so low to begin with, and having to lie to his mother had made things even worse.

It was hard for him to push the incident with the ivy from his mind. It had seemed so real, and so had the figure standing by the door with red and orange lights, like he was waiting there for a reason. Martin had had plenty of peculiar dreams before, but never one so vivid or upsetting as his own plants trying to kill him. He thought about what Dr. Fong had said about him confusing reality with—something else. Was there any truth to that, after all?

He found a parking spot by the check-cashing place. The wind was blustery near the lake; it nearly knocked him over as he made his way down the buckled sidewalk toward the meeting place. Across the road, businesses sat along the bottom of a rocky hill that led up to a pine forest. On Martin's side of the street, a sandy slope dotted with dead weeds fed down to the beach. The waves had come up fairly strong and he spotted several surfers in brightly colored wetsuits bobbing among them.

Two more surfers stood outside The North Shore, sipping coffee out of Styrofoam cups. Their boards were propped against the wall. One of them had a black eye and splotches of blood on his sweatshirt. He caught Martin staring at him.

"What the fuck's your problem, Curly?"

Martin forced himself to look away. "Nothing," he said. A gust of wind blew his hair back from his forehead. He wondered if the surfer had just finished murdering someone.

"Locals only," the surfer growled. Martin pretended not to hear. He stood up straight, brushed past the two men and opened the restaurant door.

The North Shore was dimly lit and punk rock played at an ear-splitting volume from the sound system. The place was decorated with framed photos of nasty-looking surfers from the most hardscrabble parts of Hawaii. Each man looked like a convicted felon and each photograph was scarier than the last. There was a counter where you ordered from a limited menu of burgers, sausage and egg sandwiches, coffee and pop. Then a belligerent-looking teenage girl in a tight t-shirt brought your food out to whichever grungy booth in which you chose to sit.

There was a scattering of customers in the place, but no Webb.

Martin glanced at his watch. He was five minutes early.

Someone shoved past him, hard. He struggled to keep his balance. "Hey," Martin said. "What's your problem?"

Two men in mechanics' work shirts laughed. Their hands and faces were streaked with oil and grime. They had thick moustaches and wore trucker caps.

"Shit or get off the pot, Numbnuts," one of them said.

A man sitting at a booth in the corner raised an eyebrow, almost imperceptibly. Taking it as a signal, Martin walked over to him.

He was no more than thirty and wore a half-buttoned flannel shirt and jeans. Martin had never seen him before, but it looked like he could snap a wooden plank with one hand.

"I hope you brought me good news," the man yelled over the music. His eyes were crimson and swollen and his thick brown moustache covered any trace of a mouth. He looked like a participant from the Lumberjack Olympics. There was a half-full cup of coffee in front of him. It was still hot.

"Have we met?" Martin asked.

The man gestured to the empty seat in the booth. Martin sat down reluctantly. The space was cramped and the man's massive forearms made him nervous.

"I work with Webb," the man replied. "He sent me here to retrieve a payment."

Martin looked at the man closely. There was a tattoo of a wolf's head on the inside of his wrist.

"I didn't borrow money from you," Martin said. "I borrowed it from Mr. Turner."

"Webb is busy with other important business right now. That's why he sent me."

"Were you the one following me?" Martin asked. "Standing outside my apartment?"

"You think I'd waste my time with Boy Scout Patrol? Get over yourself."

"Then who—"

Then who's been following me?

In a split second, Martin made up his mind. He sat up straight. "I went to a considerable amount of trouble to get this money," he began.

The man frowned. He spat something into his coffee cup. "So?"

"So, I make it a point not to deal with middlemen," Martin replied. He was beginning to sweat under his arms.

"You make it a point," the man repeated. "Who the fuck do you think you are? You and I both know you're just a chump security guard who got in way over your head."

"I pay my debts," Martin said. "But only to the people I owe."

"Listen here, Martin Van Lottom." The man pronounced his name like it was a disgusting racial slur. "I ain't no middleman. But I will cut your goddamn nuts off and shove 'em up your asshole if you don't pay up. Now."

"This is a public establishment," Martin said. "You wouldn't dare try anything."

The man reached across the table and grabbed Martin around the back of his head. In a split-second, he slammed Martin's face against the table—once, then twice.

Martin saw pink and green stars. His eyes burned. Blood trickled out of his right nostril.

"What now, Boy Scout?" the man sneered.

Other customers in the restaurant stared at them with passive acceptance on their faces, like they'd just seen an ordinary occurrence.

Martin knew he couldn't hand the money over to a stranger. Not after everything he'd been through.

"Fuck you," he stammered. He grabbed the cup of coffee and dashed it in the man's face.

Martin had never imagined himself to be a particularly fast runner, but he definitely held nothing in reserve as he tore out of The North Shore and down the sidewalk toward his car. He heard the restaurant's door bang open behind him and realized the man must be close behind. But he knew enough not to look back. Martin had an image in his mind of Carl Lewis racing down the track in the 100 meters, aerodynamic and focused, and he tried his best to imitate him.

Then he tripped over a buckled section of sidewalk and fell flat on his face.

For the second time in less than two minutes, pain shot across his cheeks and eyes as he slammed against the sandy concrete. A bolt of white-hot agony pierced his mouth. Raising his head, he spat out a tooth covered in blood.

Martin gingerly lifted himself to a crouching position and glanced behind him. The man with the thick moustache stood on the sidewalk, a half block back, regarding him with a look of pure hatred.

"Come back here, you fucker!" he yelled. His face was still dripping wet.

Then he reached under his shirt.

Martin had seen enough episodes of *T.J. Hooker* to know what was coming next. Operating on pure adrenaline, he scrambled to his feet and dashed across the road to his Oldsmobile. Fumbling with the keys, he finally unlocked the door and got in, slamming the door behind him.

"We know where you live!" the man yelled. He strode down the road toward Martin, slowly but purposefully. "There's no point in running! You're fuckin' dead!"

The Cutlass sputtered to life and Martin floored it down the road. The man jumped out of the way and fired one shot, shattering the driver's side mirror as Martin sped away from windswept Moosejaw and the surfers paddling among the freezing waves.

17

Chapter Seventeen—JENNY

People milled around the parking lot as Jenny pulled in next to the O'Hara house on Sunrise Avenue. They had clunky cameras strung around their necks and carried dog-eared guidebooks. Jenny spotted license plates from Wisconsin and Illinois and a yellow station wagon from Florida. Its dented bumper was covered with stickers that said things like: "I Saw Where Jeffrey Dahmer Killed You" and "This Land Is My Land—Indians Get Out!"

Jenny took a deep breath and tucked some loose strands of hair behind her ears. "I'm coming, Lance," she said. Then she put a hand on her stomach. "We're coming."

She picked up the toy and closed the car door, then made her way through the gathering dusk toward the house. It was a blue two-story Victorian, with a turret on the side, and a diamond-shaped window high above, in the attic. The house was set back from the road at the top of a grassy hill, with stone steps leading up to the wide front porch.

A blond woman with tortoise-shell glasses approached her. She wore an elaborate knitted poncho with lightning bolts on it and swayed slightly as she walked.

Jenny's chest tightened. "Hello, Silke," she said.

The Finnish film director took off her glasses and gazed at her, as if she were a sow bug on a piece of lettuce. "Where is Mr. Lance Bloomquist, architect extraordinaire?" she asked, slurring her words

117

a bit. Jenny smelled Scotch on her breath, with just a hint of Doritos.

"Lance is away on business."

"I thought you two were attached at the hip."

"Silke!" a man yelled from a green Trans Am on the street, its motor rumbling. He wore a sharp suit with a checkered bow tie. "Hurry your sweet Scandinavian ass," he said. "We're gonna be late."

"It's a pity you missed the premiere this afternoon," Silke said. "Jason Priestley has committed to do the narration when it airs on PBS. It's quite a coup to attract a star of his caliber to a project like this."

"The problem my husband and I had wasn't with the film," Jenny said. "It was with the school board bankrolling it. That money could've been spent in any number of ways to help the kids in this town."

"Too bad the city council felt differently. Regardless of the thirty-eight minute speech your husband gave."

Jenny tried to step around her, but the Finnish woman put a hand on her shoulder. She noticed the toy in Jenny's hand.

"And I see that it hasn't stopped you from buying souvenirs, she said disdainfully. "How very touristy of you."

"Take your hand off my shoulder," Jenny warned.

* * *

Nora Van Lottom stood at the top of the second floor landing inside. She was a slim, sixtyish woman with gray hair who wore a cream-colored turtleneck.

"I know who you are, Mrs. Bloomquist," Nora said. "If it were up to you, I'd be out of a job. Isn't that right? The O'Hara house would lose its funding and close. The history of Great Water would be lost."

"That's not true at all," Jenny replied. "If I could just have a second of your time. Please."

Nora regarded her for a long moment. "Very well," she said. "Let's not cause a scene."

Nora turned to the group of tourists that were milling nearby. "Go ahead and take a look at the master bedroom," Nora told them. "That's where Jack Spivey blew Benjamin O'Hara's brains out like wet confetti. Visitors say that in the dead of night, you can sometimes hear the horrific thump O'Hara's body made when it hit the floorboards."

The group trampled down the hallway eagerly, the wooden floor creaking and groaning with every step.

A heavyset woman lingered behind. "Is it true that Bridget O'Hara dreamed of her own death?" she asked Nora. She wore a t-shirt with renowned psychic Sylvia Browne's face on it. PETS GO TO HEAVEN TOO was printed in bright pink letters under it.

"Bridget's mother kept a diary," Nora replied. "She noted that the night before her murder, her daughter woke from a nightmare, screaming that the moon was bleeding. It took until morning for Lucy to calm her down. I do think it was a prophecy."

The woman smiled, satisfied. She followed the group down the hallway.

"Now," Nora said. "What is it that you want?"

"I'd like you to take a look at this," Jenny said. She set the first of her two items down on an oak table that stood next to them.

"It's a Pierre toy. Why would I be interested in that?"

"I found this in the woods, near my house," Jenny said.

Nora took the toy and examined it under the light of an antique lamp. She ran her finger along the rough wood, and examined its belly, where the rickety wheels were attached. "Why isn't there a mark?" she asked, finally. "Why isn't there a Great Water Toy Company mark?"

"I don't know. What's that?"

"All the Pierre toys made at the factory here in town have them. Otherwise they're not authentic. Where did you say you found this?"

"By Brisco Creek. That's where I saw her," Jenny said. "That's where I saw Bridget."

Nora took off her bifocals and regarded her sternly. "Don't joke with me, Miss."

"I'm telling you, I saw her," Jenny insisted. "Why won't anyone believe me?"

"I'm not one to believe in secondhand accounts of ghosts," Nora replied. "Besides, the original toy was destroyed in a museum fire in 1946. It's just not possible."

The tour group left the master bedroom.

"I could almost hear the gunshots," one bald man said, as he met them on the landing. "It's completely eerie."

"Then what happened?" another woman asked. She wore a visor with daisies on it.

"Well," Nora said. "After she heard the shotgun blast, little Bridget woke from her bedroom there —"

She pointed at a wooden door at the end of a dim hallway.

"—and she stumbled sleepily down the hall, still wearing her brand new Sunday outfit that her mother had bought for her in town, the day before. Bridget so loved the taffeta blouse and pretty knee socks that she had fallen asleep in them."

"She saw her mother wrestling with Jack Spivey here on the landing," the bald man said. "Screaming and crying, pleading for him to put the rifle down. Isn't that right?"

"And Bridget followed them out into the front yard, into the middle of the night," Nora continued. "I'll meet you out there in just a minute and we'll wrap up the tour by the old dandelion patch where Jack blasted a hole in the little girl's face."

The tour group made its way down the steps and out the front door.

"Please," Jenny said, beginning to feel nauseous again. "Have strange things ever happened near the creek? Have people ever—disappeared?"

"Well," Nora said. "A handful of them have, over the years. But only during the time of the Baptism."

"The Baptism?"

"A blood red moon, high tide and the fog converge over the lake. It occurs every thirty years or so, give or take. Didn't you see the sky last night?"

Jenny tightened her grip on the railing. "Who disappeared?" she whispered.

"Jimmy Greenjaw, the Native American boy who was a star catcher on the Blackhawk High baseball team in the 1930s," Nora said. "Marcel Duchamp, who played the calliope in the traveling circus. Ada Bloomquist. Shirley Gruber, the cross-eyed butcher..."

Jenny's heart skipped a beat. "Jimmy Greenjaw," she whispered. "And... Ada?"

"Why, your husband's sister, of course."

The floor began to spin around Jenny's feet.

"But she drowned in the lake," Jenny said. "More than thirty years ago."

"That's what the paper said," Nora replied. "But Lance was there that night. Along with Duane Calhoun and Webb Turner. The four of them were out surfing in the fog. Only those men know what really happened to her. And they're the ones who have to live with it."

* * *

Jenny got back to her car and realized she had left her cell phone on the front seat.

"Please," she said, as she saw there was a message waiting. "Please, Lance. Sweetheart—"

Jenny waited, her hands shaking, as the message finally played.

This is Diane Samuels. Eric's mother. He hasn't come home for dinner, and Pete and I were wondering if you've seen him today. Please give us a call at—

* * *

Jenny sat on a lumpy beige sofa in Diane Samuels' living room. She had just finished telling Diane and Pete about Eric's visit that morning, and about Lance. She left out the horses and Bridget O'Hara and the toy.

"Now that I think about it, Eric did mention that Lance didn't show up this morning," Diane said, as she paced back and forth on the scratched hardwood floors. She wore old Nike tennis shoes and earrings with little emerald angels hanging from them.

"I'm so sorry this is happening," Jenny replied. The room was lit by a tall halogen lamp. There were dead moths inside the plastic cover.

"Maybe he's just out with friends, Diane," Pete interjected. He sat on one arm of a yellow easy chair, picking from a half-empty Chinese food carryout carton. He wore a tuxedo shirt with ruffles, and scuffed cowboy boots.

"Eric doesn't have any friends," Diane said, pointedly. "Except for Taco Wallace, and I already spoke to him. I drove by all the surfing spots. Spivey Point. Moosejaw. No sign of him. Nothing."

"Maybe you should speak to the police," Jenny said. "They can start looking for him."

"We've already done that," Diane said. "They really haven't been much help. But Channel 10 found out about it. The assignment editor told me they'll run something on the news. Tonight, and again tomorrow."

"The kid's fourteen," Pete said. "He doesn't drink, or smoke weed. He's never been in trouble."

There was an awkward silence.

"But he's always been on the verge of it," Diane said. "We both know that's the God's honest truth. And you saw his last report card. Three C's and two D's. You would think with all the books he checks out from the library, some of it would rub off on him."

"Lance has tried to be a really positive influence on him," Jenny volunteered.

"Eric spends too much time with him as it is," Diane replied. "I mean, I'm grateful for the financial help he's given me after Duane left. But it seems like all Eric wants to do is hang out with Lance. And surf."

Jenny didn't know a thing about her husband giving Diane financial help, but she figured then wasn't the best time to ask.

"Well, Lance promised Duane that he'd look after him," she replied. "He told me that."

"We can look after him fine," Diane said.

There was another long silence. Pete shifted uncomfortably.

"You know what I'm trying to say, Pete," Diane said. "Eric doesn't need another father figure in his life. That's the role that you should be playing."

"Do you really think he would run away?" Pete asked. "All the way to San Diego? The kid doesn't have any money."

"I don't want him anywhere near Duane," Diane said. "I don't want that deadbeat son of a bitch seeing him again. Or Webb Turner, either. If that man lays one finger on my son, there's gonna be hell to pay."

"Why would Webb want to hurt Eric?" Jenny asked. Lance had never told her anything about the man, save for a few words here and there.

"He still blames Duane for the night Ada disappeared," Diane replied.

"And I hear he turned gay and is living with a dude," Pete interjected. "He's like an ex-rodeo star from Wyoming, or something. They're both super tough hombres."

"You can't turn gay," Diane said, and frowned. "Besides, that's got nothing to do with it. I know he used to be a beautiful young man, back before they sent him off to Vietnam. But I talked to a few people today who've seen Webb in the past day or two, and apparently he's gone completely off his rocker. He looks like he did when he came back from the war."

"The thousand-yard stare," Pete said. "Ready to snap in an instant."

* * *

It was near midnight as Jenny drove back along the Cove Road toward home, utterly exhausted, barely able to keep her eyes open. She guzzled half a cup of cold coffee and turned up the heater. To make herself feel better, she tuned the radio to a sports talk show that always made her think of her father. It was comforting to picture him puttering around his workbench in the corner of the basement, a rickety radio playing low as he worked on his model railroad set. An eight-year-old version of herself sitting next to him on a high stool, coloring or drawing pictures of unicorns and Smurfs on graph paper. Her father rambling on about curling or the Packers, talking back to the hosts on the radio. And periodically telling her knock-knock jokes, trying to make her smile.

And where would Mom be? Out with the girls at O'Callahan's or dozing in the yellow armchair in the den, sleeping off a hangover. Separate from us, always.

Jenny wished her father was there with her then. He'd always told her that he admired how persistent she was, how full of faith that eventually, if she kept at it, everything would work out and she would learn the answers she needed.

I've never seen you let go, Jennifer. Not ever.

When she was six years old, she stayed up all night on the living room couch, waiting for Santa Claus, refusing to fall asleep. Sometime after two o'clock, her father finally came in with an armload of presents and was forced to tell her the disappointing truth about the man in the red suit.

Jenny rounded a bend and the lights of Blackhawk Island appeared across the lake, winking distantly like forgotten stars. She only needed to cross the bridge over the creek and then she was home.

The radio suddenly switched off.

Frowning, she pressed the radio on button. A voice blasted quickly from the speakers, warbling a familiar tune from more than thirty years before:

Sharing horizons that are new to us...

Then: nothing. Jenny tapped the button again and the radio picked up another frequency: a man's voice singing, smooth as cream, as if from an antique phonograph:

I'm gonna pin a medal on the girl I left behind...

The dashboard light flickered off. The headlights flared brightly for a split second, like two exploding comets, then went dark.

"Not again," Jenny said. "Please."

She stopped the car in the middle of the road, the wind blowing the high weeds that lined either side of it. She knew the car battery had been replaced less than a month before, so the electrical system should be in working order.

The engine sputtered and died.

What in the hell is—

A figure stood in the middle of Brisco Creek Bridge. He was less than twenty feet away, cloaked with the night.

Lance!

Maybe he'd fallen after all and had woken up disoriented. Perhaps he'd spent the day wandering through the forest looking for her. Maybe—

She felt for the car door handle and pushed.

Nothing.

"Please," Jenny pleaded, shoving the handle again. "Let me out!"

The door would not budge. A gust of wind shook the car windows, as if the damp night were trying to force its way inside. Crisscrossed veins of frost shot across the glass in beveled patterns, crackling like popcorn.

The figure strode across the bridge, heading straight for her. It was a man with a ragged beard and a tunic made of bloody animal hide. He wore a crude helmet with two animal bones protruding from each side. There was a lost, ravenous look in his eyes, as if he would rip apart anyone who got close.

Jenny's stomach clenched in a horrible knot and she knew then that the man came from the same place as the little girl she had seen in the woods with half her face ripped off.

The car came to life all at once. The radio blasted The Carpenters at full volume. Both turn signals blinked simultaneously. Then the headlights switched on and cut sharp paths across the road, shining upon the figure. She saw then that its horrible face was devoid of skin; it was made of only dull white bone and its grizzled beard and desperate eyes that leered at her.

And yes, we've just begun...

Flooring the accelerator, Jenny drove the car right toward it.

The figure pointed a gnarled finger. All at once, a feeling of intense loneliness consumed her mind, as if she'd been shot through the heart by an arrow containing the most devastating poison imaginable. It spread through her body, quick as moonshine, and paralyzed her.

No one ever loved you, Jenny. No one ever wanted you. You're going to spend the rest of your life alone.

Jenny choked, struggling to breathe, trying to keep the car from going into the ditch.

No! That's not true. You have no power over me!

She wrestled the steering wheel to the left as the car shot straight toward the figure—

—which vanished just before the moment of impact. The car's right front headlight smashed against the bridge abutment as the vehicle came to rest there, its wheels spinning.

"Lance," Jenny cried, collapsing in tears. "Where are you?"

18

Chapter Eighteen—MARTIN

It was after midnight. Martin was back at work in the security office at Harborfront Stroll, working Wiley's shift. Arnold Jefferson was there, too, sitting at the desk next to him, leafing through a brochure about a dog track in Manitoba.

The lights flickered in the room. Then they went out, along with all the security monitors.

"What the—" Arnold said.

Martin felt a frigid draft on the back of his neck. He glanced behind him. The door that led to the mall was shut.

Just as suddenly, everything came on again.

"Damn computers are on the fritz," Arnold proclaimed helpfully.

Martin resisted saying something in return. He'd been thinking about the time that he and Patti went to a movie memorabilia convention in Manistique and she bought him an autographed still of Jerry Reed from *Smokey and the Bandit* for $27. It was in the top five nicest things that anyone had ever done for him.

"I'd put in a call to the tech people, but they're probably out getting lap dances at The Crystal Palace," Arnold said. "All nerds are closet perverts. I bet you didn't know that, did you?"

Since Arnold usually used the computer for internet betting sites, instead of accessing police bulletins or things actually related to their job, Martin wondered why it all mattered.

"I'll tell you something, Curly. You sure do look like shit tonight," Arnold said.

"Thank you," Martin replied. "Thanks for that support."

"What the Sam hell is wrong with you?"

"I've been having trouble sleeping. That's all."

And I've been watching over my shoulder all night for a lumberjack enforcer who wants to kill me.

"What happened to your face? Apart from your poor mama squirtin' you out like that?"

"I fell," Martin said. "I tripped and fell."

"That figures," Arnold replied. "You ain't the sharpest tool in nobody's shed."

Martin didn't want to mention that he had nearly rear-ended a muddy pickup truck on Moose Avenue on his way into work that night, after he had fallen asleep for two seconds. Thankfully the two big guys in CAT caps with a gun rack on the back hadn't stopped to have a conversation about his driving skills, or lack thereof.

"I seen it a hundred times before," Arnold said. He frequently kept talking, long after it was appropriate to stop. He took a bite of an unidentifiable gray piece of meat from a Tupperware container. Curdled gravy dripped off his chin. "It's that purple-haired girl you're running with. Women aren't worth the skin off a jackrabbit. All that grief for so little poonanny."

Martin decided not to reply. He didn't remember telling Arnold anything about Patti, let along showing him a picture of her.

"And she got you taking French, yet. You live in God bloomin' America. Speak the language like everyone else, for fuck's sake."

"My brother lives in Montreal," Martin said. "They speak French there."

"You really think you're gettin' out of Great Water? To Canada, or somewhere where they speak a whole 'nother language?"

"Sure," Martin said. "I'm only twenty-eight. I've got my whole life in front of me."

Arnold chuckled. "Sure you do. Unless you can skate faster than Mark Messier, or you get a job on a fishing trawler up the St. Lawrence, you're staying put."

Just then, Martin saw a figure on one of the security monitors. A young teenager stood outside Larry's Lobsters, under the awning, near the payphone.

"Hey. There's a kid out there," Martin said.

Arnold wiped his chin and stared at a black-and-white monitor, which gave a reading from Camera #5. "It's almost one o'clock in the morning," he said. "What's he doin' out there? Looks like one of them surfer kids. What's he doin', trying to make a phone call?"

"That's what it looks like," Martin said.

"You know those surfer kids from up the lake come down here to do methamphetamines, down there on the rocks," Arnold said. "I seen their pipes and their implements and whatnot in the sand."

"I've never seen anything like that," Martin said.

"That's because you don't look," Arnold said pointedly. "You get out there, now. You check that backpack he's got. I'm sure he's got spray cans or crack pipes, something serious in there. Don't think he doesn't."

"He looks harmless to me," Martin said.

"What about that lady who scraped her wrists up? Was she harmless?"

"That's not the same at all."

"There you go again," Arnold sighed. "Why do you always see the best in people?"

* * *

The kid saw him coming. There was nowhere for him to run except past Larry's Lobsters and down a short path to the end of the Stroll, where there was a lookout point with ancient binocular machines that cost a quarter to operate.

"Wait," Martin yelled. He ran down the cobblestone path, past the outdoor tables and trees in heavy stone pots, hung with white lights that swayed in the wind. He rounded the corner and then there was the lake and moon that hung red and low in the sky.

The kid was trying to hop over the railing, onto the jagged rocks below. His backpack slipped off his shoulders. When he hesitated, one foot over the metal bar, it gave Martin a chance to catch up to him and grab the kid by his sweatshirt. He pulled him back and shined his flashlight in the kid's face. Dirty blond hair fell into his eyes. He had a thick jaw and a long, curved nose. Martin didn't think he looked dangerous, but he couldn't be sure.

"What the hell do you think you're doing?"

"You scared me," the kid said. "I didn't think anyone was out here."

"Why'd you take off like that?"

"I don't know. I was scared."

"What's your name?"

"Eric," the kid said. He seemed petrified and numb, like he'd been walking for hours in the cold, alone.

"Do you have any weapons, Eric? Anything I should know about?"

The kid looked at Martin as if he'd just asked him if he was a purple yak. "I just have my backpack and me, that's all," he said.

"Do your parents know you're out here on the Stroll at one o'clock in the morning?"

"Affirmative," Eric said. He brushed the hair out of his eyes and took a breath. "I mean, I was just calling for a ride. I'm gonna spend the night at my dad's house. He lives over on Cranberry Street."

"I know where that is," Martin replied.

A gust of wind brought the smell of approaching winter: endless weeks of snow, icy roads and spring, long delayed.

"Are you going to arrest me?"

Martin regarded him carefully. The kid's teeth chattered and his face was pale and gaunt in the darkness.

"You haven't committed a crime, have you?" Martin asked.

130

"No."

"Then why would I arrest you?"

"I don't know," Eric said. "I don't know what the procedure is. I've never been in trouble for anything."

"You look like you're barely even thirteen years old. What're you doing out here so late?"

"My mom and her boyfriend had a gnarly fight. They were screaming and throwing stuff at each other and I couldn't sleep. So I left and I called my dad."

"It's not cool to just run off like that," Martin said. "I mean, without telling anyone. It's extremely dangerous."

"I'm gonna go live with him," Eric said. "My mom doesn't understand me, even though she has custody of me. My dad has a new wife and he's gonna move to California. It doesn't snow there, plus there are all these cool tropical plants like Bird of Paradise. So I'm hoping he'll take me back, or at least switch custody rights."

"That's an ambitious plan," Martin said.

"I'm an ambitious young man," Eric replied.

"It's going to snow tonight. You're going to freeze to death if you stand out here much longer."

"That would never happen to me, because my metabolism runs at such a high rate," Eric said. "I create heat. Kind of like a superpower."

Martin saw a hurt in the boy's eyes that was wide and deep. He didn't see the harm in making sure the kid got the ride he was waiting for. Maybe things truly were bad at home and he needed to be away from it.

"When's your dad coming?"

"He should be here entirely soon," Eric replied. "I told him I'd be in the parking lot, over by the mailboxes."

Martin considered this. "Normally, I'd call your parents myself," he said. "That's what we're trained to do. But as long as your dad's coming, and he'll take you someplace warm, then I don't see any harm in just letting you go."

Martin didn't mention that for once, he just wanted to do the thing that felt right, instead of what everyone else wanted him to do.

"Thanks, man," Eric said. "Thanks a lot. I wish all cops were as rad as you. You're the first one I've seen with a tooth missing."

Martin grinned. "Just bring me back something from California," he said. "Like a sand dollar. Or maybe a Gecko."

* * *

Arnold Jefferson was waiting for Martin outside the security office. "What happened to that juvenile?" he asked.

"His dad came and picked him up," Martin said. "It's okay, he's clear."

"Well, genius, the computers just came back up," Arnold replied. "And we got an email bulletin. A bulletin for a missing fourteen-year old kid."

19

Chapter Nineteen—ERIC

Eric had trouble falling asleep. The intense light from the strange red moon penetrated the twisted window blinds like a spotlight. And the couch cushions in Taco's living room were itchy and smelled like stale Chinese takeout. Sometime after three o'clock, he took out the letters he'd written to his father and found one written on light blue stationery that he'd borrowed from his mother's desk.

* * *

Dear Dad,

Some kids snuck beer into school and down into their lockers before gym class. Four guys did it and they were really hammered while we all played baseball outside. Mr. Augustino is so dumb he didn't even realize it. He just kept yelling at them to *catch the fuckin ball, dumbass* and *stop acting like monkeys* and *don't you know how to swing?*

We were down in the locker room afterwards changing and the guys were still drunk. They were jumping on top of each other in their underwear and burping in each others' faces. Then they started grabbing random kids and holding them down and grinding on top of them. The drunk dudes were these huge guys like Paul

133

McCoy and Sven Ackerland. It was funny at first because the kids on the floor looked so scared.

Then this guy Jack Beaudaire tackled me and I went down on the wet floor. He yells C'mere baby and give me some lovin! I was just in my jeans and no shirt and this kid is really strong because he plays football. He's only wearing underwear and his breath smells like Pabst Blue Ribbon. He sits on my face and starts rubbing his crotch against me and singing Hit Me Baby One More Time.

This horrible feeling comes over me. The only way to explain it is like being on the high dive at the swimming pool and someone trying to push you off and you don't want to go. My stomach drops and my hands go all numb. And the worst part is that I know I've felt this way before, but I don't remember when or why.

I start screaming really loud. I don't realize I'm doing it but Taco told me later that it sounded like I was being murdered. Jack stumbles off of me and all the other guys in the locker room gather around. Nobody helps me up. They just stare at me like I'm pathetic.

I didn't tell anyone about it, not Mr. Grewall or Mom or anybody.
-Eric

* * *

"Wake up, Spider."

Eric opened his eyes. Taco stood over him. He wore a long underwear top and Michigan State sweatpants. Bristly black hair stood straight up from his head like the quills of an agitated porcupine.

"What's the haps?" Eric said.

"It's almost eight thirty. My mom's gonna be home any minute," Taco said. "You gotta get your funky ass up, 'cause I ain't gonna get in trouble for harboring a fugitive."

Taco's mother worked the graveyard shift, cleaning offices in Manistique. Taco had picked Eric up last night from Harborfront Stroll, in his brother's Subaru. He'd just gotten his learner's permit and drove like an elderly woman driving her friends to Bingo.

Eric sat up on the couch, blinking in the light that crept under the gray blinds. "Don't call me Spider," he said. After he'd found a dead spider in his lime Jell-O at school once, Taco had dared him to eat it, and Eric had.

"Spider, Spider, Spider," Taco replied. "Listen up now. Eugene is leaving for work in less than five minutes. He offered to give you a ride to Webb Turner's, since it's on his way and all."

Eugene was Taco's brother. He was much older than Taco, and worked in a toll booth on the Interstate. He had questionable teeth and listened to Jethro Tull but was actually very nice.

"Drastic," Eric said.

"But let the record show that I think you're jumping into a highly dangerous situation."

"Understood. But I need to get that board back. Or at least figure out what all this is about."

"Why not forget it?" Taco asked.

"I can't," Eric said. "It makes my stomach ache."

Taco rolled his eyes. "You're a numbskull. The only things you should be worrying about are girls and waves."

Eugene ran into the kitchen. He grabbed a piece of toaster strudel from the microwave and wrapped it in a napkin. His starched polyester shirt was half-buttoned, and he wore Nike flipflops even though it was nearly freezing outside. He looked like a handsome version of Vanilla Ice.

"Webb Turner is a crazy mofo," Eugene said, as he bit into his breakfast. He picked at a scab on his elbow. "I've seen him around town and he's always drunk or looking to bash someone's head in," he said.

"He seems to have a personal vendetta against me," Eric said. "I'm not sure why."

"What does 'vendetta' mean?" Taco asked.

"He's a carp for swiping your board," Eugene said, ignoring his brother's question. "That was truly uncalled for. Doesn't he know the code of the shore?"

"A wave breaks in water that's half as deep as the wave is tall," Eric said.

"Spider," Taco said. "Listen to me. The police are gonna find you and haul you back to your mom and she's gonna be pissed. If she doesn't have a nervous breakdown first."

"Quit being a girl," Eugene said to Taco, and punched him on the shoulder. "Excuse *moi*," he said to Eric. "I gotta go find my lucky socks. Be ready to split in t-minus three minutes, yeah?"

Eugene disappeared into his bedroom, humming a Jethro Tull guitar riff under his breath.

"At least lemme get some breakfast before I leave," Eric said to Taco. "I haven't had anything to eat since last night. And that was a bag of Cool Ranch Doritos."

Taco sighed. He took a look in the cabinets, which were nearly bare. One of the doors was missing.

"We've got Oat Puffies or Cinnamon Life," he said. Then he checked the refrigerator. "Or pickle relish or baking soda," he said, and laughed. "Take your pick."

"Oat Puffies. And milk, if you've got it."

Taco set the blue box of cereal on the counter, along with a ceramic bowl and a half-empty carton of milk. "You are really insane, you know that?" he said. "Running away to freakin' California. You've never even been off the Upper Peninsula before."

Eric remembered the security guard at the mall; how pale and sad he'd seemed. "Neither have you," he replied. "But I told you, I'm not going anywhere until I get some answers."

The kitchen floor was freezing cold on his bare feet. He poured the cereal and the milk quickly, and then hopped back to the carpeted living room, still trying to straighten the sleepy edges of his mind.

"My dad definitely wants me to come," Eric added.

"Did he really say that? Or are you just reading into it?"

"You don't know my dad," Eric said. "You never met him. He runs a surf school now. He's got a wife named Misty and it never snows in California, so I'm not gonna be crying for you once the snow starts coming down and the lake freezes over."

"Look here, you little grommet," Taco said. He was taller than Eric, and wrestled on the junior varsity team at school, so Eric had to watch what he said sometimes. But he was a much better surfer than Taco, so that made things even.

"I'm just saying that catching a bus to San Diego without even telling your dad you're coming is not the most brilliant idea. And neither is hitchhiking. I had a cousin who tried hitchhiking from Detroit to Nashville. He got strangled by an escaped convict."

"Did he die?" Eric asked.

Taco laughed. "That's what strangled means, genius," he said.

There was a knock at the door. Eric and Taco exchanged a look. "That ain't my mom," Taco said. "She's got her key."

Eric put his bowl of cereal in the kitchen and grabbed his backpack. He dashed toward the bathroom, which was just off the living room.

"I ain't gonna lie for you again," Taco grumbled, as he walked to the front door of the apartment.

"Please," Eric whispered. "Don't tell them I'm here."

Taco sighed. "Spider. What am I gonna do with you?"

There was another knock, more insistent this time. Eric went into the bathroom and left the door open a little bit, so that it looked like no one was inside. He heard Taco unlock the front door.

"Hi, Theodore," Eric's mother said. "Sorry to wake you, but I had to come by to see you in person." She sounded like she had just run all the way down the street and up the stairs.

"Hello, ma'am," Taco said.

"Is Eric here? Have you seen him?"

"No, ma'am," Taco said. "Like I told you last night, not since eighth period on Friday."

Eric peeked between the hinges. His mother stood there in the dim apartment. She wore one of Pete's green flannel shirts, and tennis shoes that were streaked with mud. Her hair was pulled back in a ponytail that swung from side to side as she scanned the living room. It looked like she hadn't slept all night. Eric felt a sudden twinge of sadness. He wanted to run into her arms.

"Is your mother home?" she asked.

"She's at work."

"Listen," Eric's mother said. "Theodore. I want you to tell me the truth. Eric could be hurt. He could be kidnapped or lying in a ditch by the side of the road somewhere."

"I told you, I haven't seen him," Taco said.

Diane Samuels looked down at the floor.

"I'm sure he's okay," Taco said. "He's a tough kid, I know nothing bad would ever happen to him."

"You say that now. You say that now, but there's no way of knowing."

"Maybe he's with a girl," Taco said. "Maybe he's with a girl and he doesn't want you to know."

Eric's mother wiped at her eyes. "No," she replied. "Eric isn't interested in girls."

Taco was silent.

"Did he say anything to you?" she asked. "I mean, about his father? Did he talk about his father at all?"

The heat switched on then. Eric heard it rumbling through the heating vent next to him.

"No," Taco said. Then he glanced back toward the bathroom. "Well, sometimes. Just about how much he misses him."

"Listen," Eric's mother said. She put her hand on Taco's shoulder then. It sounded like she was about to burst into tears. "If you talk to him, if you see him, could you tell him we love him and we want him to come home? Would you do that for me?"

Eric swallowed hard.

"Yes," Taco said. "I can do that."

"And another thing. I know you might think this is personal, but I don't mind sharing it. Did he ever say anything about something that happened last winter? When I went to the hospital?"

"You mean, when you slipped on the steps," Taco said.

"Yes," she replied. "I lost the baby. I lost the baby that I was carrying. And Eric blames himself for that. He thinks he was responsible somehow. If you see him, could you tell him that it's okay? That it wasn't his fault?"

"He'll be glad to hear that," Taco said.

His mother smiled then, a thin smile of hope. That's the way she had always smiled. Eric had never known any other.

"Thank you," his mother said. "Thank you, Taco." She hugged him tightly. "You're his best friend. Thank you for being there for him."

And then she was gone.

Taco closed the front door. He stood there for a moment. Then Eugene emerged from the doorway of his bedroom.

The three of them were silent. A dog barked from the apartment downstairs.

"Thanks," Eric said to Taco. "I know that was tough for you."

"My little bro," Eugene said. "Coming through when it counts."

"I hope you know what you're doing, Spider," Taco sighed. "I really do."

20

Chapter Twenty—JENNY

She ran barefoot along the highway shoulder. Cars sped past her in the blowing snow. She waved her arms frantically and implored them to stop.

Where is he? she yelled. Where is my husband?

Drivers with blurred faces offered no acknowledgment of her presence. A semi roared past her, spraying mud and slush across her nightgown.

Stop, she screamed. Please stop!

Then suddenly, across the highway, she saw a briefcase sitting on the gravel. The leather was faded but the eagle sticker on the side was unmistakable. It was the case that her husband carried with him everywhere.

Jenny darted across the highway, cars honking and skidding out on the ice as they swerved to avoid hitting her.

She reached the briefcase and unlocked it with shaking hands.

It was empty.

No! she yelled. Where are you?

She looked around frantically, the highway cutting a path through impenetrably murky forests of pine, the cement sky pressing down like an anvil.

It was then that she saw the boy, lying face down in the drainage ditch nearby. His shirt was off and his pants were undone. His skin was the color of bone.

Jenny ran onto the grass and slipped down the short bank of the ditch to where the boy lay among the dead weeds. When she reached him, she saw his wavy blond hair, muddied and covered with a thin dusting of snow—and matted with blood. It was Eric.

* * *

Jenny opened her eyes with a gasp. She lay on the loveseat in the sunroom, covered by a knitted green shawl. Outside, flurries tumbled against the windows and melted as soon as they touched the glass.

It's morning.

Her head spun with hunger, and her legs were sore and stiff. She couldn't believe she'd slept so long.

Then it all came back to her: the drive home, the horrible figure on the bridge, smashing the car headlight. Stumbling her way back to her empty house and collapsing on the loveseat in complete exhaustion.

And now this nightmare. Or was it a premonition, like Bridget O'Hara had experienced the night before she was murdered? Whatever it was, it was getting impossible to bear all alone.

She made her way to the kitchen, her bare feet padding across the hardwood floor of the dining room. One of the glass bulbs on the chandelier lay in jagged pieces on the tablecloth. She froze.

Something's been through here. Or someone.

Jenny heard noises coming from the kitchen as she approached; a low mumbling sound, like the muffled speech of a dreamer. "Lance?" she called. She moved forward cautiously. "Sweetheart? Is that you?"

She entered the kitchen. The TV on the counter was turned on; the voices she heard were coming from the morning news. The room was colder than a meat locker.

ZZZAT! An image of a man flashed across the TV screen. He had shaggy hair and was dressed in a security guard's uniform.

"... has been suspended from his job, pending a disciplinary inquiry by the management at Harborfront Stroll," the newscaster said. "In the meantime, if anyone has seen fourteen-year-old Eric Calhoun of Great Water, please call the police hotline number on your screen..."

Eric's photograph appeared. It looked like a middle school picture; his long blond hair was carefully parted down the middle, and he wore a short-sleeved collared shirt. His smile was forced, and there was a scar across the bridge of his nose.

MISSING, the caption read.

Jenny stood there, trying to make sense of it all, her breath forming in front of her in a cloud. She wondered why the police cared about Eric, but not Lance. It didn't seem fair.

The message light blinked on the answering machine. The phone sat on a desk near the window, where she often sat and paid the bills and watched the woodpeckers at the suet feeder.

Jenny ran to it and pressed the Play button.

There was a moment of silence. Then, a barrage of deafening audio static assaulted her ears. It sounded like a thousand high-pitched voices screaming all at once.

She ripped the answering machine plug from the wall. Backing away down the hall, she found her coat and her keys and dashed outside into the cold gray morning.

Maybe he left his briefcase at the office. Maybe I'm supposed to go there and find it. Maybe I—

Flurries melted against her cheeks and eyelashes as she stood there on the gravel driveway, searching her pockets for her car keys. Then, all of a sudden, she stopped.

This isn't you. You know better than to panic. What would Mary Frann from Newhart do in this situation?

Think logically. What haven't you tried yet?

Jenny took a deep breath. The she pulled out her cell phone and dialed her husband.

All was quiet, except for the sound of the wind shivering through the pine trees, and the harsh cries of gulls on the lake, as she waited. Then she heard Lance's cell phone ringing. It was his distinctive *Ode to Joy* ringtone, coming from the forest nearby.

Her heartbeat stuttered. "Lance!" she cried. "Are you there?"

She took off running across the lawn, toward the creek that cut a path across their yard and into the forest. She stumbled through the trees, across pine needles and past dead stumps as the ring grew louder.

"Sweetheart," Jenny cried again. "I'm here! Tell me where you are!"

She reached the clearing where she had seen Bridget O'Hara the day before. The place was empty now, except for a mangy gull that picked at some weeds near the creek's edge. It brayed at her and took off into the snowy sky.

Jenny climbed atop a high, flat rock. The music was loud now, the loudest yet. She felt as if she could reach out and touch him, but there was no one there.

"Lance," she yelled, whirling around desperately. "Where are you?"

Then she saw it. Snagged on a twisted piece of driftwood nearby was Lance's lucky shirt. And next to it: a thick piece of rope, tied around a sturdy tree. The other half of the rope lay in a frayed tangle nearby.

Jenny grabbed the blue flannel fabric. It smelled of spearmint; Lance's scent. She felt the torn pocket, saw his initials written in pen on the tag inside the collar. For a moment, it was like her husband was there again.

The music stopped.

A great black dog stood at the edge of the trees, about thirty feet away. It watched Jenny with eyes that glowed like points of hellfire in the dim November morning. It was the same dog she'd seen in her strawberry patch the day before.

"Please," Jenny said. "Please, no."

Taking a step backward, she tripped and landed awkwardly on a sharp branch, crying out in pain. The hound sniffed the air and took a few menacing steps toward her. A vapor emanated from its throat; it was thick and amber-colored and smelled of sulfur.

Jenny scrambled to her feet, ignoring her throbbing palm. She knew now that she had strayed too far, that she was seeing things that weren't meant for her.

"I'll leave if you want me to," she said, her voice quivering. "Just—"

The hound roared and lumbered across the rocks toward her, leaving a trail of fire in its wake. It blackened the ground and set clumps of weed ablaze.

"Move!"

A young man stood at the edge of the creek bed. He wore a yellow t-shirt and scuffed blue jeans and gestured frantically at her.

"Move your ass! Now!"

Operating on pure adrenaline, Jenny splashed across the frigid water as fast as she could, collapsing into the stranger's arms.

"You're safe," the man said. "Look."

Jenny glanced behind her. The dog vanished in a puff of amber fire that was swept away by the wind.

* * *

The man's name was Pike and he was twenty-nine years old. He was originally from northern Oklahoma and had bright blue eyes and a surfer's build. His ripped yellow t-shirt said: I Roped A Steer At Palomino Peak. He also had a jagged cut across the bridge of his nose and purple bruises on his cheek that looked painful to the touch. He smelled slightly like body odor. Against her better judgment, Jenny decided to trust him.

She refused to go back inside her house, so Pike took her over to his van, which was parked out on the shoulder of the Cove Road. It had a rainbow airbrushed on the side and a strange weathervane-looking contraption that sprouted from the top.

He poured her a thermos cup full of butterscotch coffee and it warmed her up immediately. She sat there, looking through the passenger side at the carpeted interior of the van. There were at least three different laptop computers hooked up to a mini-bank of electronic monitors. There was a Snoopy and Woodstock sleeping bag.

A half-rotten pineapple. Three six packs of Miller Lite.

And piles and piles of books. They had titles like *Sasquatch Among Us* and *Famous Murderers of the Upper Midwest* and *Sea Monsters From A-Z*.

"Excuse the mess," Pike said. "This is pretty much where I live."

"Oh," Jenny said. She'd been through so much in the past twenty-four hours, it was hard to be surprised anymore.

"I guess I should tell you why I'm here," he said. "And why I called you yesterday."

* * *

Jenny had driven past Moosejaw Beach countless times, but she'd never stopped. It featured an eleven-foot-high iron sculpture of a moose, designed by the noted Native American sculptor Louis Freeze. The moose's antlers were completely covered with snow. She kept expecting the animal to come alive and shake it off.

They parked in a lot that offered a view of the surf as it crashed frantically in sprays of white. A single surfer stood on a dune, watching the swells.

"So," Pike said. He wore a woolen hunter's cap with checkered earflaps, presumably to keep his ears warm. He'd spent the past few minutes listening to details about Jenny's visit with Michael Graham and her dream about finding Eric Calhoun dead, not to mention their mutual speculation of whether the briefcase was a hint of where to find Lance.

Jenny hadn't asked him about the black dog. She figured she'd be better off not knowing, especially since she'd seen *Cujo* on HBO when she was little and hadn't slept for a week afterward.

Pike regarded her thoughtfully. "That's certainly a lot to digest," he said. "And you should never underestimate the veracity of prophetic dreams."

"Look," Jenny said. "Thank you for saving me from whatever it was in the woods. And the coffee, too. Thank you. But I'm sure you can appreciate how much I've been through since yesterday morning."

"Of course," Pike said.

"And that I want answers."

"Well," he said. "This might not be easy to take."

"I don't care," Jenny insisted. "How do you know Lance?"

Pike scratched his nose. "I met him here," he said. "It was last May and he tried to kill himself."

Jenny stared at him. "What the fuck are you talking about?" she asked. The words were out of her mouth before she knew it.

But her language didn't seem to bother him. "I was here surfing. I go to school at Kamachok Community College. Well, I did. Until they kicked me out."

"Are you some kind of ghost hunter?"

"Traveling paranormal investigator," Pike corrected her. "Anyhow, I was here surfing and I saw this tall older dude with a cop moustache walking straight into the lake. The surf was breaking like crazy and he was getting pounded, but he just kept walking straight in. Up to his waist, then his shoulders, then his neck."

"That couldn't have been Lance," Jenny said. "He's an excellent swimmer. He's surfed since he was seven years old."

"But it was," Pike said. "That's what I'm telling you now. I swam out to him and grabbed him and by that time his lungs were full of water and he was the color of schoolroom chalk. I used to lifeguard when I was younger and that's why I was able to save him. I paddled hard and brought him back onto the shore. There was no one around because it was like six thirty in the morning. I gave him mouth to mouth and he spat like sixteen gallons of lake water onto the sand and that's how we met."

Jenny felt herself blushing, like she'd been accused of something horrible. "Then what happened?" she asked in a low voice.

"Well, I stayed there and talked to him for a couple hours," Pike said. "I gave him some butterscotch coffee and wrapped him in a towel. Then he took me to breakfast at Bucky's Surf Shack, just across the road there. We had turkey sausage and scrambled eggs and he told me what happened to his sister and how he always felt responsible for it. He told me he wanted to die."

Jenny tried to respond, but she felt like the right words were hovering above her, just out of reach. "I never knew," she finally said.

"I'm sorry to be the one to tell you," Pike replied. "I reckon you've gone through the ringer in the last twenty-four hours."

"Lance always seemed so... normal," Jenny said. "On the outside, at least. There were times when he'd say something odd, something that made me want to ask what he really meant. But I never did."

"It's tough to ask those kinds of questions sometimes."

"I guess I've never wanted to cross the line into prying. Which is a strange thing to say about your husband."

Pike smiled at her comfortingly. "Back in 1970 was the last time the Baptism happened. That's when his sister paddled out onto the lake and most likely got sucked into the spirit world. The astral plane. Whatever you normies want to call it."

Jenny blinked. "The spirit world? You mean—ghosts?"

"That's right," Pike said. "Ghosts are the souls of the deceased who haven't yet crossed over to the other side, for one reason or another. There's a realm, in between our world and what you might know as heaven, where these souls can become trapped. Waiting for passage to the other side. People from our world—people who are alive—can get stuck there too, if they find a way in."

Jenny pictured the waiting room at her doctor's office. Then she imagined Lance sitting in a chair there, reading a magazine. She frowned. "My husband is so practical. He's an architect. All straight lines, sturdy elements supporting one another. It just doesn't seem like him to believe in any of... this."

"Well, he was sure that Ada ended up there. Along with the handful of other people from this little town who've done a disappearing act over the years. "

Jenny watched a gull dip low through the snow flurries and land on a pile of charred driftwood. She swallowed hard.

"Is he—dead?"

"No, ma'am. Definitely not. You're not really dead until you cross over the threshold for good. That's why he wanted to try to rescue his sister. I advised him against it, but—"

They were both silent.

"After all the asking around I've done, it sure seems that no one around here wants to truly believe this place is haunted," Pike continued. "Or they think it isn't their problem. Out of sight, out of mind. Which is ironic, because this town is like the San Andreas Fault of weirdness."

"I just want to know how this happened."

Pike gestured to a pile of notebooks on the floor. "Well, I've pieced things together by talking to old timers here in town," he said. "And by lots of reading. First, the blood red moon appears in the sky over there—"

He pointed to Blackhawk Island.

"—and a door opens, somewhere in the woods near your house. It's not really a door, more like an opening. A portal. People say the light coming out of it is so bright, it hurts to look at it. It's even brighter than a planetary supernova. And it opens three times over two days."

Jenny remembered the drawings on Katie Graham's wall. She nodded.

"Souls in the in-between world enter our own. They see what looks like a way out, so they take it. They're back in the world they used to inhabit, but they soon sense they don't belong here, either. So they wander the woods, waiting for someone who'll help them cross back over. Sometimes they'll even find their way back to their loved ones. Jack Spivey wrote in his diary that he was sure that his dead mother was watching him on the night of the murders. Maybe she even tried to stop him from going through with it."

"But what could a ghost do?"

"You'd be surprised what they're capable of," Pike said, and smiled grimly.

"Do they bring their personal possessions with them?" Jenny asked. "These souls?"

"Sometimes. And they might leave them behind, to show us who they are. Who they were."

"How do you know all this?" she asked. "How could you know?"

"Because I've talked to people who've seen the other side," Pike replied. "I've put a couple hundred thousand miles on this clunker, driving across the country, tracking them down. No place is exactly like Great Water. No other town has its specific history. But stories about a portal opening and what people have seen beyond it... that's the one common factor. And the ones who are really connected to that energy, they often have dreams about the future. Prophecies, you might say."

Jenny sat there in the front seat, staring out at the surf, her mind racing.

"Just before the portal closes, there's a real powerful wind," Pike said. "Like a vacuum. If you're too close, it's *adios, muchachos.*"

"That doesn't explain the horses coming down my hallway yesterday."

"You're positive that's what you heard?"

"Katie Graham saw them, too, when her mom vanished. I'm sure she was telling the truth."

"What else?"

"I saw a man. Last night, on the bridge. He was horrible."

"What did he look like?"

"Like he didn't belong here. Like he came from another time, long ago."

Pike leaned forward excitedly. "Did he look like a Viking?" he asked.

Jenny nodded in surprise. "Yes," she said. "I mean, from the pictures I've seen of Vikings in books, he definitely did. How did you know?"

Pike had a look of validation on his face. "Again, years of research," he answered. "Fueled by countless cans of Mountain Dew. And quite a few stolen library books."

"I don't understand."

"The Vikings were the men on horseback," Pike said.

"They're ghosts?"

Pike nodded.

"Why Vikings? Who are they? It makes no sense. This is Michigan!"

He smiled at her. "As a matter of fact, I have a pretty good idea of why."

"Wait," she interrupted, remembering the rope tied to the tree in the woods. "Is that what happened to Lance? Did he go through the portal? Get sucked in?"

"It sure looks that way," Pike said quietly. "Lance knew the time of the Baptism was coming this weekend. I helped him do the research. Months and months of it. We met at his office and looked at Jack Spivey's diaries, old newspaper clippings, tide charts, everything. And yesterday marked exactly eighty-two years since the O'Hara murders. That was pretty much a dead giveaway that this weekend was fixin' to be chaotic."

"Are you saying Lance wanted to leave?"

"Oh, no," Pike said. He put a hand awkwardly on her shoulder. "Of course not. He was gonna try to get her out. He was gonna try to rescue Ada."

A curtain of steaming anger descended then. Jenny knocked his hand away. "You helped him," she said. "You knew it was dangerous and you helped him leave."

"No."

"I'm his wife, goddammit. I had a right to know."

"I would've stopped him if I could. It's just... I ran into some trouble yesterday."

"What's that supposed to mean?"

"I spent the night in jail in Youngstown," Pike said. "Had too much to drink and I—"

Jenny got out of the van and slammed the door behind her. She set off across the parking lot toward the main road, her breath steaming in front of her, flurries blowing in her face.

"Jenny," Pike called. "Wait up, please."

"Go away," Jenny said. "Leave me alone. You didn't care about Lance. You used him so you could get off on what he told you. All your theories about ghosts and astral planes and dead Vikings. If you thought it was dangerous, you never should've helped him."

Pike reached her. His cheeks were bright red and he looked genuinely sorry.

"When I talked to him on Wednesday, he said that the plans were off," Pike said. "That he was taking you to Chicago for a romantic night and he was going to recommit to your relationship. Make you his number one priority instead of spending all his time thinking about Ada and what he could've done to save her."

"He should have told me," Jenny said, shivering. "I don't want to be one of those people you mentioned, someone who spends the rest of their lives missing the person they loved. Waiting thirty years for the chance to see them again."

"That's the curse of Great Water," he said. "No one's found a way to end it for good."

"I don't have time to be talking about curses. I need to get my husband back."

21

Chapter Twenty-One—MARTIN

Martin was in the offices of Valiant Security, on the other side of town. It was 9:30 in the morning and he still had the thirteen hundred dollars meant for Webb Turner in his pocket. The hard-backed chair he was sitting in and the four cups of coffee he'd consumed overnight were the only things keeping him awake. Every time he closed his eyes, there was comforting darkness, but only for a few fleeting seconds. Then the deep red moon, the one that hung so low on the lake the night before, loomed in front of him. It seemed far away at first. Then, without warning, it sped toward him like an approaching freight train. A feeling of intense panic came with it, like he was barreling toward a horrible fate that he couldn't prevent.

A man named Mr. Norris sat across from him, staring at Martin with a mix of distaste and contempt. He took a sip from his coffee mug. It had a painting of a crying Indian on it.

"It's the moon," Martin declared. It felt like a private revelation, like he'd solved a particularly difficult algebra problem in an empty classroom.

Mr. Norris was clearly confused. "Say what?" he spat.

"I said, it's the moon," Martin replied.

"Haven't you been listening, Van Lottom?"

Mr. Norris was the chief administrative officer of the company. Part of his left earlobe was missing. Martin wondered if he had survived a grizzly bear attack, or if he had just been born that way.

"Yes, but—"

Mr. Norris wiped his chin and put the mug down on top of some employee files on his metal desk. "I told you, you're suspended for two weeks. Without pay."

"I can't—"

"What? You can't afford it? Well, maybe you can ask your mother for money," Mr. Norris smirked.

A pain slashed across Martin's stomach; he gripped the arm of the chair until it subsided. "The kid said that his father was picking him up," he whispered.

"This was a fourteen-year-old who was reported as missing earlier that night," Mr. Norris said. "You and your supervisor were provided with that information. Why didn't you act accordingly?"

"I never received it," Martin said. "Our computers were down."

"Bullcrap. Arnold Jefferson said that you knew about this kid but you still let him go."

"That figures," Martin said.

"Would you care to repeat that?"

Martin knew it was pointless to argue about it. "You mentioned a disciplinary hearing," he said.

"That means that we'll be asking you some tough questions," Mr. Norris said. "To find out what happened between you and Eric Calhoun early this morning. Then we can determine whether you should be terminated from your position."

"I've never been fired from a job before," Martin said.

"There's a first time for everything, now, isn't there?"

Martin didn't reply. He was thinking how much he wanted to call Patti then, to call her and have her tell him that everything was going to be okay.

"We've turned a blind eye to your behavior on the job," Mr. Norris said. "You've been with us, what? A little more than a year? And all of your co-workers have unflattering things to say about you. You hardly ever talk. You don't believe in the mission objectives of our company. You consume large coffees and soda pop the whole time and stare off into space. I've tried to provide you with the names of people who can help you."

"I'm fine," Martin said.

"That's what Jack Spivey told the guys who worked with him at the dock. Just before he lost his marbles."

"Jack Spivey was a mentally deranged killer," Martin countered.

"Well, you look like absolute dog crap," Mr. Norris said. "So I don't think you have far to go to reach that point. If I were your superior officer and you showed up to work in that condition, your carcass would be out on the street before the magpies began to sing."

"I—"

Mr. Norris leaned forward. "Yes?" he asked, a warning edge in his voice. "What is it?"

Martin was silent. Mr. Norris chuckled and leaned back in his chair. "Has that purple-haired filly been giving you problems?"

Martin regarded him warily. "What?"

"Your lady friend. I remember her from the company pizza party two weeks ago. She wore that tight halter top that showed off her bosoms. What was her name? Petunia?"

Martin bristled. "Patricia," he said.

"That's it. Purple Patti. How is that girl?"

Martin lunged out of his chair and grabbed Mr. Norris' paisley tie, pulling the older man's face close to his. Caught off guard, Norris choked out a few unintelligible words as Martin twisted the fabric tightly, constricting his airway.

He stared into Norris' suddenly panicked eyes, enjoying what he saw there. "Don't ever mention her name again," Martin growled. "Got it?"

Mr. Norris nodded quickly, his face turning the color of a nasty bruise.

"I don't let my women be disrespected, least of all by a limp-dick pencil pusher like you," Martin said.

Norris nodded again and Martin released his grip. The older man coughed twice, rubbing his neck. Then a sly smile crossed his face.

"There's the fight I've been looking for, Martin Van Lottom," he said. "Looks like you got some spunk in your jizz after all."

* * *

Flurries tumbled down from the sky as Martin made his way across the parking lot to his car. The office park was empty because it was Sunday. The wind blew steady and cold. Whitecaps glinted on the lake.

Martin tried to process what had happened back in the office. He couldn't remember ever grabbing anyone so violently like that, not even Lars when they were playing *WWF SuperSlam* as kids. It felt like something had been awakened inside him that would keep hovering just beneath the surface like a predatory crocodile. Something that had never been present until that weekend and the blood red moon.

He had nearly reached his car when he saw a battered orange Volkswagen turn off the main road and enter the parking lot. He caught a quick glimpse of a man wearing an eye patch, sitting in the passenger's seat.

The car came to a screeching stop; a woman got out and ran up to him. Martin knew who she was, even before she spoke.

"What the fuck happened last night?" Eric's mother asked. She wore paint-spattered jeans and a red wool scarf.

"Listen," Martin said. "Let me explain."

The man wearing an eye patch and cowboy boots got out of the car and came over to them.

"We've been to the police," Pete said to him. "We know what happened between you and Eric last night. We know that you were the last person to see him."

"I thought you were a security guard. I thought you were supposed to keep people safe," Eric's mother said. "Why did you let my son go, you bastard?"

Pete grabbed Eric's mother by the shoulder, gently but firmly. "Diane," he said.

"No, goddamn it," Eric's mother said, pulling away. Tiny flecks of spit flew out of her mouth. "You let me talk, Pete. I want to hear what this man has to say. I want to hear his excuse."

Martin looked at her. Her hair was graying around her ears, but her eyes were sharp.

I could tell her that I admire that kid. He wants to get out of this crummy town and find something better. I wish I had that. I wish I had choices.

"There is no excuse," he said finally. "Eric said he was going to spend the night with his father. He said that you and your boyfriend had a fight and that he was going to see his dad."

"Pete is his father," Diane said.

"Diane," Pete said.

"You're the only father I want in his life," she insisted.

"How can you blame me for this?" Martin asked. "Eric's the one who lied to me."

Eric's mother slapped him hard across the face. Martin stared at her in shock, his cheek tingling in the cold.

"What were you thinking?" Eric's mother yelled. "Can you tell me that?"

"I wanted to help him," Martin said.

"Someone needs to teach you the difference between right and wrong," Eric's mother replied. "Because you're obviously a complete moron."

"You can't talk to me like that."

"I knew your father. George Van Lottom was crazier than a shithouse rat."

Martin took a step toward her. "You take that back."

"He flashed those girls in the park. Those girls were Eric's age. They were just children. What kind of a pervert was he?"

"You better get your facts straight," Martin said.

"You're insane," she said. "Like father, like son."

"Diane," Pete said. "That's enough, goddammit. There's no need to get personal."

Pete pulled Martin aside. "Look," he said. "Look here. We've been looking all over town for Eric since last night. We haven't slept. We've called his friends and people who might have seen him but nobody knows anything. So we're a bit concerned. I hope you can appreciate that."

"Sure," Martin said. "Yes, I can."

"And if something happens to our boy, well—"

They stared at each other.

"I'm gonna put you in the hospital," Pete finished. "Permanently."

I'm sorry, Martin thought. He tried to speak the words out loud, but his throat felt heavy and tight.

Eric's mother turned to him. She leaned against the side of the Volkswagen for support. One of the windshield wiper blades was missing.

"My son is gone, and it's all your fault," she whispered. "It's all your fault." She sounded like an old nun, praying the rosary in church. Her hands shook violently.

Pete pulled her away. "Diane," he said. "That's enough now. We know where Eric's headed. He's going to California. There's no need for any more of this. Not now." He opened the passenger's side door and helped Eric's mother inside. She sat there, staring straight ahead, shifting tree branches reflected in the windshield. Martin couldn't tell if she was crying.

22

Chapter Twenty-Two—ERIC

Webb Turner lived in the deep woods across the road from Lighthouse Park. This was most definitely not a surprise. The forest was a place most townspeople knew not to enter unless they knew the quickest way out. It was a sprawling maze of deformed pine trees and rutted dirt roads, with houses hidden among them—mostly one-story bungalows with high metal fences and fancy motorcycles parked out front. The convicted felons who lived there had nicknames like Butch and Salamander and The Minotaur.

Taco had taken on a paper route the previous summer. He had nervously enlisted Eric's help on the first day, after he learned that he had customers in the forest. The boys found a dead cowbird in a muddy wheelbarrow on the front porch of their very first house; its stomach was torn out. This was a signal to dump the remaining newspapers in a ditch and get the heck out of Dodge. The local paper was typically less than eighteen pages, and half of it was classifieds, so it wasn't an enormous loss.

The lake appeared out Eric's window as Eugene drove down the Cove Road. Whitecaps flashed in the morning light.

"Time to rock and roll," Eugene said. He slowed as they approached their turnoff.

"Shaka," Eric replied.

Lighthouse Park was on a hill that climbed sharply up from the road and overlooked the harbor. It was on the State Register of Historic Places, but Eric wasn't sure why. There were a few uncomfortable benches along the path that wound up the slope, as well as a rusted statue of Randolph Brisco, one of the town's founding fathers. The lighthouse, long out of use, had a part-time docent and a small gift shop that sold Jack Spivey keychains. Eric had loved to climb the winding, wrought-iron staircase as a kid, but now, the building just looked like a decrepit old man drinking alone at a bar, long after the lights had been turned off. And the place had become infamous recently because a rich lawyer from town had been arrested for indecent exposure there—with two girls Eric's age, no less.

Eugene pulled his car over to the gravel shoulder near the park entrance and switched off the cassette player. He had popped in the soundtrack from *Rocky*, to get Eric geared up for his mission. Eric was surprised that he owned music other than Jethro Tull.

"Now, Calhoun," Eugene said, gazing across the street, sizing up the woods like an opposing fighter. "Are you sure you're ready for this confrontation?"

"As ready as I'll ever be," Eric said. His heart raced. He felt like he'd chugged a twelve-ounce Mountain Dew too fast.

"Do you know any martial arts?" Eugene asked. He took one last drag on his cigarette, then flicked it out the window. "Do you have a black belt, like yours truly?"

"I don't typically wear belts," Eric said.

"What about a weapon?"

"Affirmative," Eric said. He showed Eugene the knife that Taco had insisted that Eric take with him. It looked like it was made for slicing celery. Normally, Eric practiced a policy of strict non-violence, but he was beginning to reconsider. Sometimes he heard Rose's sobs when he closed his eyes.

"What's that thing? You plan on making a salad or something?"

"Not even."

"Then I'm definitely coming with you," Eugene replied. "The guys at the toll booth are just gonna have to wait."

* * *

The woods were so thick that Eric could not see the sky. A coating of dead pine needles and mud covered the ground, as if there were no longer any need for grass or flowers or things that grew.

"How much further?" he asked. They had been walking for almost ten minutes. The dim light made it seem like sunset.

"Shut your trap and let me concentrate," Eugene said.

"I think we're actually in Siberia," Eric said. "We learned about that place in Geography last week. Maybe there's a gulag back here somewhere."

He took another step and immediately slipped on a patch of snow. His Nikes were soaked instantly.

"Definitely Siberia," Eric confirmed.

"If you think this is a big joke, then why don't I leave you here and let you find this scumbag yourself?"

"Sorry. I get this way when I'm nervous."

Cardboard street signs were nailed to the trunks of trees like strange crucifixions. They came to a fork in the road. After a long moment of internal debate, Eugene followed a spray-painted arrow that pointed left and led down a narrow, bumpy road.

"How do you know this is the right way?"

"This guy I know works at Larry's Lobsters. He deals with Webb all the time. Took me back here once to pick up a package."

"What kind of package?"

Eugene shot him an annoyed glance. "You've got a lot to learn, Cub Scout," he said.

"I could've found my own way back here, you know."

"Is that right?"

"I made it this far without the cops finding me," Eric said. "Except for that lame security guard at the mall last night. But he doesn't count."

"Listen to Mr. Tough Guy over here. Are you hyped up on Dr. Pepper again?"

"Just because I'm quiet doesn't mean I can't take care of myself."

Eugene's glare softened a little. "Listen. If you want to know the truth, I always felt bad that your dad skipped out on you," he admitted. "That's why I'm here."

Eric shivered in the cold. "I don't want anyone to feel sorry for me."

"Dudes need a dad in their life. Mine left a long time ago and I didn't make things easy on my mom. I was a real holy terror. Thankfully I got my shit together a few years ago. Now I can look after you and Taco."

"Lucky us," Eric said sarcastically.

There was a sudden rumble in the forest. Eugene grabbed Eric by the collar and pulled him behind a thick yew bush. They crouched in the mud as a figure on a motorcycle emerged from a bend in the road and sped past their hiding place with a roar.

Eugene poked his head up. "Holy fuck," he said. "I think that was Webb. I'd know that Ninja bike anywhere."

"How're we gonna get the board back now?" Eric asked, brushing off his knees.

"Leave that to me."

Webb Turner's bungalow was rusted and low to the ground. It lay in a clearing near a pitiful creek. An old black sedan sat up on cement blocks nearby; the passenger door was gone. Envelopes and flyers from the Price Slasher were stuffed into a black metal mailbox. Someone had spray painted FUCK OFF on the side of it.

"You'd think a bigtime drug dealer could afford a few home improvements now and then," Eugene said.

Eric shrugged. He was thinking the same thing.

"He must have a secret mansion in Traverse City," Eugene added.

"Maybe this town just feels like home to him."

"No sane person would want to stay in Great Water," Eugene replied.

"You and I both know this town is just one long *Cops* episode. Except if you're from Goosebeak, but what is that, about point two percent of the population?"

Eric laughed grimly. No sane person would want to stay in Great Water, but it seemed like no one was ever able to leave, either.

Except his father.

Flat pieces of shale lay half-buried in the dirt and snow; they led from the clearing to the front door. A speckled bird poked in the mud around a clap-board shed that stood down by the creek. Eric thought it was a chicken, but he wasn't entirely sure.

"So, what's your plan?"

"Check for an open window. Plan B, smash one with a rock. Climb inside and grab what we need, then get the hell out of here."

"I thought you said you outgrew that juvenile delinquent phase," Eric said. "How about we see if anyone's home first?"

"Are you serious?"

"Better that than breaking and entering and getting our nuts shot off by whoever's inside."

Eugene sighed. "You're braver than I thought, Calhoun," he said.

Squirrels chattered at them from the trees as they made their way down the path and up three steps to a narrow porch. The doorbell was covered with gray duct tape and a cardboard shamrock was taped to the screen door. The heavy wooden door behind it was wide open. Eric glanced at Eugene, who shrugged his shoulders.

"He must've left in a hurry," he whispered.

Eric knocked on the metal. The chicken or whatever it was squawked and disappeared into the creek bed. Eric realized then that as usual, he hadn't thought this mission through. He could only remember how defenseless he'd felt when Webb had attacked Rose. He never wanted to feel that way again.

Eric was about to knock on the glass a second time when Eugene shook his head. "Let's just go in," he said. "Grab that board and get the hell out of here."

Eric took a deep breath. Then he opened the door and stepped inside. There was a living room of sorts, piled high with boxes and stacks of magazines. A football game blared on a black-and-white TV, just inside the door.

"Hello," Eric called.

Eugene punched him on the shoulder. "I can see you haven't done this before," he whispered. "Close your mouth and let's just get what we came for, all right?"

It was dim in the living room and the carpet was rust-colored and smelled like vomit. A ratty couch was covered with stacks of newspapers, bound together with frayed cord. Next to it was a coffee table with a broken leg, covered with plastic bags full of white powder.

Eric heard sobbing from another room, up ahead. He froze in his tracks and exchanged a worried look with Eugene.

"I told you I didn't want you to go," a man's voice said. The words were slurred. It sounded like it was coming from the kitchen.

To Eric's right was a doorway that led to a short hall. A surfboard was propped up against the wall, under a single light bulb that hung from the ceiling. The board was long and low-nosed and had three curved fins.

Eric walked carefully across the living room, the sound of his steps muffled by the noise from the TV. He reached the hallway, grabbed the board and turned it over.

It was the color of clover.

"This isn't it," he whispered to Eugene.

"We ain't leaving here without it," he whispered back.

The two of them peeked around a corner and into the kitchen to get a good look at the man who was there, crouched on the floor. He was no more than thirty and wore a half-buttoned flannel shirt and jeans. He had a bruised, swollen eye and blood on his chin.

"You think I don't know what you went through?" the man mumbled. He was carefully picking up the pieces from a shattered glass picture frame. Tears streamed down his face. "Why would I ever leave you?"

Broken dishes covered the linoleum in a puddle of milk. Grocery bags sat on the table, and food lay on the counter, still not put away. There were bags of hamburger buns and lunchmeat and plastic cartons of chicken wings from the Price Slasher. Eric didn't know who the man was, but he looked like he could snap a wooden plank with one hand.

"He'll be right back," the man said to no one in particular. "He just went to get some cigarettes and then he'll be back, that's all. Webb ain't going to no creek. He ain't leaving."

He turned Eric's way. Eric stepped back behind the wall before the man could spot him.

"I told you no," the man yelled suddenly. "What the fuck are you doing?"

Eric and Eugene dashed down the hallway, under the single light bulb, and into a bedroom. They stood behind the door, breathing quickly. Eric's heart beat a mile a second. Eugene looked scared.

Eric scanned the bedroom. There was no window, only a twin bed with a busted mattress and sheets that had French guys riding unicycles on them. There was an aquarium on the floor with three large hermit crabs inside: two alive and one dead. And taped to the wall was an ancient poster of an attractive couple sitting on rocks by the seashore; they had shaggy hair and the woman wore a flowing white dress. CLOSE TO YOU | CARPENTERS was lettered above them in blue.

Eric listened at the door. All he could hear now was the noise from the TV; it was the second half of a tight game between the Packers and someone else.

"I'll talk to him," Eugene whispered. "He's drunk, he can't hurt us. I'll find out where Webb went."

"No," Eric said. "We both will."

Eugene finally nodded. Eric opened the door cautiously and peeked out. The hallway was empty; so was the living room. They moved across it and found the man lying in a heap on the kitchen floor, staring straight up at the ceiling. He wasn't moving.

"Hey," Eric said. There was no answer. Eric poked at the man with his toe; he didn't move.

The man held a photograph; the shattered pieces from the glass frame lay around him. The image was black and white and very old. A young man with thick brown hair and sunglasses and a rifle stood on top of a hill. He wore Army fatigues and dog tags and flashed a V sign with his fingers. There was thick jungle behind him.

"I told him I didn't want him to go," the man whispered. He stared straight at Eric and Eugene with bright blue bloodshot eyes.

Eric's heart stuttered. "Go where?" he asked. "Why did he need the board?"

The man grabbed Eric's ankle and held it tight. His grip was freezing cold. There was a tattoo of a wolf on his wrist.

"Let him go," Eugene warned. "Let go of him now."

"She was talking to him," the man said. His voice had a drawl, like from an old cowboy movie. "Sending him messages on the TV. That's what he said. That fucker's lost his mind."

"Where did he take the board?" Eric asked. He thought for a moment that the man would die, still clutching his ankle with a frigid grip that he could never pry off.

"She told him she was waiting for him in the light. What am I supposed to say to that?"

"Who? Who was the woman?" Eric whispered.

"The only girl he ever loved," the man said. "His butterfly baby."

23

Chapter Twenty-Three—JENNY

Jenny drove past a sign that read: Bloomquist Design, Inc., the name etched in black letters on a white marble slab. She turned right onto a loose gravel driveway that led off the Cove Road and into the trees, to the old Whispering Pine cottages, which Lance had purchased a while back and converted into his local offices for himself and junior partners.

She parked the car, got out and started across the snowy gravel toward Lance's office. Behind the cabin was a short beach, scattered with pieces of driftwood. Whitecaps flashed on the lake beyond.

A man stood in front of a dented Oldsmobile Cutlass, parked in one of the visitor spaces off to the side. One of the car's side mirrors was shattered. "Mrs. Bloomquist!" he called. He raised one hand tentatively, like he was hailing a cab but didn't have enough money for the fare.

It was Martin Van Lottom. Jenny hadn't seen him since July, when Lance had him and a dozen other people involved in the Toronto outdoor garden project over to their house for drinks and a congratulatory barbecue. Among his many talents, Lace was a magician on the grill, particularly with honey lemon chicken.

Jenny had forgotten how tall Martin was. He'd always struck her as a genuinely nice person, but he perpetually had a lost look in his eyes, like he'd spent his whole life only making left-hand turns.

"I told you before, remember? Please call me Jenny."

"Hi, Jenny," he replied, and smiled bashfully.

"What're you doing here, Martin?"

He looked absolutely horrible. His eyes were bloodshot and there were substantial bruises on both of his cheeks. There was dried blood above his lip and he hadn't shaved in at least a week. His security guard uniform hung on his gaunt frame like frayed clothes on a scarecrow.

"I have a lunch date with Lance," he replied. "I apologize that I look a little bedraggled, but I had to come straight from work, and I didn't have time to change. He told me to meet him here, but I knocked and nobody's here. I didn't know what else to do but wait."

"You look like you've been in a fight."

Martin looked down. He kicked at the gravel. "Kind of," he said. "It's a long story."

It was clear he didn't want to discuss it. "When was the last time you spoke to Lance?" she asked.

"Not since Tuesday," Martin said. "Why? Is there something wrong?"

* * *

The main room of the cabin was hazy with afternoon light filtering down through the skylight above Lance's enormous drafting table. There were cupboards stacked with pencils and enormous rolls of drawing paper. Charts and maps covered the walls, along with photographs of Lance and Jenny in different locales around the world, from the Australian Outback to the surfing beaches of Costa Rica.

"So what're you looking for?" Martin asked. Back in the parking lot, Jenny had told him that Lance was missing. She didn't mention anything about ghosts.

There was a long silence. "Did you go to the police?" Martin asked, not sure if she'd heard him.

"Of course," Jenny said. "But they didn't want to help. Not until at

167

least two days have passed."

She wanted to add that all of the police's attention seemed to be focused on Eric, but she didn't want to make Martin feel guilty. After all, the news report she'd heard that morning didn't give his side of the story of when he'd run into Eric at Harborfront Stroll.

"Do you think he left something for you here?" Martin asked. "A clue? Or a note?"

Jenny glanced around the room. "I'm not sure," she admitted. But then she saw it, and her heart sank.

Sitting in the middle of Lance's desk was his worn leather briefcase.

Jenny ran to it and twisted open the rusted metal clasps. Inside the briefcase was a VHS tape, a legal pad and manila folders full of old newspaper clippings and Polaroid photographs.

The photos were all shots of their property and the woods around it. There were numerous pictures of the clearing by the creek. Others were of the area under the bridge where Brisco Creek emptied into the lake, as well as the beach around Spivey Point. Scribbled on the backs of them were dates; most were that year, some the year before, or earlier.

Jenny took a closer look at a Polaroid of a tiny church with a stained glass window of a little girl, reaching up to angels high above. She recognized it as the site of Jack Spivey's old cabin on Blackhawk Island.

Another yellowed newspaper clipping from 1970 read: *Local Girl Disappears in Fog at Spivey Point.*

The windows shook against the wind that blew hard off the lake.

"Are you okay?" Martin whispered. Jenny had forgotten he was standing there, next to her.

"What does it—what does it all mean?" he asked.

Wiping tears from her eyes, Jenny picked up the legal pad. It was filled with astronomical diagrams and tidal charts and journal entries, scrawled in Lance's messy, looping cursive. Most detailed Lance's expeditions in the woods, or his trips to Blackhawk Island. Some were observations about Jack Spivey's life.

168

Spivey was a lot like me, one of the entries read. *I know that now. Listening to the wind in the pine trees and the cries of the loons helped him get to sleep at night. It just reached the point where he couldn't bear to be alone. The voices in his head were just too loud.*

* * *

There was a VCR hooked up to a TV in a small conference room. Jenny closed the door and pulled the drapes.

"Are you sure you want to see this?" Martin asked.

Jenny nodded. "He left this for me," she said. "I have to."

She inserted the tape in the VCR. The image flickered to life. There was Lance, sitting on a rock on the beach, Blackhawk Island looming in the distance behind him. It appeared to be a late autumn morning; the lake was gray and restless.

"This is Lance Caleb Bloomquist," he said. "I am of sound mind and body. And this is my living will."

He stopped to glance out at the water, and Jenny thought she saw a tear in his eye.

"I'm entirely aware of how crazy all of this may sound," he said. "But I believe every word of it. For most of my adult life, I've been investigating strange phenomena in the town of Great Water. Events that occurred after the Jack Spivey incident of 1918.

"I lost my sister on this lake, and I know now that she did not drown. Ada was taken away from this physical world, the world we know, into another reality. The reality where some deceased souls actually live and exist."

The waiting room, Jenny thought.

"During The Baptism, some say that the armies of the dead make three rides on horseback," Lance continued. "On a route across Great Water, to gather living beings and take them away to the other side. The last ride comes just before midnight on the third night."

Lance turned away from the camera then, and Jenny knew he was trying to compose himself.

"My sister was taken in this way," Lance said. "And I'm going to try to get her out. No, I won't try. I'm going to do it."

Jenny closed her eyes. Martin put a comforting hand on her shoulder. She could tell he was trying to process everything, just as she was.

"Jennifer," Lance said. "Jennifer, I love you. You turned my life around, and I owe everything to you. But I always felt empty. It's dark and deep and it never went away. I tried to live my life as best I could, but it was too much of a struggle.

"I give it all to you. The house, my business, everything. It's all for you. I have no other family. Ada was my only family. And Duane and Webb. But the three of us, that's only a memory now. And Eric is the only way I have to remember it. So I want you to give him the boards. The boards of the Three Kings. It's time he learned the truth. He has to know that his father wasn't the horrible man that everyone makes him out to be. Duane was actually a pretty righteous dude, back in the day. So, I want you to look after Eric and make sure he's safe. Can you do that?"

Lance paused for a moment.

"I love you," he said. "Thank you for everything you've done for me."

The TV screen went black.

* * *

Martin made her a cup of chamomile tea. The mug had a photograph of the Chemosphere home on it. It was on the side of a mountain in Los Angeles and it was Lance's favorite house. Jenny thought it looked like a home for astronauts.

"Just drink it," Martin said. "My mom says chamomile helps get your thoughts in order."

Jenny took a sip. She had to admit, it tasted perfect. It reminded her of sitting by the window in her house, listening to a Vivaldi concerto on the radio as she watched the snow fall.

"So, your last shot is tonight," Martin said. He sat on a chair in the reception area, thinking.

"Right around midnight is when the portal opens for the last time," she said.

"Trying to get him out would be way too dangerous," Martin said. "I hope you know that."

"We don't know for sure if he..." Jenny's voice trailed off. "We don't know what really happened to him," she finished.

"But you told me you found the frayed rope, tied to a tree. And his shirt. I know it's tough to hear, but obviously he went after her."

Jenny put down her cup. "I'll find Pike and see what he thinks. He'll help me. He already feels bad about not being able to stop Lance in the first place."

"I don't want you to go."

Jenny smiled. It felt good to have someone actually express concern for her. "I appreciate it," she said. "But don't you have your own problem to worry about?"

"I don't know what you mean," Martin replied.

"It's not too late to find Eric."

* * *

Martin said goodbye and drove off down the road, leaving her alone in the cabin. It was hard for Jenny to tell if her words about Eric had made any impression on him at all. But she felt grateful that someone was there when she watched the tape. She knew she wouldn't have been able to handle it alone.

She lingered near the doorway of Lance's office for a while, trying to soak in its homey atmosphere, hoping that it would give her comfort. Jenny even found herself wishing that he would magically materialize at his desk, immersed in blueprints and plans, and greet her with a smile. But everything remained the same.

171

Jenny sighed and pulled on her coat. She opened the front door, took two steps out and found a shaggy-haired man standing on the walkway, just a few feet in front of her.

"Where the fuck is Lance?"

Jenny felt for the door behind her. The man was so close that she didn't have enough room to open the door and get back inside. He was around fifty years old and more than six feet tall. He wore mud-splattered jeans, work boots and an old Army jacket on top of a white t-shirt.

"Who are you?" Jenny asked, her voice wavering. He was unshaven and had dark green eyes that sparked with danger. His hands were huge and looked like they could snap her neck easily.

"I went to your fancy house and rang that fancy doorbell but nobody was there," the man said. His voice was deep and rough, like the men who worked in the lumber yards. "Where's Lance at?"

Jenny saw a motorcycle parked behind him on the gravel driveway. There was no one else within shouting distance. She stood up straight and thrust out her chin. "You haven't told me who you are," she persisted.

"Your husband and I go way back. He's the only honest man in this godforsaken shithole of a town."

"Lance is away on business. And I'd like for you to leave."

Jenny reached for the door handle, but the man shot out a hand and grabbed her wrist. "You're lying," he said.

His grip singed like a hot stove burner. "Let me go," she stammered.

The man smiled crookedly; his uneven teeth were stained yellow with nicotine. "My apologies. My manners are usually top-notch. It's just that I came to say my goodbyes. I've kinda been making the rounds since yesterday." He released his hold on her wrist.

"I'll be sure to tell him you stopped by," Jenny replied nervously, her hand inching toward the door handle again.

The man stared past her through the trees, toward the whitecaps glinting on the lake like shattered glass. A vacant look came over his

172

face. "The waves are hitting so hard," he said. "I wish he and I could go out for one more session together."

"You surf?"

He regarded her warily. "Don't act so surprised. The Three Kings ruled these beaches, back in the day. Ask anybody."

"Wait," she said. "Are you—"

"Webb Turner," he finished. "At your service." He spat a glob of tobacco juice on the steps.

Jenny wondered how much she should tell him about Lance. She decided to stick with her original story.

"I can tell by your perplexed expression that Lance doesn't ever talk about me."

"Not much. I mean, I know you and Lance and—"

"The Three Kings wanted to rule forever," he said. "We swore a blood oath to do it. There was nobody who could touch us out on those waves. Fuck, anything's possible when you're eighteen."

"What happened?" Jenny asked.

Webb glared at her, his expression clouded with anger. "What do you mean, what happened? Viet-fucking-Nam happened. Ada fucking happened. Everything got tossed around and inside out and nobody came out of it the same."

Jenny's heart stuttered. "I'll tell Lance you stopped by," she said. "But you have to leave now."

"Look," he said. "Look here." Webb reached in his jacket pocket and pulled out a white, sealed envelope. He handed it to Jenny with shaking hands. "I ain't all bad, despite what people in town might say," he said. "I'm just trying to survive so I did it the best way I knew how. I thought I had a man who loved me but it turns out he wasn't worth nothing."

Jenny took the envelope. "What's this?" she asked.

Webb seemed to be tuned to a different frequency altogether. He swayed back and forth on his feet unsteadily, like he was crossing a rickety bridge over a deep chasm. "Ada was the only one who ever loved me," he whispered. "And pretty soon I'm gonna be with her again. So you take that and give it to Eric's mom. That boy didn't ask to be born into this mess. I made a shitload of money these past few years, existing the best I could. But none of it means anything if it can't go to good use. There's enough in there to provide for that kid for a real long time."

24

Chapter Twenty-Four—MARTIN

Patti wouldn't return his calls, so Martin decided to go see her, post-haste. She lived in a drafty apartment above a tattoo parlor, in a particularly lower-income neighborhood of town. There was a junkyard across the street from her place, and an auto body shop called Ronnie Raccoon Motors. The sign out front had a raccoon wearing a top hat and tails, dancing on the hood of a car. Martin didn't think animals should ever wear clothes.

He drove past her apartment and parked around the corner on a residential street called Heron Lane. Rusted trailer homes sat back from the road at the end of rutted dirt driveways. Some of the yards had lawn gnomes out front, or bird feeders that were made of fake white marble.

A dog with bristly red fur, pus-filled eyes and a bandaged leg crawled out from under an old Chevy that was up on cement blocks across the street. It ambled up to Martin's car, sniffed at the tires, and then went off in the opposite direction.

Martin sat there for a moment. He took a few deep breaths, but his heart still thumped in his chest like techno music from a crowded dance club. He wanted so badly just to curl up on the front seat of his car and sleep; let the numbing cold surround him until all the aches were gone.

Maybe Valiant Security wouldn't fire him, he thought. And more importantly, maybe Webb's henchman would forgive and forget, if Martin was able to avoid him for long enough. He would just have to find out where Webb lived and drop a check in the mail for him, including all accrued interest, of course. He'd work harder and longer and earn the money to pay his mother back, just like he promised her at the O'Hara house. And once he started moving forward, earning a good living with full health benefits and maybe even accidental death and dismemberment, maybe things would be okay again.

Martin wanted his own family. The night before, he had seen the hope in Eric's eyes and it had moved him like nothing had for a long time. And now he'd seen Jenny probably lose the person she loved most in the world. Martin desperately wanted a family of his own, but he needed someone to show him the way.

* * *

"It's Martin," he said. Wind whistled under the window on the landing outside Patti's apartment door. The window pane was cracked. There was an orange kite stuck in the telephone wires across the alley.

"Just a minute," came a muffled voice from inside.

"C'mon, Patti," he said. "I'm freezing my tail off out here." Death metal music thumped through the walls of the tattoo parlor below.

Then the door opened. Patti's hair was now the color of stale cornflakes. "What're you doing here?" she asked, glaring at him.

Martin leaned over to kiss her, but Patti turned so that his lips met her cheek instead. She smelled like cheap beer and Chinese food.

"What did you do to your hair?"

"I needed a change," she said. "What happened to your face? Did someone hit you?"

"I really need to talk to you," Martin said.

A Mexican man with a shaved head sat on the futon. He wore a red t-shirt inside out, and khaki pants with ripped kneecaps. His thick arms were crisscrossed with veins. He was watching a Korean soap opera.

"Who're you?" Martin asked.

The man turned to look at him. "Is this the guy?" he asked Patti.

"This is Martin," she confirmed.

"Who is he and what is he doing here?" Martin whispered to Patti.

"Hey, fuck you, *compadre*," the man said.

"Pedro, I'm just going to talk to him in the kitchen for a second, okay?" Patti said. "You just watch your television program."

Patti took Martin in the kitchen, which was dingy gray and had a floor that sloped to one side. There was a hot plate and a sink that dripped water constantly. Poetry word magnets were scattered across the refrigerator; two of them held up a menu from Chang Wang. Snow flurries melted on the window that overlooked the junkyard across the street.

"What's going on here?" Martin asked. A sharp ache had developed in the pit of his stomach.

"Lower your voice, okay?"

"Who the heck is this guy? He looks like he's tweaked out on meth," Martin said. "Geez-o-pete."

"Just be quiet for a second," Patti said. "Please."

Martin glanced over and saw a six pack of empty beer cans in the wastebasket.

"Are you drunk right now?"

"Of course not. But listen. I need you to listen, all right?" She peered down at the floor and traced a line in the linoleum with her toe. "I'm with Pedro now," she said quietly.

"What?"

"I met him at a Bloody Lizard concert last week. He works on a fishing boat in Alaska. They go all the way to Siberia and back. He makes a real good living. We're going to move to Dutch Harbor and I'm going to open my own tattoo parlor and sell handmade totem poles."

"What're you talking about? When did this happen?"

"We saw each other last night and we met and we decided to do this," she replied.

"Last night?" Martin asked. He glanced up and saw Pedro standing at the door.

"Hey, no hard feelings," Pedro said. "Things change, you know?"

"This is a private conversation," Martin said. "I'd appreciate it if you'd leave us alone."

Pedro stared at him with narrowed brown eyes. "Fine," he said, and cracked his knuckles. Then he went back to the TV.

"I know this is a lot to handle right now," Patti said.

"I love you," Martin said.

"Martin, we went out on two dates," she said. "And the last one was two weeks ago."

"But you're my girlfriend," Martin insisted.

"You need help," Patti said. "You need to see a doctor. I don't think you understand that."

"Why do people keep saying that?"

"Because it's true. You've dreamed up this whole scenario between us that doesn't exist. It never existed. You've told everyone that we're together and we're not. We never were."

The room began to spin. Martin grabbed hold of the counter.

"Well, you've pulled the rug right out from under me," he said. "Serves me right for thinking you were different." He walked unsteadily across the kitchen to the door that led to the living room. "I didn't think you could ever hurt me," he said. "Not like this."

* * *

Martin drove for at least half an hour, down winding streets of bare November trees and identical gray apartment buildings that had names like Stonecross Manor and Pinewood Court. Then he realized that he didn't know where he was going, so he pulled over and shut off the engine.

The frigid silence overtook him then, and he replayed Patti's words in his head, like a rickety 8-track.

You've told everyone that we're together and we're not. We never were.

Truthfully, he wasn't bothered by the fact that she'd found someone new. Martin had been dumped before, most spectacularly by Whitney Bianchi on the night before Senior Prom. What frightened him was that he really had believed—and felt, deep down—that he and Patti had a history together. The idea that his mind might be operating with its own agenda, devising its own reality, was horrifying. He wanted to be in control; he needed to feel like he was making his own decisions. Living his own life, not being lied to or lying to himself.

He remembered Pearl at Harborfront Stroll the morning before, how she seemed nothing like the cheerful, positive woman he'd always known. It was like someone was inside her. Altering her perception of what was real.

If what I had with Patti wasn't real, then what is?

He held his right hand in front of his face. His nails were bitten down to the cuticles and his fingers shook with a slight tremor. Then the tips began to tingle. The sensation was pleasant at first, like they were thawing out inside, after a long winter walk.

Then his fingers began to disappear.

Martin's heart exploded in his chest. He gaped in disbelief as slowly but surely, his fingers vanished, as if someone was erasing him.

Help!

He couldn't tell if his scream was out loud or only in his mind, but in it, he heard all the desperation and hurt that had accumulated in his heart over the past two days.

Martin glanced at his left hand. His fingers were already gone, up to the knuckles.

Help me! Please!

He glanced around desperately. There was a feeble park across the street, no bigger than an afterthought. It was a square of dead grass about the size of someone's front yard, along with two rusty benches and a swing set. A boy about ten years old, dressed in a black sweatshirt and a ski hat with furry ear flaps, sat on one of the swings, kicking at the snowy dirt.

Martin laid on the car horn with his elbow. The hollow blare echoed through the musty interior of the Cutlass. "Hey!" he yelled. "Over here!"

The boy looked up and then cocked his head, as if he didn't understand a question that only he could hear. Then he got off the swing and began walking toward a nearby house.

No. Come back! Please!

Martin glanced down. Both of his hands were gone. He felt like a child's drawing, a mistake that someone wanted to begin again. His wrists and forearms began to fade and vibrate, like television static.

Maybe I should just take a few deep breaths. Try to relax. Accept it.

He stopped screaming and closed his eyes. The crimson moon loomed in front of his dark consciousness like some kind of deity in an ancient Aztec painting, an all-knowing presence that had complete control over everyone and everything it touched.

Martin cowered in front of it, ready to accept his fate.

I'm history. I'm gone.

He took a deep breath, then another. Then he listened. He listened closely and realized that the moon had something else in mind for him. It was offering him a potential way out.

* * *

Martin banged on the door to Patti's apartment. The orange kite was gone from the tree outside. His conception of time seemed completely askew; he wondered if it was even the same day. Or was it a week later?

Make it right, a voice inside him whispered.

"Open the darn door, Patti," Martin yelled. He wore a bright green ski mask that he'd found on the back seat of his car.

He put an ear to the door and listened. The television blared the

180

theme song from a long-cancelled show about a wholesome family who was raising a little girl who happened to be a robot. Martin typically avoided the program at all costs.

He pounded on the door again, harder this time. Someone from the tattoo parlor downstairs yelled for him to shut the fuck up. There were no voices from inside the apartment, no indication that anyone had heard him. Or cared.

They're in there. Both of them.

Every vein in his body constricted; his heartbeat accelerated like a car from Pole Position. A curtain of red lowered in front of his eyes, like he was wearing special tinted glasses in a science fiction film. It felt comfortable and right, like he finally had the power he needed.

Martin took a few steps backward. He pictured Sergeant T.J. Hooker standing outside a perp's door in a tenement house hallway. With a warrior's cry, he strode forward and kicked at the door with all the strength he could muster.

It burst open with a crash, like a mighty pine tree toppling in the woods. Fueled purely by rage and adrenaline, Martin pushed aside the splintered doorframe, charged into the dingy apartment and found Patti and Pedro seated at the kitchen table, shooting up with methamphetamines.

Pedro wore a wool watchman's cap and a faded tank top with Hulk Hogan's face on it. He contemplated Martin and blinked twice. A needle syringe stuck out of his arm like a giant pin in a pincushion.

Patti bounded to her feet, like she'd been shocked by a hidden buzzer. Her eyes were glued wide open and there was a bloody track mark in the inside of her forearm. "Hey," she sputtered. "What do you—"

Martin pushed her hard; she stumbled backward against the table and knocked over a paper plate full of something that looked like a crushed icicle. The plate flipped onto the floor and the drugs spilled everywhere. Pedro gave an alarmed yell; he finally staggered to his feet and glared at Martin.

"What the fuck are you wearing that mask for? Get out of my house, *pedejo.*"

Martin glanced around the kitchen; all he could see was pulse-pounding red. A heavy ceramic pitcher, half-full of lemonade, sat on the counter. Martin seized it with two hands and charged across the kitchen. Before Pedro could react, Martin smashed it across his temple, sending Pedro sprawling to the floor and splashing lemonade everywhere like a Jackson Pollack painting.

Patti screamed.

A deep welt was already beginning to form on Pedro's right cheek. The man moaned and tried to get up, like a boxer under a ten-count.

"I make the rules!" Martin yelled. "Do you hear me now, fuckface?"

He kicked Pedro as hard as he could. The blow caught him right under the chin and sent one of his teeth flying out of his mouth in a bloody arc.

"Martin!" Patti yelled. "Stop it, please!" She pulled at his shoulder; Martin shoved her backward again with newfound strength.

"I trusted you!" he hollered at her. His voice sounded hoarse and desperate. "You told me you loved me!"

"No," she whispered. "I never—"

"Why did you leave me? You left me alone and now I've got no one. Why did you leave me, Dad?"

The look on Patti's face was pure confusion. "Martin," she pleaded. "Just put the pitcher down. Calm down and we'll talk about it."

Pedro grabbed Martin's leg just below the knee; he was making another attempt to stand. "I'm gonna kill you," Pedro wheezed. "You're fucking history, do you hear me, *cabron*?"

Martin heaved the pitcher and connected with the top of Pedro's skull with a sickening THUMP. His bloodshot eyes rolled back in his head and he collapsed onto the linoleum. He twitched once, then lay completely still.

Patti screamed again; even in Martin's state of pure rage, he recognized that she was truly afraid.

Good, he thought. *You should be.*

On his way out the door he smashed the TV with a lamp, short-circuiting Vicki the Robot's face in a shower of sparks.

25

Chapter Twenty-Five—JENNY

Jenny drove back toward town in the fading light of the afternoon. The Packers game played on the AM radio but she didn't hear a word of it. She could barely contain her anger at Lance. It bubbled up inside her, rocketed through her veins and spilled out of her like water from a thawed winter pipe.

That jerk didn't want me to try to stop him. Doesn't he trust me? I thought spouses weren't supposed to keep secrets from each other. I guess I'm naïve. Or maybe just stupid?

He'd had his chance when he stood at the bedroom window that morning. She knew now that he'd been debating whether or not to tell her.

Maybe he didn't think I'd believe him?

Jenny didn't care if it was traveling through a portal into another dimension or embarking on a new career as a pastry chef. Lance could've talked to her and explained it all. They'd had dozens of discussions about all kind of subjects, and although she could be a bit hard-headed sometimes, she was always open to new ideas, including the possibility of worlds beyond their own. She'd seen at least four episodes of *The X-Files*, for Christ's sake. Jenny figured that should count for something.

She let loose with a scream then, a shriek of pain and abandonment that started deep in her heart and shot through her body like a jolt from a hypodermic needle. It nearly shattered her eardrums and ruptured her vocal chords, but after about eleven seconds, she felt a weight lifted off her chest. She took a deep breath and gripped the steering wheel tightly.

Okay. Time to think about this logically. What are my options?

The thought of following Lance over to the other side terrified her. She knew that much, at least. According to what he'd said on the tape, the opportunity would be there for her, just before midnight, when the horrible riders came through one last time. But she wasn't sure if she wanted to go, or even try to save him. Not without help.

Not without Pike.

She had the phone number of his motel written in her spiral notebook. Although he typically slept in his smelly van as he traveled across the country, he'd mentioned that he needed a hot shower and a firm bed for the night, at the Big Break Inn in Great Water.

Maybe she was a little bit rough on him at Moosejaw. He knew all of this ghost business best, so maybe she could call him and—

She rounded a bend in the road and saw her father, sitting on a dead tree stump.

"Daddy," Jenny said, running up to him, after she'd pulled the car over and parked. "What're you doing out here?"

Her father was dressed in purple sweat pants and slippers, and wore his favorite checkered robe. He turned to look at her, a look of faint surprise on his wrinkled face. His cheeks were bright pink.

"Charlotte?" he asked.

"No, Dad, it's Jenny. I'm your daughter."

"I was just out for a walk. I was walking for a while."

"You know you can't be out by yourself," Jenny said. "You must've been walking for half an hour at least, to get all the way down here. Look at you. You're freezing."

She put her arm around her father and brought him back to her car. His slippers made scuff marks in the snow.

"What happened to your headlight?"

Jenny ignored him. "Where's Mom?" she asked, as she opened the passenger door and helped him inside. She slipped in next to him and cranked up the heat.

"She's meeting a friend at O'Malley's," he said, and coughed deeply. His hands shook as he reached in his pocket for a tissue. "She didn't say who it was," he said. "She never does."

"Oh, Daddy," Jenny said. She brushed his rumpled gray hair back from his forehead, trying to hide how furious she was.

"Don't look at me like that."

"She always leaves you alone. It's just not right."

"Your mom takes care of me."

"You call this taking care of you?"

"We play Crazy Eights. We watch Turner Classic Movies. And she doesn't mind when I watch the World War II shows. I know she hates them."

"She's out getting plastered right now," Jenny said. "She'll come home drunk and stumbling around and yell at you for no reason."

"I don't know," he said. He peered out the window at the snow. A thin layer of it covered the grass and loose gravel that lined the side of the road.

"It's true," Jenny said. "Someone has to say it."

Jenny watched him stare straight ahead, and she was reminded of the countless times that her parents would argue bitterly at the dinner table when she was a child. Her father would end up sitting alone in the den, his face lit by the TV, unwilling to admit any wrongdoing.

"I should come around more," she said. "I can make you that macaroni casserole you love. The one with the caraway seeds."

"Don't start with that again."

"It's true," Jenny said. "I miss you. I want to see you."

"You're busy. You've got volunteering and traveling. And you've got a huge house to take care of. Why would you want to spend your time taking care of a sick old man?"

"You're sixty-one," Jenny said.

"I'm an old fart," he replied, and coughed. "My postal carrier days are long behind me. Besides, you should be out ballroom dancing and doing cultural things. Learning to scuba dive. All the things I could never teach you."

"You taught me a lot," Jenny said.

Her father stared at her with bleary eyes. "Where is she?" he said.

Jenny swallowed hard. "She's out with a friend," she replied. "You told me that, remember?"

"Okay," he said. "I remember."

Jenny wondered then if she should tell him everything that had happened, and if he would even understand.

"I'm gonna hold you to your promise, you know."

"Promise?"

"I'll need a good maintenance guy," Jenny said. "Once I get the bed and breakfast up and running, that is. And no pro bono work. I won't allow it."

She saw a spark of recognition in his eyes. "Well then, I'm your man," her father said. He leaned his head back on the seat and stretched out his legs a bit.

Jenny smiled for the first time that weekend. "Do you want me to take you home?" she asked.

"Nope," her father said. "Let's just sit here awhile. I like watching the snow."

* * *

O'Malley's Pub was downtown on the waterfront, near the rickety docks where the fisherman brought in their catches. It was the main drunken commiseration spot for the swarthy, acne-ridden men who worked at the toy factory.

The pub was an absolute hole in the wall that smelled of mold and dead trout. As Jenny made her way inside, past the Terminator 2 pinball machine and the jukebox playing a yowling Randy Travis tune, she spotted her mother sitting in a corner with a man in a beige turtleneck. He had his hand on her breast and she was drinking a Miller Lite from a bottle, whispering in his ear.

"Mother," Jenny said pointedly.

They both looked up. The man was barely thirty years old and had a thick beard that made him look like a Russian spy. He stared at her with a blank expression.

"Come to retrieve me, have you?" her mother asked, wiping at her mouth with a napkin. She still wore her faux fur coat.

"I came to let you know that Dad was wandering on the road, alone," Jenny said. "In the freezing cold in his slippers and robe. While you were here sticking your tongue down the throat of some Russian gangster."

"Clyde is a graduate student," her mother said. "And a philosopher."

"Who's this?" Clyde asked. His eyes were extremely bloodshot.

"This here is my firstborn and only," her mother replied.

"Did you hear a word I just said? About Dad?"

"I heard you," her mother said. "But it's getting harder and harder to believe anything you say these days."

"Can we get out of here"? Jenny asked. "I'd like to discuss this in private."

The jukebox switched to Bad Company's *Feel Like Making Love.*

"Unless you've come to tell me that they've found your precious husband, dead, I've got nothing to say to you," her mother slurred. She took another swig of her beer. "I'm sorry about your father. Maybe Grace fell asleep watching The Oxygen Channel again. It's true what they say, you really can't get good help these days."

"Maybe if you weren't plastered off your ass half the time, you'd be able to take care of him yourself," Jenny said.

Clyde was looking from one woman to the other, transfixed. "You're married?" he asked no one in particular, and grabbed another fistful of beer nuts.

"Maybe if you weren't such an ungrateful daughter, you'd be around more often to help," her mother said.

Jenny's heart clenched. "Do you want to repeat that?"

"Go off and marry some rich old guy and forget about the only person who gave you everything you have. The only person who gave you food, a place to live, clothes for your back. Go ahead, I don't care. For all I know, you married Lance for his money. Lucky you."

Jenny stood there, seething. "How the hell can you do this to Dad?" she whispered.

"I met your father for the first time in this very bar, thirty years ago," her mother replied, smiling with lipstick-stained teeth. "Apparently you don't know him as well as you think."

"I do know that you're a drunk and a slut," Jenny said. "And I'm ashamed to be your daughter."

* * *

She walked to the end of Harborfront Stroll and stood at the dark green railing, watching the waves lapping against the rocks below. The wind blew snow flurries around her in a cacophony of white. She held the Pierre the Bear toy in one hand. It was quite cold at the edge of the lake and her hands were freezing.

Jenny examined the rough-hewn wooden edges of the toy, the crudely painted eyes and toothy grin. But the two sections of the bear fit together perfectly, like a handshake. She imagined Jack Spivey in his cabin on Blackhawk Island, sitting at a table, whittling it by the light of a flickering candle. Did he know at that point that his affair with Lucy O'Hara was over? Was the toy one last expression of love for Lucy and a hope that he could still somehow be a part of her family?

Jenny threw the toy as far as she could, into the lake. It landed with a hollow *thunk* in the waves, more than thirty feet away. For a moment, it floated on the water like a nondescript piece of driftwood. Then it sank out of sight.

* * *

A man in bright orange overalls was hanging giant plastic candy canes from the light posts in the parking lot at Harborfront Stroll. He leaned at the top of a heavy metal ladder and listened to instructions from a rail-thin woman who stood on the ground, holding a coffee mug.

Jenny stopped on the cracked blacktop and watched them. Great Water had a long tradition of ushering in the Christmas season early. The winter was so unendurable, bleak and infinite, that the town needed something to last them until April, like Frederick and the mice in the children's story. She figured that five weeks of Advent wreaths, plastic mangers and caroling reindeer were the best the residents could provide.

The smell of hash browns and dead fish filled her nose as she stood there, boats bobbing in the choppy waters of the marina, gulls circling low overhead. She tried to push thoughts of her mother from her head and focus on what to do next.

An older man in a security uniform walked past; he had patchy gray hair and carried a supersized plastic cup full of bright pink soda. There was a rip on the backside of his dark blue pants. A stitch of white flashed beneath.

Jenny ran up to him as he unlocked the driver's side door of an ancient Dodge Charger and tossed a Tupperware container inside.

"Excuse me," Jenny said.

The man turned and regarded her. His cheeks hung low and thick around his neck. A shiny name badge above his shirt pocket read: Arnold Jefferson.

"Why hello," he said, looking her up and down. "What can I help you with?" he said. Snowflakes blew into his face and melted on his fleshy jowls.

"It's about a missing child."

Arnold Jefferson chewed on an ice cube and then spat it into the plastic cup. There was a dancing turkey on the side of the cup; it read:

Happy Holidays from Your Friends at DeeDe's Bait Shop.

"You mean Eric Calhoun?"

"That's right," Jenny said. "I saw something on the news about it, and wanted to see how I could help."

"Well, you're gonna be inclined to speak to the police about that," Arnold Jefferson replied.

"The police?" Jenny repeated.

"Yes, ma'am. That surfer kid's long gone. Some trucker pervert's probably snatched him by now, taken him across the bridge down south. Or maybe up to Canada. You know all them truckers are perverts."

Jenny decided not to dignify his response with a reply. "What about Martin Van Lottom? He's a friend of mine. I know he feels terrible about what happened."

Arnold took another guzzle of soda and crunched an ice cube between his jagged yellow teeth. "Well," he said. "Hmmph. If you say so. But Marty won't be coming back to work for a while, if ever. The fact of the matter is, he let that kid go. And that's a cardinal sin in our business. I've worked security for more than thirty years. Believe me when I tell you that."

"So you think Eric's found his way to the highway by now? To the truck stop?"

"Maybe so," Arnold Jefferson said. "Maybe he hasn't left town yet and he's waiting for the right time to make his move. I reckon he knows that everyone's looking for him."

"I get the feeling you don't care one way or the other," Jenny said.

Arnold frowned. "Don't get me wrong. I hope they find him. But I seen too many of these stories end, shall we say, unhappily. There aren't many happy endings in Great Water."

Arnold Jefferson got into the Charger and gunned the motor. Jenny stepped back as he pulled away, past the man in orange overalls hanging candy canes and the woman with the coffee cup, barking orders. He drove past a group of fishermen and then rumbled down the road, the rusty tailpipe clanging against the blacktop.

Jenny turned on the heat in her car as soon as she got inside. She rubbed her hands together, struggling to get warm. Flurries plummeted from the sky as she watched shoppers stride back and forth across the parking lot, dressed in muddy trucker jackets and heavy winter boots.

She picked up her cell phone and dialed Martin's apartment. The phone rang five times, then six.

"Hello?"

"It's Jenny."

"What do you want?" He sounded like he'd been crying.

"Arnold Jefferson thinks Eric's heading for the highway," Jenny said. "I think you've still got a chance to find him."

"That guy doesn't know his ass from his elbow. Besides, I screwed up and there's no going back. That's all there is to it."

"Of course there is. You know as well as I do that our local cops have no idea what the hell they're doing. Take a drive down the road out of town. Check the rest stop. Park there and watch everyone that leaves."

"It won't do any good."

"I want at least one of us to find the people we lost," Jenny said.

She hung up the phone and dialed Pike.

26

Chapter Twenty-Six—MARTIN

Martin ran down the hall of his apartment, stumbling like an inebriated dockworker. He reached the bathroom and crouched over the toilet to vomit, but nothing came, only a chill that shook his body and made his eyes burn.

The mask of crimson rage had dissipated as soon as he'd staggered down the steps from Patti's place and into his Oldsmobile. He sat there in the front seat, trembling like a delusional man with a 106-degree fever, struggling to understand what he'd just done. Wondering where he'd gotten the frightening strength to attack Pedro so violently. The answer came in the face of Jack Spivey, which slowly materialized in his mind like a black-and-white police artist sketch, eye patch and all. Martin realized then with a shock that he understood the blind anger and acute desperation that the man must have felt before he strode to Sunrise Avenue with a shotgun. Their situations were too similar to ignore.

Time ticked by and eventually he started the engine and drove home.

So, as he lay on the moldy tile of his bathroom floor, staring up at the expensive blue shower curtain that his mother had bought for him almost a year ago in a vain attempt to improve the décor of his apartment, the thought of killing himself cut a path to the front of his mind.

He thought about Pearl that morning, slashing her wrist on the broken window glass. The resignation in her eyes, how ready she seemed to embrace it.

He knew that death could be painful, but perhaps only briefly, like getting a tetanus shot, or slamming his fingers in the car door. But it meant that he would not have to feel the sharp ache in his heart ever again. And the part that made sense, the thing about it that made his heart glad, was that he would see his father on the other side.

Grabbing the corner of the sink, he pulled himself up on his stiff, unyielding knees and watched his reflection in the mirror. His eyes were sunken and red, rimmed by deep circles the color of bruises. He was pale and unshaven.

The degree of his ugliness overwhelmed him. Martin opened the medicine cabinet so that he would not have to look at himself any longer.

He picked up a bottle of shaving cream. There was a circle of rust on the shelf beneath it.

Martin threw the bottle as hard as he could against the tiled wall inside the shower. A BAM sound shook the tiny room as the plastic can rattled down into the tub, rolling up and down until it finally settled against the drain.

A straight razor sat inside a cracked drinking glass. Martin picked up the blade and ran his finger gently across it. He looked at his left wrist, which was narrow and crisscrossed by thin blue veins.

I'm sorry.

He took the razor and pressed it lightly against one of the veins. Martin closed his eyes and the faces of his family flashed in front of him in a whir of color. Deep in the clouded corner of his mind, he heard the echoing sound of a stampede of horses, thundering closer and closer.

Then he heard his father's voice:

Martin.

Martin opened his eyes, expecting to see his father standing next to him.

"Dad?"

But he was alone.

Martin glanced down and saw the razor in his hand. He dropped the blade in the sink like a scalding hot frying pan. Then he sat down on the edge of the bathtub.

"Please help me," he said to the empty room. "Please."

The only sound was the thumping of loud hip-hop music from the apartment above him, and the dripping of the faucet in the tub.

Martin choked back a sob. "Dad," he said. "Please tell me what to do."

But there was no answer. Martin took a deep breath. Then he wiped off his wrist with a towel. The spot of blood on the white terrycloth was bright red and perfectly round, like the period of a sentence that wasn't ready to end.

There was a sharp knock at the door. Martin pulled on a sweater, his heart racing. He opened his apartment door and found his mother, Lars and Delphine standing in the hallway.

"Surprise," Lars said, and threw his arms around Martin. "How are you, bro?"

Lars wore a black leather blazer with a checkered Western shirt. His closed-cropped blond hair accentuated his bright blue eyes and flawless bone structure.

"Hey," Martin said, as Lars released him from his bear hug. "Hello. I mean—what are you guys doing here? You caught me completely off guard."

"Delphine and I are taking you and Mom out to brunch," Lars said. "I got the week off work, so we're in town through Turkey Day. The station owes it to me, I've been sweating like a pack mule for 'em all year anyhow."

It appeared to Martin like his brother's teeth had been whitened professionally. He knew Lars could not have achieved results like that using ordinary toothpaste.

"Isn't that great?" Lars asked. He squeezed Martin's neck, then slapped his cheek lightly. "Man, I missed you so much! How've you been?"

"Awesome," Martin said, and forced himself to smile. "Everything's pretty much status quo," he added.

Lars watched him closely. It seemed to Martin like he stared through his thin sweater and his skin and muscles and into his heart, and for a moment, Martin thought his brother could see everything that had happened that weekend.

"What's wrong?" Lars asked. "Where's your tooth?"

"It's nothing," Martin answered. "I'm entirely okay."

"*Bonjour*, Martin."

Lars stepped aside as Delphine kissed Martin on both cheeks. She smelled like a combination of rose petals and pine cones.

"*Comment allez-vous*, Delphine?" Martin said.

Delphine tossed back her auburn hair, which was ramrod straight and quite luxurious. Martin noticed she had acquired a pair of horn-rimmed glasses since he'd last seen her.

"I am fantastic now that I see you," she replied.

Martin remembered the dream he'd had about Delphine, where they'd had sexual intercourse in the elephant compound at the Manistique International Zoo. The dream had been so vivid that he'd written down as many details as he could remember on the back of his unpaid electric bill, under the bathroom nightlight.

"Thank you," Martin replied. He felt his penis stir between his legs.

His mother stared at him with concern. The older woman wore elegant gray slacks and a jade necklace that Martin knew her father had given her years ago.

"Did you make an appointment to take your car in?" she asked.

"Tomorrow," Martin said.

"What's wrong with that heap of junk?" Lars asked.

"A corroded undercarriage," his mother said.

"What the heck is that?" Lars asked.

"I'll explain later," Martin told him.

His mother frowned. "Well, you better go get cleaned up. We're going to 99 Olives out on the Old Highway."

"From what I understand, it's khakis and button-down shirts or they don't let you in the door," Lars said, and laughed.

* * *

99 Olives was a brand new Greek restaurant about twenty minutes from town. They drove through thick pine forests and past shallow, frozen ponds rimmed with dead reeds. They passed campgrounds and a propane store, then a service station with a rusted-out Buick sitting up on concrete blocks out back. There were quite a few vehicles up on concrete blocks in Great Water.

Martin sat in the back seat of his brother's luxury class BMW, listening to his mother chat with Delphine about potpourri and cashmere sweaters and Canadian TV. Surprisingly, all he could think about was Eric. Patti and Pedro felt like a sunburn that was still fresh, and Martin was waiting to see how sore it would become. Losing Eric, however, sliced deep, and Martin had no clue how to stop the bleeding.

They came to a shopping center with a U Buy It and a Pizza Shack and a fishing tackle store. Lars made a left-hand turn and found an excellent parking space in front of the 99 Olives restaurant.

"I hear their Mediterranean cuisine is exquisite," their mother said, as she opened the car door.

Martin didn't know the difference between Greek and Mediterranean food, if there was one.

"It beats cheeseburgers at the Cozy Kitchen, right, Mart?" Lars said, and winked at his brother in the rearview mirror.

The restaurant smelled like chlorine. There was a bar with a video screen that was playing a 1960s Gladiator film. On screen, shirtless men wearing sandals battled with swords and shields in the middle of a dusty arena. The bar stools were painted orange. There were paintings of olives everywhere.

"This is wonderful," his mother said. She squeezed Martin's hand as the host led them to their table. They passed an enormous vault in the middle of the restaurant, bounded by glass walls. Dozens of wine bottles were stacked on shelves inside, and from time to time, waiters entered the vault through a heavy door and exited carrying a bottle, wrapped in a black cloth.

They sat down and a waitress named Melanie, who wore a tight white blouse and no bra, told them the specials. They were all dishes with that ended with the letter "a."

"I'll be right back with your drinks," Melanie said, after they ordered. She had perfectly manicured nails.

"Thank you," Delphine said pointedly.

Melanie gave Lars a long look up and down. "Sit tight," she said, and licked her lips, ever so slightly.

"We'll do that," Lars replied, and frowned. Martin knew that his brother appreciated the attention, but would never be unfaithful to any woman he was with. Lars had told him that eleven different women and one man (named Elliott C.) had sent him their undergarments in the mail, after he had started work at the television station.

"Everyone is so friendly here," their mother proclaimed, after Melanie had retreated into the kitchen, down a long hall lined with black-and-white photos of Greek landmarks made of old stones, like the Parthenon and the Acropolis. Martin only was able to identify them because of the plaques underneath each image.

"Well, I bet you're wondering why we brought you here," Lars said, and grinned. He looked at Delphine, and she nodded. "*Oui*," she said, and gripped his hand tightly.

That's when Martin saw the ring. The modest diamond flashed and caught the light, and Martin realized how perfect it looked on her slim, delicate finger.

"I—" Lars began.

"Lars and I are to be married," Delphine exclaimed. She tossed her hair and sat up straight and for a moment, Martin saw the dark shadow of her perfect breasts underneath her pale gray sweater.

Lars grinned sheepishly at Delphine. "Sweetheart," he said. "I wanted to—"

As Martin stared at his brother's cleft chin and perfect white teeth and his mother, beaming and teary-eyed, wearing the jade necklace that brought so many memories of happier times with it, the sounds of the restaurant blurred into a humming drone of static, and suddenly Martin's stomach was riddled by a brilliant jolt of pain.

"And," Lars was saying, "I want you to be my best man. I want you to stand up there next to me, in April, when this thing shakes down. What do you say, bro?"

Martin sat there in his seat, clutching the table, waiting for the jagged wave of hard pain to subside. His mother put a worried hand on his arm. "What's wrong?" she asked.

He rose to his feet, knocking his utensils to the floor with a clatter. People at the bar turned to stare at him. "I'm gonna throw up," he said.

Lars grabbed his shoulder. His grip was forceful, prying. "Martin," he said. "Did you hear what I asked you?"

"Let go of me," Martin replied. He shoved his brother away. Lars lost his balance and stumbled backward. He tripped over a chair and his elbow hit a nearby table, spilling a glass of water onto his slacks.

Delphine screamed. It sounded like the yelp of a delicate toy poodle.

Martin felt the bile rising in his throat for the second time that afternoon.

Lars got to his feet. His cheeks were red and there was an enormous wet spot on his leg. The look on his face was one of profound disappointment. Martin had seen it countless times before.

Martin vomited on the floor then. His stomach heaved until he had nothing left. "I'm not going to the wedding," he said, his voice barely above a whisper.

Everyone stared at him: the patrons at the nearby tables, the bartender, the waitresses. Melanie stood nearby, balancing a tray of drinks, her chest rising up and down with each quick breath.

"You're sick," his mother said. "We have to leave. We have to get out of here now."

"Don't pretend like there's nothing wrong," Martin said. The stench of his vomit was everywhere.

His mother drew back her hand. "What're you talking about?" she asked.

"You don't care that he's gone," Martin said. "You don't even talk about him anymore. You washed all his clothes, his blankets. You got rid of the smell of him before he was barely cold."

His mother's face fell. "How dare you," she said.

"I'm never going to forget Dad," Martin said. "You may want me to, but I can't."

"No one wants you to forget him," Lars said.

"You seem to have done a good job of it," Martin countered. "You're getting married to the hottest woman on the planet. You're a fucking TV star. What do you care?"

Lars put a hand on his shoulder. Martin could see he was struggling to control his temper. "Just take it easy," he said. "Relax. We'll take you home."

"I don't want to go home," Martin said. "I hate staring up at that white ceiling in my fucking apartment and thinking about how everything went wrong."

He staggered to his feet and ran through the restaurant, weaving through a maze of tables with bouquets of bright marigolds and empty place settings. The drone of static in his ears grew louder and he suddenly saw the glass-walled wine vault. Dozens of bottles sat undisturbed on racks, the liquid inside catching the light in flits of purple.

Martin opened the heavy door. It was quiet inside, and cool. He flopped down on the hard linoleum floor and stared up at the bottles that stretched above him like Christmas ornaments.

Martin heard people pounding on the door. Their voices were

muffled, as if coming from behind layers of soft, white cotton.

He closed his eyes then. Martin closed his eyes and finally went to sleep.

27

Chapter Twenty-Seven—ERIC

"I need to take care of this alone," Eric insisted.

"Negatory," Eugene replied. They were in his car again.

"Just listen to me for a second—"

"It was stupid for us to go in those woods in the first place. That dude could've had a gun and blown our heads off. That wouldn't have been an optimum situation, Calhoun. I'm far too pretty to die."

"What're you even talking about?" Eric asked. "I know where Webb is and I know he's got the board. I just want to talk to him. That's all."

"You thought that cowboy in the kitchen was a charmer? I guarantee Webb will have no problems splitting open your head with a machete."

"This isn't Jason Vorhees we're talking about."

"Webb Turner's ten times worse," Eugene said. "Besides, Jason Vorhees isn't even real."

"Look, you're always harping on Taco to be a man. When did you finally step up and start taking responsibility for yourself?"

"When we had to go on food stamps and my mom was working two jobs just to put TV dinners and grape soda on the table for us."

"Well, this is my moment," Eric said. "Can you at least grant me that?"

"You think you one bad shreddah, is that it?"

"The reef affects the shape of the waves," Eric answered. He could tell by Eugene's expression that he'd made his point.

* * *

Eric didn't say a word on the drive from Lighthouse Park to Spivey Point. Before Eugene dropped him off, Eric found the stash of letters in his backpack and recognized one, written on notebook paper torn from a three-ring binder.

* * *

Dear Dad,

This is probably the last letter I'm going to write. It feels like I'm talking on the phone with just the dial tone on the other end. I think about you all the time but I can't tell if doing this is making a difference.

I went to the doctor for the first time in a while, four years at least. Mom just got a new job and she has insurance now. So she wanted to take me for a physical. She said I probably missed some shots and immunizations or however you spell it and she didn't want me to get measles.

This guy Dr. Prentiss seemed okay. He had a fuzzy beard and spectacles like people wear in old-timey movies. He asked me a lot of questions and looked in my eyes and my mouth and made me say Ah.

Then he asked me to take off my shirt and I did. He listened to my heart and said it sounded good. He asked me stuff about puberty and how I was adjusting to all the changes. I said I wasn't. Then he told me to take off my underwear. I was lying on that table on top of that white paper cover thing and the room was really cold.

This seemed okay I guess, because he's a doctor and he has to be sure I don't have like cancer or something growing down there. But as soon as he said it, my heart started beating really fast. Dr. Prentiss said What's the matter? I tried to talk but I couldn't. So he said It's okay Eric, you can trust me. And I'm not going to hurt you.

I started shaking then and crying really hard and I kind of curled up into this ball. The doctor kept saying What is it what's the matter? I tried to talk but nothing came out.

-Eric

* * *

He stopped at the top of Brisco Creek Bridge. Up ahead was the opening in the pines where the Bloomquists' gravel driveway met the Cove Road. It had finally stopped snowing.

Eric walked across the bridge, his heart beating faster. Dark water flashed through the cracks in the slats beneath his feet. The wooden deck was splintered and peeling off in jagged strips of pine.

He reached the other side and put his backpack down in the snowy weeds along the side of the road. He noticed a Kawazaki Ninja motorcycle propped against a tree stump.

Eric heard moaning then; a deep, sad sound coming from the creek bed below. He grabbed a sharp stick from the ground and walked cautiously down the sloping bank. A paper sack from the Price Slasher lay upside down in a tangle of dead blueberry bushes. Then he saw a beer bottle smashed on a rock, its pieces catching the gray light that flickered through the pines.

Webb Turner sat on the ground, a few feet from the swirling dark waters of the creek. The butterfly surfboard was propped up against a stump nearby.

A gun lay at the edge of the water. Eric stopped, then sucked in a breath.

Webb focused on him with weary eyes. Sweat dripped down his cheek. "Come closer," he said. "Let me take a look at Duane Calhoun's boy."

Eric was too afraid to move.

"I hear you're a real shredder. I hear you surf even better than your daddy."

"Who told you that?"

"Lance fucking Bloomquist," Webb replied. "I hear he's been training you to be a real soul surfer."

Eric was silent.

"Knowing Lance, he's probably teaching you about geese and dandelions and shit. Am I right? That codger hasn't changed."

"How do you know him?"

Webb laughed. It was a dry, rasping noise, like an ancient radiator. "Me and him go way back," he said. "The three fucking kings. Me, your old pops, and Lance. Inseparable high school hellraisers."

Eric couldn't imagine that his father—or Lance—could ever be friends with someone like this. "I don't believe you," he said.

"Well, that figures," Webb replied.

"Look," Eric said. "I don't know what you have against me or my dad. But I'm taking that board back."

"You ain't taking jack shit," Webb said. "Fuck you and your lying bastard of a father."

The back of Eric's neck bristled. "What did you say?"

"Duane stole my woman right out from under me," Webb said. His breathing was ragged; his chest rose up and down rapidly. "He married Ada Bloomquist when he was nineteen. They moved to fucking Detroit and they didn't even care that I went to Nam and served my country. Then they came back to town and I was supposed to act like everything was okay?"

Eric felt his chest tighten. "My dad was married before?" he said softly.

"Indeed he was. A whole storied past you obviously knew nothing about."

Eric tried to picture his father in a tuxedo, walking down the aisle of a church with the woman called Ada. The edges of the picture bled dark.

"Some amigo he turned out to be," Webb said. He spat some blood onto the muddy rocks. "You know your dad was there, out on the lake, the night the fog took her? He could've saved her. He heard her calling and calling but he just paddled back to shore."

He's talking crazy. Everything's spilling out of his scrambled mind and he thinks he's making sense.

"Me and Lance heard her," Webb continued. "We were on the rocks and we heard her screaming but by then she was gone. The wind was too strong. That fucking warm wind that smelled like it came from hell itself."

Eric took a step forward. "You hit Rose," he said. "I was there, I saw it. Do you always go around beating up women?"

Webb smiled. One of his front teeth was missing. "Most of 'em deserve it," he said.

Eric reached in his pocket and felt the knife handle.

"Why didn't you stop me, Eric Calhoun?"

Eric felt his face redden. "I could kick your ass if I had to."

Webb laughed. "Is that fucking right? Who taught you how to fight? It sure wasn't your dad, 'cause he didn't stick around long enough to do it. Must be those tweakers from Moosejaw. Is that who you're hanging around with now?"

"Any man who puts his hand on another woman isn't a man," Eric said.

"Did Lance teach you that?"

"No," Eric said. "My mother did."

"To start with, Rose is a filthy whore who has boned every man in town, including yours truly," Webb replied. "So she had it coming."

"Take that back."

"Try and make me, you little punk."

Before he knew what was happening, Eric charged down the bank toward him, the dull paring knife clutched tightly in his hand, intent on hurting Webb, making him pay for all the confusion and stomach aches and lonely nights he'd spent since his father left. Webb scrambled for his gun and fired it. There was a flash of metal and a shattering boom and then Eric felt a blistering pain in his right ear, like it had been ripped from his head. He lost his balance and toppled into the icy water of Brisco Creek. The knife flew out of his hands, onto the creek bed.

Webb was on top of him in a second, holding him just below the surface of the water with a linebacker's grip as Eric kicked vainly at the rocks and weeds, struggling to breathe. Blood spread into the water around his head.

Suddenly Webb hoisted him up and Eric choked for air, his clothes soaked and sticking to his body. Webb gripped his shoulders tightly; he had Eric's legs pinned underneath him.

"You got more fight in you than any of us ever expected," Webb said. "You know that?"

"Let go of me," Eric sputtered. "You son of a bitch, let go of me now. You shot me!"

Webb turned his head to take a look. "Ah, it's just a nick," he said. "You'll live. I seen a lot worse, believe you me."

Eric struggled underneath Webb's heavy weight. The water was freezing.

"You were a mistake," Webb said. "I bet you never knew that, did you? Your dad only asked your mom to marry him because he knocked her up."

"What're you talking about?" Eric said. His wet, matted hair was in his eyes.

"It was in the back of a '79 Ford Pinto. I think Lynyrd Skynyrd wrote a song about it."

"Are you trying to be funny?"

Webb laughed bitterly. "Now that Pinto's lying in a junk heap in the woods. Your dad set it on fire to collect the insurance money."

"Bullshit," Eric said. His ear throbbed with pain.

"Why do you think your dad split? That's what he does best."

"My dad's married now. He's in California and he runs a surf school. He finally got out of here, which is more than I can say for you."

"Oh, I'm leaving," Webb said. "Tonight's my last chance. Me and the blood red moon."

He hurled Eric's knife into the deep water below the bridge with a heavy splash. Then he did the same with the gun. Webb heaved himself to his feet and grabbed the surfboard. It took a second for Eric to realize what he was doing.

"This is where it happened," Webb said. "This is where we went into the creek with our boards that night."

Eric stood there, blood trickling down his neck, too dazed to fully comprehend what was happening.

Webb pointed a shaky finger under the bridge, out toward Spivey Point and Blackhawk Island. "He was with her," he said. "Duane was with her, and he lost her. He lost her in that massive surf that was crashing in the fog."

For a moment, Eric saw something in his blue eyes, a hint of kindness behind the anger.

"Eric," Webb whispered. "Are you gonna turn out like him? Be a coward who runs? Or will you stay and be a man? Be a man like Lance?"

And with that, he grabbed the board and waded into the creek, out into the middle, where the water was fast-moving and deep. Eric heard him suck in his breath sharply, and he grew very pale.

Webb hoisted himself onto the board with one last effort and began to paddle. "See you on the other side," he said. He let the current carry him under the bridge and past the dead plum tree until he was only a speck among the whitecaps on the lake.

Eric shivered violently as he stood in the freezing shallows of the creek. His teeth chattered a staccato beat and strange tears stung his eyes as he realized that recovering the butterfly surfboard no longer mattered. Webb had taken it to a place where he and the board would never be seen again.

28

Chapter Twenty-Eight—JENNY

The Big Break Inn was a one-story venue on the outskirts of town, across the road from a small strip mall that featured Fancy Tan and the Chang Wang Buffet. Less than a mile down the way was a heavily industrial area with sterile-looking warehouses and the Great Water Toy Factory. Jenny was familiar with all the accommodations in the area, as well as the gossip associated with each place, because of her job at the hotel. The Big Break, which was popular with surfers from out of town because of its extremely affordable rates, had gained unfortunate notoriety earlier that year. A popular city councilman named Rupert Stoyakovich had been discovered there with a woman with a wooden leg who was not his wife.

As Jenny pulled into the parking lot she saw Pike's van double-parked outside a room at the far end. She knew he might be upset with how she treated him at Moosejaw, even though she did have reason to be angry. Although it had always been difficult to ask people for help, she figured she had to swallow her pride and enlist his assistance in rescuing Lance.

Rubbing her hands together to get warm in the evening chill, she knocked hard on the door of Room 12. Hazy light peeked out from behind thick rust-colored curtains. She heard the sound of the TV from inside.

She was about to knock again when the door opened. A figure wearing a silver beekeeper suit stood in the doorway.

"I think I have the wrong room," Jenny said.

The person carefully lifted off the hood of the suit.

"I was wondering when you'd get here," Pike said. He grinned.

* * *

Every light inside the motel room was on and there was a spool of heavy industrial cable on the floor.

"I have seasonal affective disorder," Pike explained, off Jenny's puzzled look. "And I filched that cable from a road crew in Toledo."

"What do you mean?"

"I stole it. Temporarily, I mean."

Jenny didn't know where to begin. She felt like she was staring at a jumbled pile of jigsaw puzzle pieces.

Pike put the hood of the suit on a night table. "Why don't you come on and sit down," he said. There were old maps of Michigan and Great Water spread out on the bed. Something resembling a bungee jumping cord was coiled on a chair. "I'm preparing for tonight," he said. "I've never tried out this suit before, but I got a real good deal on it."

Jenny still stood by the door. "Well, I came here to apologize," she explained.

"There's no need to," Pike interrupted. "You have a right to be angry. I was lucky to have been there on that beach when Lance went into the lake."

"You took advantage of him."

"You're absolutely right. And I'm truly sorry."

They were both silent. Two truckers in heavy boots clomped by outside. One hocked an enormous glob of tobacco juice on the ground.

"I feel a little ridiculous talking to you wearing this thing," Pike said. "Excuse me for a second, okay?"

Jenny nodded. Pike picked out a clean shirt and jeans from a duffel bag and went into the bathroom.

The TV was turned to a movie on HBO. Hilary Swank was dressed as a boy. Jenny didn't think she looked too convincing. She took off her coat and draped it on a chair. There were framed, faded photographs hanging on the walls—men surfing the lake, catching fairly large waves. She guessed they were from 1980 at least, maybe older.

"I'll explain everything in just a minute," Pike said from behind the door.

Jenny stopped at one of the photos hanging above the night table. A handsome, long-haired man in his 30s stood at the end of the jumbled rocks of Spivey Point, wearing jeans and a Hawaiian shirt. He had one hand on his surfboard and waved at the camera jubilantly with the other.

It was Lance.

Jenny's heart sank.

Well then. I love you more.

"Are you hungry?" Pike called from the bathroom. "I might have some leftover pretzels."

Jenny picked up one of the maps. It showed the land right around her house. A line was drawn in red magic marker from the woods nearby, across Spivey Point and the lake, and ending at Blackhawk Island.

It was like her house was right in the middle of the Bermuda Triangle.

Pike came out of the bathroom. His hair was neatly combed and his eyes were a beautiful bright blue. He wore jeans and a flannel shirt. Jenny hadn't realized how handsome he was.

"Sorry about this crazy getup," he said, placing the beekeeper suit on the bed. "I'm figuring out the best way to approach my rescue. That's what the cable's for, too."

"Your rescue?"

"I'm going to get Lance tonight. I screwed up. I shouldn't have believed him when he told me he wasn't going after Ada this weekend. I thought I'd convinced him not to try."

"He isn't your responsibility," Jenny said. "He's mine."

"I'm sorry, but it's too dangerous for you to attempt a mission of this magnitude."

Jenny glanced at the bungee cord. "Mission?" she repeated. "What is this, *The A-Team*? Besides, have you ever done anything like this before?"

"Technically, no," Pike admitted. "But I have to try. I've done the research, as you can see. I've talked to librarians and historians all over Michigan. I know exactly where the portal originates, and the route the spirits take."

"So what, you're going to pop in there and grab him, and that'll be it? You saw that frayed rope in the woods."

"That's why I've got this industrial-strength cable," Pike said.

"Are you listening to yourself? Do you know how ridiculous this sounds?"

"Lance wasn't careful enough. He wasn't ready."

Jenny felt like she was trying to navigate down a river full of plunging rapids. The room began to sway.

"Maybe you better sit down," Pike said gently.

"I don't want to sit down, goddammit! You aren't going after him. If anyone goes, it should be me!"

Jenny's legs buckled. Pike took her arm and guided her into a chair. "When was the last time you ate?"

Jenny remembered the pan of sausages on the stove; the breakfast abandoned the morning before. "I can't remember," she admitted.

"In that case, sit tight. Can I interest you in some Combos or M&M's? I spotted the vending machines over by the laundry room."

Jenny managed to smile. She blinked back tears. "M&Ms sound perfect," she said. "Peanut, if they've got them."

Pike crouched down next to her. He patted her knee awkwardly. "It's okay," he said. "Just let it out."

"I'm pregnant," she finally said. The voice sounded disembodied to her, like a PA announcer at an empty bus station.

Pike grinned. "Well now," he said. "That's outstanding news!"

"You're the first person I've told," Jenny said, the words pouring out. "There's no one else to share the news with. And I'm so scared about my dad. I don't know if I should call the police or have him move in with us—with me—so that I can watch him. I need to talk to his doctors and find out what's really going on. And of course my mom just doesn't care. I finally told her what I thought of her and it felt great in the moment, but it just doesn't make things any better. And I want them to be the way they were!"

"Whoa now," Pike said. "I think this talk might involve more than M&M's. I think I saw Mr. Pibb in the pop machine. How's that sound?"

* * *

Jenny had to admit that the can of Mr. Pibb really hit the spot. She sat in a chair and Pike sat on the edge of the bed across from her.

"Are you sure you're feeling better?"

"My stomach has settled a bit," Jenny said. "Thank you. I've just been running nonstop since yesterday morning. It all caught up to me at once."

"But you haven't changed your mind about wanting to go with me tonight."

"We need to do this together."

"All right," Pike said. "But I meant what I said about this being dangerous. When you saw that spirit on the road by the bridge—"

"It communicated to me," Jenny said. "It didn't speak, but I felt—like it wanted to hurt me."

"Those Vikings started all of this. It all originated with them."

"I still don't understand why."

"People have uncovered evidence of Viking explorers in the upper Midwest," Pike said. "Michigan, Minnesota, North Dakota. They've found whole ships, buried. Artifacts like weapons and bits of armor. And they date back to the fourteenth century."

He paused, letting this sink in.

"That's ridiculous," Jenny said. "Vikings came to America before

Columbus?"

"I know how crazy it sounds. But I've been researching this for a long time. I've even been to museums in Norway. Cost me an arm and a leg for the plane ticket. I've seen tapestries and ancient manuscripts and talked to descendants of—"

"Pike, listen—"

"A Viking scouting party was around Great Water sometime around 1402," he continued. "Twelve men, at least. And they were all driven insane by the blood red moon. There might even have been cannibalism involved."

"That's enough."

"People around here think it was the Jack Spivey incident that started it all," Pike said, leaning forward excitedly. "But it stretches back hundreds of years. All this paranormal activity has to do with the moon and the tides and the particular tilt of the earth on its axis. Every thirty years or so, it all lines up. And it's only this town, this place on a tiny corner of Lake Michigan, that's affected. Like a guy's bald spot that always gets sunburned."

"You're saying we're like this town inside a snow globe? Every so often someone picks it up and shakes it and everything goes haywire?"

"It's like a perfect case study," he said. "A paranormal G-spot, if you'll pardon the expression."

Jenny crumpled up the M&M's wrapper and tossed it in the trash can. "I told you, I don't want to be your lab rat," she said.

"Don't misunderstand me," Pike said. "Horrible things happen here, clearly. Yes, ma'am. Some people have even told me about a so-called curse. There are residents here who are more susceptible to depression. During The Baptism, it intensifies. There have even been suicides. I've interviewed dozens of people. Old timers who barely have any teeth. I've got it all on tape."

Jenny thought of Martin. "What can they do to stop this—curse?" she asked.

"Unfortunately, nobody really knows. Sometimes with these types of situations, you need to do extraordinary deeds to overcome it. Prove that you're stronger than the evil forces that have their hooks in you."

The TV proclaimed that *Shakespeare in Love* was coming up next. Jenny leaned back in the chair and tried to relax. "I'm actually glad you were there on that beach," she said. "To stop Lance. To listen to him, and to help."

"Thank you," Pike said. "Any regular person would've done the same."

He glanced around the room. "I know how all this must look to you," he said. "Beekeeper suit, lassos made of cable. But I've been traveling around the Midwest for all my adult life, researching paranormal phenomena and helping good people like you. I've changed lives, I really have. I've fought carnivorous giant rats in the sewer of Cleveland. Helped get rid of a poltergeist in a church orphanage. Even assisted at an exorcism."

"That seems like small potatoes, compared to what we've got in Great Water," Jenny said.

"Darn right," Pike said, and grinned.

29

Chapter Twenty-Nine—MARTIN

Martin opened his eyes. It was dark; a thin shaft of light crept under the door in front of him. As his eyes adjusted to his surroundings, he realized that he was in his bedroom, the room where he had slept as a child.

He stretched and rose to a sitting position. His head pounded. The digital clock on the nightstand read 6:08 PM.

Martin reached over and turned on the lamp. His mother had converted the room into a sewing and crafts workroom. A brand new sewing machine sat on his old desk. There was fabric piled everywhere, and boxes of pine cones and beads. And to add insult to injury, she had replaced his posters of Cindy Crawford and Johnny Cash with framed quilts and quaint watercolors of Lake Michigan.

Faint strains of laugher and baroque classical music found their way through the crack in the door. *They're here*, he thought, as the events of that afternoon tumbled through his head in a rush. *They're downstairs, probably having desert and coffee, wondering about me.*

What happened with Pedro and Patti played in front of his eyes then, like a horrible TV rerun. Or was it a dream?

Martin slid out of bed and got shakily to his feet. He realized he was wearing one of Lars' t-shirts and a pair of his father's old checkered flannel pajama bottoms. Every joint in his body ached. He figured that there was no sense in him staying up there, hiding. He might as well take each thing as it came.

* * *

Lars and Delphine were sitting at the kitchen table when Martin appeared in the doorway. His mother was at the counter, tending to the coffee and arranging cookies on a plate. They were all in the middle of laughing about something.

There was abrupt silence as they turned to stare at him. He felt like a museum exhibit.

"Hello, dear," his mother said, finally. "How're you feeling?"

"Hey, Ralph," Lars said.

Martin smiled. Back in high school, Lars had come home intoxicated from the Spring King's Kaper Dance and vomited all over his mother's antique dining room table. Martin had called him "Ralph" for a solid month after that.

"Takes one to know one," Martin said. "Thanks for taking care of me."

"I don't think they'll be asking us back to that place anytime soon," Lars said.

"The menu was extremely overpriced, anyway," his mother added.

Delphine scrutinized Martin carefully. "We cleaned the vomit from your face," she said.

"I'm really sorry about that," Martin replied. Even the thought of Delphine treating him with tenderness was not enough to get him excited. Every organ in his body felt numb.

"Your clothes are in the washer," Mrs. Van Lottom said. "And the manager at the restaurant was very nice. A little officious, but very nice. He had an unusual moustache."

"I just told him you were sick," Lars said. "Not from the food or anything."

They continued to stare at him. Martin decided to move into the room and sit down at the end of the table, next to his brother. He felt a

217

little better, sitting down. The room smelled like cinnamon.

"Would you like some coffee?" his mother asked. "I have Sanka or chamomile tea. And chocolate sugar drop cookies."

"Nothing right now," Martin said. "My stomach isn't quite up to speed yet."

His mother poured coffee for Lars and Delphine and set everything out on the table. Baroque classical music played from the radio on the counter.

"So, I've decided to turn over a new leaf," Martin said.

"How do you mean?" Lars asked.

"Of telling the truth," Martin said. "Of being completely honest with all the people I care about."

His mother ran her hand across the counter. "Really," she said.

"That sounds like a sound policy," Lars said.

"So, Delphine," Martin said. "I think I'll start with you."

She regarded him curiously as she sipped her coffee. "*Oui?*" she said, and tossed back her hair.

"I had a dream once."

Delphine raised one eyebrow. "What did you dream of?"

"I had a dream that we had sexual intercourse in the elephant enclosure at the zoo."

Lars spit his coffee onto the table. "Dude," he said.

"Martin," his mother said, and frowned.

Delphine smiled, ever so faintly. "*Oui?*" she offered.

"It was amazing," Martin said. "You were dressed in this green zookeeper's uniform. And when you let your hair out of your ponytail, it cascaded everywhere, onto the straw."

"Straw?" Lars asked.

"The bottom of the pen is covered with straw. Don't you remember, we went there on a field trip when you were in fifth grade. I was in third."

"I don't think this is an appropriate topic of conversation," his mother said.

"I think it's hilarious," Lars said. "It seems like no one in this family wants to laugh anymore."

"This is my home and I make the rules," their mother said. "And we won't discuss sex, not in the kitchen. It's the most holy room in the house."

"I wrote down all the details I could remember on the back of an unpaid electric bill," Martin said. "Usually you forget dreams as soon as you have them, but this one was very vivid."

Delphine blushed. She took a nibble of a cookie, and bits of sugar scattered onto her chin.

"What do you think?" Martin asked.

"I am very flattered," Delphine said shyly. "But I'm frightened of *les elephants.*"

Lars laughed. "You could've told me about this, bro. How come you didn't?"

Martin looked at the floor. "I just—" he said. His voice broke off. He thought of the white terrycloth towel, then; the one with the tiny red spot of blood that was sitting on his bathroom sink.

Lars reached over and took his hand. "Dude," he said. "It's okay."

Martin peered up at him, blinking tears away. "Those things I said at the restaurant," he said. "About the wedding, about you. I didn't mean any of them."

"You hurt all of our feelings," his mother said. She stood at the counter, sipping her coffee, apart from the other three of them.

I meant what I said about you wanting to forget about Dad, Martin thought, but he didn't say it out loud. Instead, he turned to Lars.

"I want to come to the wedding. I want to be your best man."

"Sure thing," Lars said. "I wouldn't have it any other way."

Martin looked away. Heavy darkness pressed against the kitchen curtains. He took a deep breath. "Mom. The second thing is that I lied about my car."

"I knew it," his mother replied.

"The truth is that I borrowed money from Webb Turner and I needed to pay him back."

His mother put down her cup. It missed the counter and shattered on the floor.

"Who's Webb Turner?" Lars asked.

"Did I hear you correctly?" Mrs. Van Lottom asked. Her hands shook. She seemed unsure whether to clean up the shattered ceramic or not.

"I was shot at and his enforcer slammed my face into a table, twice," Martin said. "And he probably still wants to kill me. So we should make sure all the doors are locked."

Lars gaped at him. "You borrowed money from—"

"The biggest drug dealer in town," his mother finished. "Hattie Templeton works down at the courthouse and she tells me everything."

"But they've never been able to pin anything on him," Martin said. "That's why I figured it might be safe. I mean, relatively speaking."

"What in the world is wrong with you?" his mother yelled.

"I'm going to pay you back, Mom," Martin said. "Somehow, I will."

"There are criminals in Great Water?" Delphine whispered to Lars.

"Plenty," he replied. "This town is one giant cesspool of depravity."

Martin swallowed hard. "Dad really would've been disappointed in me," he said.

"Never mind your father," Mrs. Van Lottom said. "I thought I raised you better than that. I really did."

There was a long silence. Delphine took another bite of her cookie. Mrs. Van Lottom began to clean up the broken cup pieces.

"Mom," Lars said. "Why don't you ever talk about Dad?"

"Because he's gone now," she admitted, after a while. "He's gone and I have my life to live."

"But what if I can't forget him?" Martin asked.

"Do you mean forget Dad, or what happened in Lighthouse Park?" Lars asked.

Martin looked up at him. "What do you mean?"

"Sometimes I have trouble separating Dad from the way that other people saw him," Lars said.

"You mean, a crazy pervert," Mrs. Van Lottom said.

"Mom," Martin said, shocked.

"It's perfectly fine. You can say it," she replied, dumping the shattered cup in a trash can under the sink. "I certainly hear enough about it in the produce section at the grocery store. People whispering at the library."

"I don't think of him that way," Martin said. "Not at all."

"Martin," his mother said. "It's important that you know this. Just before your father died, we were in the hospital room together. It was late at night and he told me what happened in the park that day."

"You mean, that those girls made up that story."

"No, he said it was true," his mother said quietly. "He exposed himself to those girls. And he asked them to touch him."

Martin put his face in his hands. Delphine covered her mouth in surprise.

"No," Lars said.

His mother folded her hands in front of her. "When I want to talk to George," she said. "When I want to remember him, I go to a place that holds good memories. Sometimes I go out in the back yard, where his hammock used to be. Or I sit in the coffee shop downtown where he used to meet me on his lunch breaks. I think about him and then I remember his face. Sometimes I talk out loud. I don't care if anyone hears me."

Then she smiled.

"You should try it," she said. "I'm sure he's ready to listen."

* * *

Martin and Lars sat in the kitchen, finishing up the last of the plate of chocolate sugar drop cookies. Their mother had lain down on the Persian-inspired couch in the living room because she wasn't feeling well. Delphine was in the spare bedroom, speaking on the phone to her parents in Montreal. Martin didn't want to think about what she might be telling them.

"There's something else, isn't there?" Lars asked.

Martin's coffee was cold, but he still took another sip.

"There is no Patti," he admitted. The words tumbled out of him like spiraling dominoes.

"What do you mean?"

"I told everyone that I had this girlfriend, this new amazing woman in my life. But the truth is that we went out on two dates, and that's it."

"I don't get it. Did you tell people that on purpose?"

"That's the thing," Martin replied. "I didn't. I just—it's hard for me to tell the difference between what's real and what isn't sometimes. Like, all weekend I've felt like someone's been following me. I know they're there. But when I look around—nothing."

Real concern showed in Lars' eyes. "There are people you can talk to about this," he said. "Therapists. Grief counselors."

"Doctor Fong already referred me to a shrink at Goosebeak. There's no way I'm gonna waste my time with her. Or money I don't even have."

"I'll come with you. We can do it together."

"What do you need a therapist for?"

Lars laughed. His perfectly white teeth flashed. "You'd be surprised," he said. "Maybe if we talked more often, you'd know the truth."

"I guess you're right," Martin said. "It's probably high time for me to get my own email address. I hear AOL is pretty affordable."

"Welcome to the twenty-first century," his brother said.

They listened to the Vivaldi sonata that filled the room. It felt strange to Martin to feel close to someone again. *It doesn't feel so bad, after all*, Martin thought. *Just different.*

"So what're you gonna do about your job?" Lars asked.

"You heard about that?"

"Of course. Mom saw it on the news and told me everything. Did they ever find that kid?"

Martin's heart sank. *Eric.*

"I need to borrow your car keys," Martin said. "And your cell phone, too." He knew exactly what he needed to do.

"What're you talking about?"

"Please," Martin said. "I'm sure there's still time."

* * *

Lars drove a black 1999 BMW 328i. It took Martin more than three minutes to figure out how to adjust the seat and find the switch for the headlights. After that, he was out and gone, driving out of Goosebeak to the Cove Road.

He knew that it would be nearly impossible to find Eric. But his family—well, Lars, at least—had given him a second chance, and he wanted to make good on it. Martin also felt ready to accept the consequences of what he'd done to Pedro. He'd just have to wait and see what happened.

Traffic was heavy because hundreds of people were heading to the holiday lighting ceremony later that night at Harborfront Stroll. It was a huge event that drew people from the nearby towns, as well as extra police and security. Martin thought Eric might take advantage of that and try to sneak out of town then.

He kept his eyes peeled to the side of the road as he drove. The car behind him honked sharply as the stoplight ahead turned yellow. Martin instinctively pressed the accelerator and sped through the intersection, passing right by a police cruiser stopped at a frontage road that led down to the beach. The light turned red as Martin went through it, and he saw the cop turn on his siren, make the turn and accelerate behind him.

"Shit," Martin said.

He reluctantly pulled over to the side of the road. There was barely enough room on the sandy shoulder for the car. A steep hill to his right led down to the lake.

Martin rolled down the window and put his hands on the steering wheel. He had seen enough episodes of *Cops* to know what to do.

The cop who approached wore a black leather jacket with fur around the collar. He walked with a Steven Seagal strut. As he came up beside the driver's side of the car, Martin recognized his shaved head and biker moustache.

"What's your hurry?" Officer Slater asked. Even underneath his jacket, Martin could sense his enormous strength.

"I'm so sorry—" Martin began.

"Hold the phone. It's you, from the doctor's office. Yesterday morning."

"I'm trying to find Eric Calhoun," Martin explained. "The boy who went missing."

"I know who he is," Slater said. "Do you know something I don't?"

"I feel bad about letting him go earlier. I want to find him and make things right."

"I can appreciate that," Slater said. He spat a glob of tobacco juice on the gravel as a car sped by on the opposite side of the road. It was freezing with the window open. "I just don't see why you have to go disobeying traffic laws while you're doing it," he continued. "You wouldn't want to get in a traffic collision and damage this beautiful vehicle of yours."

"It doesn't belong to me," Martin said.

Slater raised an eyebrow.

"It's my brother's. Lars Van Lottom."

"Ah," Slater said, after peeking inside and doing a thoroughly obtrusive visual inspection. "That's a ten-four. Well, you best take excellent care of it, then."

"I will," Martin promised.

I guess Patti never went to the cops after all.

He was about to close the window when the police officer spoke again.

"Do you know a man named Bates?"

Martin shook his head.

"There was an incident this morning at the adult establishment he owns. The Crystal Palace. We're trying to bring him in for questioning."

"What kind of incident?"

"Let's just say he might be on his way out of town, much like your boy Eric," Slater said. "If you spot a light blue 1967 Chevelle, you give me a call, pronto." He passed Martin a business card. "Meanwhile, keep both eyes on the road. This is gonna be a crazy night."

30

Chapter Thirty—ERIC

Eric walked for nearly an hour in the gathering darkness, following the two-lane road that led out of town, toward the truck stop and the highway beyond. His ear was wrapped in one of the black dress socks from his backpack. It felt to him like a bit of the cartilage, the stuff that hung down from his ear, was missing. Thankfully it had stopped bleeding.

I've been shot, he thought. The novelty of it had worn off, but he realized now that if the bullet had hit a fraction of an inch closer, he wouldn't be alive.

His feet ached right through the soles of his black Nikes. His fingers were numb, long past the point of wiggling. All he was left with was a hard ache in his stomach, like the time he had eaten the shrimp walnut salad from Chang Wang—only this pain was worse.

He cried a little, just a few tears that made his vision blurry and then froze on his cheeks. It hadn't made him feel any better; only lonely and small, like a snail crawling up the bark of a fifty-foot tree.

A light blue Chevelle pulled up beside him, its tires crunching on the gravel shoulder. Bates, the owner of The Crystal Palace, leaned over and rolled the passenger side window down.

"What the hell happened to you, Eric?"

Eric peered inside the car, surprised. "Hi," he said. "I'm okay. I'm just...walking."

"You've got a sock on your ear," Bates said. He reached and opened the door for Eric. "Get your tail in here. Have you been crying?"

"I don't need a ride," Eric said. He felt the heat radiating from the front seat; it beckoned to him like a fresh grilled cheese sandwich.

"You ain't fooling anyone. Get in."

Eric stood there a moment. A gust of wind blew hard across the road then, sending snowflakes fluttering into his face. His lips felt chapped and he wondered if his left big toe had gangrene and would need to be amputated.

He finally opened the door and slid onto the front seat next to Bates. He placed his backpack on the floor by his legs.

"I'm going for a little drive and I need some company," Bates said. "You don't have to tell me what happened if you don't want to."

Eric nodded. Bates gunned the motor and they set off down the road again.

Eric regarded him warily. Even in the gloom, he could see that Bates' eyes were wide open, like he'd drunk six gallons of black coffee. He wore a rumpled suit and there was a yellowish-purple bruise on his right cheek. "Where are we going?" Eric asked.

"South," Bates replied. He drummed his fingers on the steering wheel, lightning-quick. "How's that sound?"

The words SAN DIEGO flashed across the road in front of them, then vanished like neon fog.

"Pretty excellent, actually," Eric said.

Bates sped up. He inhaled deeply through his nose, then wiped his nostrils with the back of his hand.

Eric buckled his seatbelt. "Are you okay?" he asked.

"All systems go," Bates replied, and grinned.

The forest thinned out and dropped away and then there were fields; sloping expanses of grass covered with a dusting of snow. And up ahead were the lights of the Travel Plaza and the highway that led along the north shore of the lake toward The Bridge and the Lower Peninsula.

I'm really doing this. I'm really leaving.

Eric's heart beat faster as he tried to imagine his father's face when he knocked on the front door of his cottage. He might look a little different, maybe twenty pounds heavier, and less hair. But the hug would be the same. And maybe he still ate a pack of Butterscotch Lifesavers a day.

"What're you smiling at?"

"You came by at the perfect time," Eric said. "That's all."

They sped past the Travel Plaza and approached the toll booth. Eric was relieved to see that Eugene wasn't on duty. Bates took the ticket from the elderly woman inside the booth, which was decorated by a plastic wreath and candy canes. The woman was dressed in a heavy Michigan State sweatshirt and gloves with the fingers torn out. She told them to drive careful.

They merged onto the highway. "I've been thinking about you ever since you came by yesterday," Bates said. He was speaking extra-fast, like one of the Animaniacs.

Eric glanced at him. "What?" he asked. "Why?"

"I'm sorry I was such a jerk," Bates said. "I've just been under a whole lot of pressure lately. Running a business, you know. But seeing you made me remember what good times we had together."

Eric thought hard, but his mind was a smeared eraser swipe on a blackboard. "All I remember is watching *The Lion King* and getting ice cream," he said.

They were going quite fast down the highway now; there was nothing but dark fields on either side.

"Well, you were a real sweet kid," Bates said. "I loved spending time with you."

Something in his voice made Eric's stomach drop. "What do you mean?"

Bates reached over and put a hand on Eric's leg, just above the knee. "I mean, I liked getting to know you," he said. "I love my Crystal Palace girls," he said. "Don't get me wrong. But you tasted just as nice."

Eric flinched.

"You always knew how to cheer me up," Bates said.

"What are you talking about?"

"Like wild mountain honey," Bates said. He ran his hand over Eric's crotch, and squeezed it.

Eric pushed his hand away. His stomach lurched. "What the heck is wrong with you?" he stuttered.

"I'm paying you a compliment. Don't be so sensitive."

"Please," Eric said. "Please just watch the road."

Bates smiled. He brushed at an imaginary spot at the end of his nose, over and over again. "Just need to get clean," he said. "Clean up, clean up."

Eric glanced out the window. He wondered if he could open the door and jump out. Or did William Shatner only do that on *T.J. Hooker*?

"I'm a fighter," Bates said. He threw a quick left jab above the steering wheel. "The cops try to lay all kinds of raps on me, but I always beat 'em. I'm gonna beat this one, too. Just need a little time to think."

"Look," Eric said. "Just pull over and let me out. I'll walk the rest of the way."

Bates laughed. "Walk where? We're in the middle of fuckin' nowhere. Besides, I'm gonna need you to keep me warm tonight."

Suddenly, a black BMW pulled up next to them on the two-lane highway. Eric caught a glimpse of the Harborfront Stroll security guard behind the wheel, gesturing wildly at them to pull over.

"What in the blazes," Bates said. "Will you look at this kook."

He made an obscene gesture at Martin.

"I know him," Eric said.

A green sedan approached from the opposite direction. Martin accelerated ahead of them, cutting into the same lane as the Chevelle. As the sedan passed, Martin threw on the brakes, causing Bates to stop suddenly to avoid hitting him. The Chevelle skidded to the right on the snowy highway and rumbled to a halt on the shoulder.

"Jesus Christ," Bates said, and smacked the steering wheel.

Martin exited the BMW and ran toward them, nearly losing his footing on the snowy gravel. Bates got out of the car, followed by Eric.

"What the fuck is your problem?" Bates yelled.

"You're kidnapping a juvenile who's been missing since yesterday morning," Martin said. "How about that for starters?"

"He's the one who wanted a ride," Bates said. His eyes twitched. "I mean, goddammit, I'm just trying to do the kid a favor. I'm heading out of town and I just needed some company. That ain't exactly kidnapping, now is it?"

"His family's looking for him," Martin said. "They're frantic."

"Shove it up your ass," Bates yelled. He spun around and glared at Eric. "Tell this yokel that you want to come with me. Go on."

Eric stared at Martin. The security guard had a changed air about him, like he'd fought the school bully and won.

"Don't say a thing," Martin warned him. "Keep your mouth shut."

The headlights of passing cars made shadows dance around them. A truck blasted its horn as it sped past.

"Get back in your yuppie car and get the fuck out of my face," Bates said. "I oughta break your nose for practically sending me off the road."

Eric felt like his feet were frozen in place. Everything seemed like it was moving in slow motion. He noticed that the moon was perfectly full and white, instead of the blood red color it had been in town.

"I know who you are," Martin said to Bates. "You got in a whole mess of trouble tonight, didn't you?"

Bates kicked at the snow. "That's none of your concern," he said.

"Officer Slater will tell you differently. They've got an APB out for your sorry ass."

"You don't know shit," Bates said. He wiped at his nose again.

Martin turned to Eric. "Get in my car. You're not safe out here. Not from men like this."

His voice was surprisingly forceful and clear.

"But—" Eric said.

"Do as I say," Martin said. "And maybe I'll let this son of a bitch be on his way."

* * *

"When we get inside, you're going to call your mom," Martin said, as they walked across the parking lot toward the entrance to the Travel Plaza. He had inspected Eric's ear and had proclaimed himself amazed that it had stopped bleeding.

Eric stopped. Thoughts were tumbling through his head, too fast for him to process.

"What's wrong?" Martin asked. "Are you worried about Bates? The cops will be on him before he reaches the next exit."

"It's not that."

"Your mom and Pete are worried sick," Martin said. "You need to call them."

"You know my mom?"

"She found out what happened last night at Harborfront Stroll. She and Pete paid me a visit."

"I—"

"What is it?"

Eric spotted Cassiopeia far above them in the night sky; Lance had taught him all the winter constellations. Eric wondered if she'd been watching over him the entire weekend. Protecting him. "I don't know if I want to see them," he finished.

Martin frowned. "You aren't making any sense," he said. "You're fourteen years old. You can't just decide to up and leave Great Water. Your mother's your legal guardian. She's responsible for you. What if that Bates guy had taken you away from here? God knows what he would've done to you."

Eric remembered the feel of Bates' hand on his leg. "I think he was high on something," he said.

"He runs The Crystal Palace. What do you think that place is—a library?"

"I could've taken that guy down," Eric said. "I could've chopped him in half if he tried anything."

"Explain that to your mother when she gets here. You tell her that and see if she agrees."

They stood there, next to a row of newspapers and pop machines that stood outside the entrance. Eric was about to open his mouth to reply when he realized he was right.

The restaurant inside the Travel Plaza was called The Come Again Diner. A TV high above the counter was tuned to the second quarter of the Vikings game. Truckers sat on stools, eating plates of runny scrambled eggs and wheat toast sopping with melted butter. Trunk slammers ate cheeseburgers and curly fries.

They were about to head inside the diner when Eric touched Martin's arm. "I need to use the restroom," he said.

Martin regarded him with concern.

"I won't take off. I promise."

"All right then," Martin replied. "I'll be right here."

Eric walked quickly past the gift shop and pushed open the door to the bathroom. His stomach lurched again. He dashed across the garish yellow-tiled floor, ran into a stall and vomited into the toilet.

* * *

They got a booth in the corner and Martin told him to order anything that he wanted. Eric ordered a grilled cheese sandwich and a Cherry Coke. Martin didn't order anything. He handed the menus back to the waitress.

"Hey," Eric said, after the waitress left. "Your hands are shaking."

Martin blushed. "No, sir," he said. "I'm fine. Really."

Eric looked at him closely. There were nasty bruises on his cheeks.

232

Snowflakes were still melting in his hair. One of his front teeth was missing.

"Thank you," Eric said. "Thanks for what you did back there. You were extremely brave."

"You're welcome. I screwed up once, and I had to make things right."

A group of truckers erupted with cheers as the Vikings scored a touchdown. Then Martin seemed to remember why they were there. "Hey," he said, and handed Eric a cell phone. "It's time for you to make that call."

"But what if she's not home?"

"Someone will be there," Martin said. "They're waiting to hear from the police about you."

"I just wanted to see my dad again," Eric said.

"I know."

"I didn't mean to make her worry."

"That's what mothers are best at. I'm speaking from experience, of course."

Eric closed his eyes. He imagined himself curled up underneath his favorite purple comforter, listening to the sound of the rain on the roof. Finally home.

He picked up the phone and dialed. He pictured his mother springing off the couch and running into the kitchen to answer it, the cord twisted and bunched as it hung below the receiver.

"Hello," she said. "Eric?"

He felt the tears well up. "Mom," he said. "Mom, it's me."

* * *

While they waited for his dinner, Eric told Martin about going to the cottage in the woods with the drunken man inside. Then he told him about Webb Turner.

"You're lucky you got out of there with just a hole in your ear," Martin said.

Eric pushed the ketchup bottle back and forth across the table. The waitress brought him his soda, with a striped red straw that bent at the top. Eric took a sip. He waited until the waitress had retreated behind the counter.

"I'm sorry that I lied to you last night," he said.

Martin sighed. "I shouldn't have believed you," he replied.

The ice cubes shifted in Eric's soda glass. Tiny bubbles traveled to the surface and dissipated in a soft fizz.

"I got into a lot of trouble because of it," Martin said. "But it's okay. Sometimes you need to sink real low before you notice how twisted up everything is around you."

Eric thought of his mother in Taco's apartment that morning, the tremble in her voice that was usually so calm and clear. "Sometimes I feel like one of those hound dogs," he said. "The ones that people chain up in their back yards, instead of letting them live inside. All solitary and muddy and howling at the moon."

"Whatever it is, it can be worked out," Martin said. "You just gotta speak up and tell people what you're feeling." Then he smiled awkwardly. "That's easier said than done. Believe me."

The waitress brought his food then. She peered at Eric over the edge of her enormous glasses. A charm bracelet jingled on her wrist. "You okay, sweetheart?" she asked.

Eric nodded. "Safe and sound," he said.

"I recognized you from the news," she said. "I was going to have Earl call the cops, but I figured you already have," she said to Martin.

"My mom's on the way," Eric said. "She'll take me home."

* * *

Eric's mother ran across the dark parking lot of the Travel Plaza. She took him in her arms and held him tight. She smelled like cigarettes and Oil of Olay. Splotches of red and yellow paint dotted her jeans.

"It's okay, Mom," Eric said. "Don't cry."

"You've never even been out of Michigan," she said, brushing the hair back from his forehead. "What were you thinking?"

"I wanted to see Dad."

His mother smiled sadly. "I'm sorry about the letter. I really am." For a moment, she seemed like the pale woman with sunken eyes in the hospital bed, the woman who had lost her baby.

"It's okay."

"I'm sorry about everything."

Pete stood apart from them, shuffling back and forth in the cold. His eyes were puffy and he wore cowboy boots and jeans with ripped kneecaps. "We thought we lost you, Little Chief," he said. It looked like he wanted to hug Eric, but he didn't.

"I'm okay," Eric said. "Martin bought me dinner."

"Where is he?" his mother asked.

Martin stood by Lars' car nearby. The wind blew his hair in his face. He lifted one hand to wave.

Eric's mother gestured him over. Martin reluctantly walked across the blacktop toward them. His tennis shoes made tracks in the slushy snow.

Diane Calhoun wrapped him in a firm hug. "Thank you for saving my son," she whispered.

"I'm really glad I got a second chance," Martin replied. He hugged her back.

* * *

Eric paused at the bottom of the steps that led up to their apartment. He shut his eyes, and for a second he saw his mother, lying at the bottom, twisted in a heap, screaming.

Sweetheart!

Eric felt his breath catch in his throat, like he'd just missed getting dinged by a massive wave. The familiar ache in his stomach swelled and spread.

"Sweetheart."

Eric opened his eyes. His mother and Pete stood next to him. They both seemed exhausted, but there was a different air about them now, an undefinable shift in the geography of their hearts.

"It's time to move on," his mother said.

"We're ready to, if you are," Pete said. "Eric," he added shyly.

"I thought—" Eric began. Then he stopped, because there were no words to express what he wanted to say.

His mother took his hand and led him up the stairs, past the clay pots filled with dead marigolds, and the old blue lawn chair with the busted seams. She unlocked the front door, and he followed her inside.

The apartment looked the same. The sink was full of dirty dishes and there were open boxes of Chinese takeout on the sofa. The Great Water White and Yellow Pages lay spread in the middle of the linoleum floor in the kitchen. His mother took off her jacket and threw her purse on the sofa.

They stood for a moment in silence. Eric focused on the room. The gray paint was peeling off the wall in jagged flakes. The cuckoo clock was still broken. He heard the faucet dripping in the bathroom and felt the familiar draft from under the front door. A wetsuit hung from a hanger, under a lamp. His Algebra textbook and pencil case were still on the coffee table, where he'd left them.

And, on top of the mantel was a picture of Eric and his father, standing at the top of Bearclaw Street, surfboards under their arms. His father wore pastel board shorts, his beer belly sticking out under his white t-shirt. He had a raggedy Fu Manchu moustache. Eric, barely six years old, stood next to him with tousled blond hair and bare feet, clutching his father's hand.

Eric had never seen the photo before. "Where'd you get this?" he asked.

"It was in the top drawer of my dresser," his mother said. "Buried underneath."

"Dad looks like a walrus," Eric said.

Pete laughed.

"I figure he belongs up there," his mother said. She tried her best to smile, but Eric could tell it was one of the hardest things she'd ever done.

31

Chapter Thirty-One—JENNY

It was after ten that night and Pike was in the living room of Jenny's house, doing final equipment preparations for their rescue mission. He wore a miner's helmet with a light affixed to it and had been guzzling Mountain Dew for the past hour.

Jenny cleared her throat from the doorway. "I've got some business to take care of," she said. "Upstairs."

Pike glanced up from a map of the area that he'd spread out on the coffee table. "Hey," he said cheerfully, flashing her a crooked smile. "Everything will be fine. Try not to worry."

"I hope so," she replied. But there was a distinct tremble in her voice.

Jenny went upstairs to the small room that served as her study. She opened a filing cabinet and thumbed past folders labeled TAX RETURNS and RECEIPTS. Then she found one labeled WILL. Sitting down at her desk, she opened the folder, frightened that she had reason to examine the document that she'd put together such a short time ago.

It left her entire estate to Lance.

Jenny knew that it was too late to change the will. And imagining her mother's glee at getting her hands on the house and all of Lance's money made her skin burn. She cursed herself at not including a provision for her father.

She glanced at a framed photo of her and Lance on top of the Empire

State Building. Was he brave for attempting to rescue his sister? Or foolish? He knew the risks involved, but why didn't he trust Jenny enough to tell her? It was clear now that marrying Lance had been like jumping into a swimming hole without knowing how deep it was. Now she was in way over her head.

He hid everything from me. Now he might be lost forever. Does he even deserve to be rescued? And can I take the risk of our baby being lost, too?

The sharp edge of those thoughts made her wince, like she'd sliced her finger with a kitchen knife. She felt like she'd committed a kind of betrayal of her husband by even thinking them. But then, sitting there in the quiet, Jenny realized that she was considering all sides of the problem for the first time. She took a breath, then picked up the phone on the desk and dialed her parents.

"Hello," her mother answered briskly. "Whatever you're selling, I'm not interested."

"It's me," Jenny interrupted.

"What do you want, Jennifer?"

"I want to speak to Dad."

"Don't you have something to say to me first?"

The old urge to apologize—to do everything her mother asked—surfaced. Jenny pushed it back down firmly. "No," she answered flatly. She felt her mother bristle on the other end of the line.

"Fine. I think he's watching television." Her mother put the phone down with a dull thud.

That might be the last time I ever talk to her, Jenny thought. She realized then with a shock that she didn't care.

Jenny waited for more than a minute. A daddy longlegs crawled across the small potted ivy plant on the windowsill.

"Jenny?" her father finally said.

She felt her breath catch in her throat. "Hi, Dad," she said. "Did I wake you up?"

"I was just watching a program on the Bedouin people of Egypt. It was really fascinating."

"Dad," she said." I know it's late, but I just wanted to call and tell you—tell you how much I love you."

Her father chuckled. "I know that, sweetie," he said.

"And if Mom ever tells you to do something you don't want to, I want you to speak up. She doesn't always know what's best. Okay?"

"What do you mean?" he asked. "Why would she—"

"Just promise me. Promise me you'll speak up."

"I delivered mail for thirty-one years," he said. "I've battled blizzards and pit bulls. I'm tougher than I look."

There was a long silence. Wind rattled the windows. Jenny felt tears form in the corners of her eyes.

"Is something wrong?" her father asked. "Tell me what it is."

"I just love you, Dad," Jenny said quickly. "I love you so much. Goodnight." She hung up the phone and lifted up the potted plant; underneath was a single key. Jenny picked it up and went into the bathroom, then dropped it down the toilet. It vanished out of sight.

* * *

"How's everything going?"

Pike looked up from the sofa. Jenny noticed that he'd fixed himself a sandwich of cold cuts and pickles. "We need to leave in approximately t-minus fifteen minutes," he said. "I'll need help carrying the cable into the woods and settling it all up."

"I'll be ready," Jenny said.

"I helped myself to the ice box. Sorry about that."

Jenny sat down in an upholstered chair next to the fireplace. "Not at all. I should probably eat something too."

"I was gonna videotape the operation. I thought it might be important to document it. But then I realized it would be disrespectful. I mean, considering the circumstances and all."

Pike had taken off the miner's hat and folded up the maps. The beekeeper suit was laid out on the back of a chair. He looked to Jenny like someone who was embarking on a round-the-world voyage and couldn't wait to launch.

"What got you started in all this?" she asked.

"What? You mean paranormal expeditions?"

Jenny nodded. "I've been curious this whole time," she said. "It's not exactly a common job around here."

Pike glanced at the floor. "Well, it's not a story I've told many folks," he said.

Jenny sensed pain in his voice. "I didn't mean to pry. You just seem so... committed."

Pike sighed. He leaned back on the sofa. "I grew up in northern Oklahoma," he said. "Tornado country. I shared a bedroom with my little brother when I was a kid. One April when I was ten, my mom rushed into our room in the middle of the night. She was yelling that a twister was coming and we needed to run down to the basement pronto."

Jenny had never been in a tornado; she'd only seen specials about them on the Weather Channel.

"What happened?"

"Jim was only six. He was so scared, he grabbed his stuffed Pooh Bear and took off. About thirty seconds later, I heard the basement door slam closed. I didn't holler after him because I wasn't fully awake yet, you know? But I figured he was safe down there."

His voice shook.

"It's okay," Jenny said. "I don't mean to make you relive this."

"It's all right. I guess it's good for me to get off my chest. I helped my mom get my sister up. We grabbed some pillows and flashlights and we heard the town tornado siren blasting. We were about to head to the basement when suddenly, there was this ripple."

"What do you mean?"

"I was in the kitchen. The lights were on. It was thundering like crazy outside. And all of a sudden, the sink, the stove, the air... quivered. Wavered. Like someone had tossed a big stone into the middle of it. It only lasted five seconds, maybe six. Then things were normal again."

Jenny thought of Katie Graham and what she'd seen in the woods.

"We all ran down to the basement, but Jim wasn't there."

"I don't understand."

"There was no sign of him. I found his Pooh Bear on the floor by the furnace. But that was it. There were no windows, no way for him to leave the basement except the way he came. And me or my mom would've heard." Pike gave the sofa armrest a squeeze. "We would've heard."

Jenny got off the chair and sat down next to him. "I'm so sorry," she said.

Pike looked up at her. "I just want to help folks," he said. "Sometimes I don't go about it the right way. But I mean well."

Jenny stared at him. He was just inches away and his breath smelled like pickles and Mountain Dew, but he was quite handsome.

Pike leaned over and kissed her. His lips felt soft and tender, and a spark zipped through Jenny's heart.

He brushed a few strands of hair away from her face. "We need to get moving," he said.

"Okay," Jenny said. "I just have one more call I need to make."

* * *

She went in the kitchen and dialed Michael Graham's number. She wanted to tell him that she was going after Lance.

The phone rang six times, then seven. Then an unfamiliar man's voice answered. "Hello?"

"Hi. I apologize for calling so late," Jenny said. She found herself pacing back and forth, in front of the sink. "Is Mr. Graham there?"

"Who is this?"

"My name is Jenny Bloomquist. I'm a friend of his."

There was a long pause. Snow flurries blew against the window. It was pitch dark outside.

"I'm sorry to tell you this," the man said. "But Mike is dead."

Jenny stopped. "What?"

"The cops are still putting it all together," the man said. "But it looks like Mike took little Katie and drowned them both in the lake. They found their bodies earlier tonight."

"I—"

"I have to go," the man said. "I'm sorry."

* * *

They stood in the foyer. Jenny felt like her heart was beating at three times its normal rate.

"I still don't understand how this is going to work," she said, pulling on a heavy winter coat. Pike wore an old Army jacket and his furry trapper's hat.

"I decided the beekeeper suit wasn't the best idea," Pike said. "Katie Graham and other people have said how bright the light is when the portal opens. But it's a might naïve to think that wearing a special suit or sunglasses will protect me from all that energy pouring out from the other side."

Pike immediately noticed her frightened expression. "Listen," he assured her. "I'm the one going in. You'll be completely safe. You'll be in the woods nearby. Here in the physical world."

"You mean, with those cannibalistic Vikings roaming around?"

"Spirits can't hurt you."

"That's bullshit," Jenny said. "You weren't on that bridge with me last night. He crashed into my mind. He knew me."

"Don't give them that power," Pike said. "Don't let them in."

"Oh, it's as simple as that, right?" Jenny asked, as he handed her a heavy-duty flashlight.

"Look. I'm scared, too. But everything is gonna go great." Pike reached out and touched her cheek. Although she was as frightened as she'd ever been, his touch felt reassuring.

She took a deep breath. "I hope so," she said.

"Now," Pike said. "We've got this." He indicated the roll of flexible industrial cabling on the floor. "I've picked out a really strong tree close to where the portal is going to open," he explained. "We're going to wrap the cabling around it, and attach it to this harness." He indicated the bungee jumping harness around his waist. "You'll be harnessed to that same tree, and you'll assist if the cable becomes tangled as I go in."

"Why are you going after him?" she asked. "He barely even knows you."

"Souls stuck in the in-between world are drawn by familiar presences," Pike said. "Lance and I have spent plenty of time together. He'll see me and move toward me and I'll grab him. I'll pull three times on the cable, and that's when you'll know to start pulling us back."

"I'm not strong enough to pull the both of you," Jenny stammered. "Think about this."

"I'm not letting you go in there," Pike said. "And that's final. Now we need to hurry. It's gonna be midnight soon."

* * *

Jenny and Pike walked down the Cove Road and over Brisco Creek Bridge, to the embankment where she'd followed the path into the forest just one day before. Wind blew wisps of snow across the blacktop. Off to their right, the waves struck the rocky shore of the lake, approaching in fast sets of swirling white.

Pike carried the roll of cable. They both had harnesses around their waists. Their flashlights cast jagged beams into the night.

Jenny stopped suddenly. She could hear nothing except the rustle of pine needles, and the faint, mournful call of an unfamiliar bird.

"What is it?" Pike said. His breath formed in a cloud in front of him.

Jenny thought of her father, sitting on the stump by the side of the road. "I just realized I didn't leave a note or anything," she said. "I didn't tell people where I was going. I didn't say goodbye."

"Come on now," Pike said. "There's no need for that. You'll be home before you know it." The wind blew the collar of his jacket up as they started walking again. "Hey," he said. "I shouldn't have kissed you. That was real wrong of me. I'm sorry."

Jenny considered this. "I liked it," she finally said. "I'm glad you did."

Pike locked eyes with her in the darkness. "So am I," he said. Then he smiled.

They made their way down the slope and through the forest, the path lit by the strong light of the blood red moon above. The snow was less deep under the dense cover of the trees. On one side of them was the creek, which was frozen and silent; on the other, the woods grew even thicker.

Pike glanced at his illuminated watch. "We need to hustle our tails. Come on."

They followed the creek until they reached the spot where Jenny had found the frayed rope and Lance's lucky flannel shirt.

"Now," Pike said. He set down the cabling and pulled out an electronic meter. He waved it around the clearing until it started to light up and buzz. "Here. This is the spot."

All at once, Jenny felt a blast of warm wind through the trees from the direction of the lake. It carried with it a symphony of sounds that filtered through the forest. For a few seconds, she heard the lilting notes of a calliope, clear and tuneful. That music swirled around her and vanished into the snow, and was replaced by a man's voice, scratchy and deep, singing in French.

Jenny felt her heart twist as she spun around in the darkness, trying to determine where the sounds were coming from.

"Hurry," Pike said. He carried the cable over to a sturdy oak tree and wound it around the trunk again and again.

"What should I do?"

245

"Make sure your harness is squared away. You're gonna secure yourself to this tree. "

The singing grew amplified then, as if someone had flicked a switch on an invisible speaker beside her. Jenny caught a glimpse of an elderly man, withered and frail and dressed in a checkered jacket and pink bow tie, shuffling through the woods not ten feet away from her, up ahead.

"Pike!" she yelled, terrified.

The elderly man turned. Half of his face was missing, his jawbone glinting dull white underneath a frayed mass of bloody skin.

Jenny screamed.

Nous allons, the man whispered. *We go now.*

"Don't pay him no mind!" Pike called. "These spirits have been lost in the forest all weekend. They're just lookin' for a way back home. Now you get yourself fastened up! Quick!"

"This is crazy! This isn't going to work!"

"Just trust me and do it!"

Jenny's pulse raced. She saw faces in the darkness, elderly women and teenage boys and even infants, dressed in clothes from other times and places, staggering through the woods as the warm wind swirled around them. They reached out to her and moaned tremulously as they wandered past, walking straight through trees as if they were insubstantial.

"What're you waiting for?" Pike yelled. He wrapped the other end of the cable around his waist.

Then Jenny heard the horn, echoing through the forest.

They're coming.

The ground shook as dozens of thundering hooves rumbled through the woods toward her. Jenny imagined them stampeding across the dark lake, from the direction of Blackhawk Island, across the beach and under the bridge and through the forest to where she stood. That was the route that Lance had drawn in his notebook; he called it the Spirit Highway.

Jenny.

It was Lance's voice, clear and strong. But she didn't hear it—she felt it.

"Lance!" she yelled. "Where are you?"

She knew the riders were drawing closer with each passing second.

"Jenny!" Pike yelled. "Get to the tree!"

The air in front of them rippled. The outline of a door, bordered by amber light, materialized in the darkness.

This is it. It's really happening.

"I can't let you go in!" she yelled. She rushed over to Pike and grabbed for the harness that secured him to the cabling.

"What the hell is wrong with you?" he hollered, as they struggled awkwardly with the cable. "Let me go after him!"

"Lance won't come to you!" she yelled. "I'm going!"

Light streamed from the door in brilliant rays of orange and yellow. Spirits moved past them, drawn to the portal like moths to a porch light.

Jenny unhooked Pike with a burst of effort and secured herself to the end of the cable. She pushed him toward the oak tree and he stumbled across the snowy clearing. "Grab a hold and lower me through!" she yelled.

Pike stood there, hesitating, sheer terror etched across his face. "No!" he cried. "Please!"

The thunder of stampeding horses reached a crescendo and the wind became a gale, gusting through the forest in the direction of the door to the other side. In a split second, Pike was swept off his feet and into the portal, his startled scream echoing through the woods.

Jenny stood there a moment, horrified, as she was buffeted by the wind that smelled of burning sulfur. Screaming, she grasped the cable with both hands and tried to pull herself toward the oak tree. The gale was stronger than anything she'd ever fought against, and she struggled to make progress toward safety.

She ventured a glance behind her. The light streamed from the door like a supernova. Snow and pine needles swirled around it, pelting her face and stinging her eyes.

Is Lance there, right on the other side? Waiting for me?

Her hands screamed from the scrape of the cable. Thoughts pounded through her head. She thought of her mother, standing impatiently in her fake fur, in front of the police station. Not caring one bit about what had happened to Lance. Sitting in the bar in the arms of another man.

She pictured the meadow full of daisies, close to where she wanted to build her bed and breakfast. She would have to do it alone at first, but her father would help, as he promised. He would be there in the delivery room when she had her baby. He would be there through it all, as much as he could.

Jenny knew then that she could make it on her own. She had to try.

She turned away from the portal and focused her attention on the tree. She reached, grabbed a hold with one hand. Pulled.

She hadn't made it two steps when the stampede of horses reached her. Six Vikings with gnarled hair and beards crusted with blood appeared, each riding dark brown horses with shaggy manes and bared teeth. They circled Jenny and the tree and glared down at her, impervious to the gusting wind.

The leader—the man Jenny had seen on the bridge—sneered at her. His mount pawed the earth and lunged at her hungrily. Seeing him up close, Jenny was even more afraid of his face, devoid of skin but still somehow capable of human expression.

Come with us, Jenny. We'll take you to your husband. We promise.

Jenny steeled her nerves. "You have no power over me!" she stammered.

Lance came along so easily. We grabbed him before he knew what was coming.

"Leave me alone!" she yelled. She lost one hand's grip on the cable and stumbled back a few steps. She felt it straining against the wind, threatening to snap.

Why not come join us on the other side, where it's silent and warm? I've got a whole lot of friends who're waiting to love you... you and your sweet little child.

"Go to hell!" she yelled.

The lead Viking smiled, showing two rows of bloody teeth.

As you wish.

The rider grabbed for her with a shriek. Jenny instinctively lunged to her right. The wind ripped at her, tore at her clothes, but she hung on to the cable for dear life, screaming the whole time as the rider finally surrendered, following the other Viking ghosts into the golden door and the celestial light beyond.

32

Chapter Thirty-Two—MARTIN

Martin drove through swirling snow flurries to the marina. The parking lot was bustling with townspeople who were headed to the lighting ceremony on Harborfront Stroll. Young couples walked with their arms around each other. Children squealed and skidded in the snow.

Martin pulled into a space just as someone was leaving. Instead of following the crowd to the shops, he walked down to the marina and boarded the ferry to Blackhawk Island. His father was buried there, in a tiny cemetery near a church where Jack Spivey's cabin used to be.

Even though it was bitterly cold, he climbed the stairs to the upper deck of the boat, then went to the rail that separated him from the churning black water below as the ferry made its way across the bay.

The buildings of downtown receded as the boat drew Martin farther away from land. Great Water hugged the coastline desperately, as if the dark forests that pressed against it wanted to push the town into the lake. Martin spotted the hills of Goosebeak and the beaches of Moosejaw and far on the outskirts of town, the woods where Jenny lived. Everything seemed so small, so close together. Martin felt ashamed that he'd spent his whole life in a tiny place that still seemed so overwhelming to him.

Lars got out of here. Why can't I?

There were a few other people standing on the deck. "Look," one man in an overcoat said. He pointed back toward land.

All at once, the marina came alive with hundreds of points of white light, from the masts of the ships to the storefronts, all reflecting off the water. And far off in the distance, Martin heard hundreds of voices singing "O Come All Ye Faithful" in the night.

For a moment, he felt his father standing next to him, heard his heavy breathing, smelled his familiar scent of cigars and peppermint.

Isn't it beautiful, Marty?

Martin looked. There was no one there.

Suddenly, a blast of warm wind blew strong across the lake, from the direction of Blackhawk Island. Martin heard the sound of a calliope, as if from a carnival long ago. It made him think of women wearing petticoats and men with perfectly groomed moustaches.

Then he saw a parade of human shapes, glowing white and gold and floating a few feet above the water, coming from the island and gliding toward Spivey Point and the woods beyond. There were children and adults and old people, and they hovered together, above the waves. They shimmered and vibrated like the Northern Lights. Then they were gone.

* * *

After the ferry docked, Martin walked up a winding street in the thick darkness, past seafood restaurants and sweet shops and toy stores with Pierre the Bear displays in the window. There were a few couples strolling about, looking in the windows, wearing mittens and Packers jerseys.

Martin left the village and wandered farther up the hill. He passed scattered cottages, set back behind picket fences and bounded by thick pine trees. Then he came upon a simple stone church that sat on a tiny plot of grass. A stained-glass window—depicting a little girl, her arms stretched up to the clouds, angels reaching down to her—cast brilliant points of amber and royal blue into the night. The doors of the church were open, even in the cold. Martin's father was buried in a cemetery just up the hill, behind it.

Martin stood on the street, staring up at the stained glass image of Bridget O'Hara. Her hands were outstretched to meet the waiting angels.

He thought about Jenny and wondered if she'd found Lance.

A blast of warm air came from inside the church, blowing his hair back from his forehead. Then invisible fingers, a gentle tickling in his heart, pushed him gently forward.

Martin walked across the short sidewalk and stepped inside. Although empty, the church was filled with glowing golden light from dozens of candles everywhere. The altar was decorated with red and yellow poinsettias.

And standing on the steps—just beyond the first row of pews—was his father.

Martin stopped breathing.

George Van Lottum looked just how Martin remembered him. His beard was red and full, and his hair lay in unruly wisps across his bald head. His eyes were bright behind thick bifocals.

Hello, son.

"How—?"

His father smiled. *I've been watching you the last few days, Marty. I've been real close.*

"I never thought you were listening," Martin said, the words tumbling out of him. Tears streamed down his cheeks. "Dad, I screwed everything up. I made a huge mess of everything. I—"

A warm breeze blew through the church again. His father flickered for a second, like a candle flame.

I'm only here for a moment, Marty. But while I'm here, I want to give you this. I want to give you this gift.

Then he was gone.

"Give me what?" Martin asked softly.

It was quiet. Then a gull cried, far down by the lake. Martin peered up at the stained glass window, at the image of the little girl reaching up to heaven, and felt his father's love come through, clear and strong.

Martin closed his eyes. Memories surrounded him then, remembrances of times past when he felt his family's love, and when he loved himself. He held on to them tightly at first, afraid that they would disappear and he would be left with the cold, dark ugliness that he knew so well.

But—miraculously—they stayed with him. Martin realized then that that was his father's gift: he would have the memories forever.

* * *

The Christmas lights of Harborfront Stroll shimmered in the night as the ferry drew closer to the mainland. Martin looked closer and saw that two lights were flashing at regular intervals: blue and red, blue and red, cutting a revolving path through the darkness. He leaned over the rail of the boat, the frigid water of Lake Michigan churning beneath him, and realized that he'd find out soon enough whether all the things he'd done that weekend had consequences after all.

But strangely enough, he didn't feel scared. This time, he felt ready.

33

Chapter Thirty-Three—ERIC

Eric watched a bit of television after a very late dinner, which Pete made—spaghetti and meatballs and salad with blue cheese dressing, his favorite. Then he went into his room and sat on his bed. He thought about calling Taco, to tell him that he hadn't been abducted or killed by Webb Turner, but he didn't feel like talking. He didn't feel like studying for his Algebra test either.

There was a soft knock at the door.

"Come in," Eric said.

His mother stood in the doorway. She had taken a shower and changed into a red sweater with snowflakes on it. "Hey," she said.

"Hi."

Eric cleared a place for her to sit down at the edge of his bed next to him. He sat with his back against the wall, his pillow in his hand.

"I just," his mother began. Her voice sounded small, like a little girl's. She crossed her hands in her lap. "You must have a lot of questions," she finally said.

"Well, yeah," Eric said. "To start with, I want to know why we never talked about Bates."

"You were just a little boy. Barely eight years old."

"That's my point," Eric said. "Why was I even left alone with him?"

"Your father and I fought about that constantly," she said, her face reddening. "I asked him to confront Bates about it and he did. Of course that fucker said he never touched you. So your dad believed him."

Eric realized it had been many months since he'd heard his mother curse. He traced the seam of the pillowcase.

"I knew something was going on," she said. "I could sense it."

"I don't remember a thing about what happened back then," Eric said. "I really don't. I just remember him babysitting. Taking me to see *The Lion King*."

"Sweetheart—"

"But when I got in his car tonight, I just got this sinking feeling. I felt ashamed and I hadn't even done anything wrong."

"That's right. You sure hadn't."

"So, Dad took his side. How'd you feel about that?"

"I honestly loved your dad once. And him and I, we worked, for a while. We clicked."

"Why'd he leave?" Eric asked. "Was it because of Bates?"

There was a long pause. Eric saw the pain in her eyes. "That was part of it," she admitted.

"What about Ada Bloomquist?"

"Your dad never talked about what happened that night. But it tore him apart. He told me he had nightmares about it for years. And it broke up the Three Kings."

"Seems like those guys were pretty popular around here."

"Everyone thought they would really make something of themselves as surfers. Webb was kind of like Snacko Thompson, really flashy turns. Lance was the shaper, the engineer. And your dad was the steady one, classy. The gentleman."

"That's hard to believe," Eric said.

"I know," his mother said. "They even showed this surf film in the high school auditorium back then. *Kings of the Earth*. The three of them starred in it. My brother took me. It cost a dollar fifty to get in. That was the first time I really got a look at your dad. I think that's when I fell in love with him."

Eric thought about this. He had never asked how his parents had met.

"I was glad Lance was there for you," she said. "After your dad left. I know how much you needed it."

Eric looked at the map of the United States that hung next to his bed. California seemed even farther away now. San Diego was a dot at the very bottom.

"I really screwed up," he said. "I'm sorry. I didn't mean to make you worry."

"You're a teenager," his mother said. "I figure if I cut you some slack, you can do the same for me."

* * *

"Sweetheart. Wake up."

Eric opened his eyes. He saw the dark outline of his mom, standing in the doorway. She wore her robe and her hair was frazzled from sleep.

"Someone's on the phone for you."

He glanced at the red digits on his alarm clock. It was 12:47 in the morning. He'd been dreaming of snorkeling at a pink coral reef; tiny puffer fish and bright anemones were everywhere. Now he was back in his cramped, drafty bedroom.

"Who is it?"

"Lance's wife. I told her you were asleep, but she insisted on talking to you. She sounds pretty upset."

Eric stumbled out of bed and took the cordless phone from his mother. She waited there a few seconds until he shooed her away and closed the bedroom door. With all the commotion and rollercoaster of emotions that had happened since he got home, he'd managed to completely forget about Jenny.

He turned on his desk lamp and sat down. "Hello?"

"Eric? Are you okay?" Jenny sounded like she going to break down into tears.

"I'm fine. Sorry for—for everything. Are you all right?"

"I'm just here in this empty house and it's so quiet. I needed some good news, you know?"

"Lance isn't there?"

"I don't think he's coming back."

Her voice cracked, then there was silence. Eric could almost see the tear dripping down her cheek.

"Do you want me to come over?"

"I just needed to hear your voice."

"I'm safe and sound," Eric said. "I know that you were worried. But I'm okay."

"Good," she said. "That's good. Thank you."

She hung up.

Before he realized what he was doing, Eric threw on a sweatshirt and his charcoal-checkered Vans. He kept his long flannel pajama bottoms on.

He opened his bedroom door carefully. The hallway was dim; a thin shaft of moonlight bled through the blinds. He tiptoed past his mother's door. It was open just a crack.

"Eric? Is she okay?"

"Yes," he whispered. "She just wanted to check on me. Go back to sleep, Mom."

As he rounded the corner into the main room, he saw Pete lying on the couch, watching TV with the sound turned low. He had his eye patch off and his uncovered eye looked completely normal.

Eric gaped at him in surprise. "What—" he stuttered. "Why don't you—"

Pete brought one hand up to his eye self-consciously. "Little Chief," he said in a low voice. "What're you doing up?"

"That was Jenny Bloomquist on the phone. I need to go see how she's doing."

Pete sat up straight on the couch. "Are you sure that's a good idea?"

he asked. "It's almost one o'clock. Can't it wait 'til the morning? I mean, after the sun comes up?"

"She sounds really bad. I feel like I owe this to her."

"Maybe I should go with you. Just so your mom doesn't worry."

"It's all right," Eric said. He walked into the room and sat down in the worn-out yellow recliner next to him.

"Why do you wear that patch all the time?" Eric asked. "Your eye looks completely regular to me."

Pete ran his fingers through his moustache. Then he scratched at his belly button underneath his Led Zeppelin t-shirt. "It is," he said.

"Then why do you wear it?"

"I just thought it would make me stand out," Pete said. He turned off the TV, and they sat in darkness, with only the light from the VCR clock casting a feeble glow on their faces.

"You mean, when you go on auditions?"

"Just in general," Pete said. "It makes me more memorable."

"I'd say you already are," Eric said.

Pete grinned. "Thank you kindly, Eric," he said.

"I know you love my mom a lot," Eric replied. "I always wanted her to find someone who did."

* * *

Eric rode his bike down the Cove Road, which had been plowed so that only a thin layer of snow covered the blacktop. The blood red moon sat low and heavy in the night sky, which was fathoms deep and sprinkled with hundreds of stars.

He crossed Brisco Creek Bridge and caught a glimpse of Spivey Point. The waves crashed in steady and strong, whitecaps breaking on the rocks, the lights of Blackhawk Island blinking far off in the darkness. Leaving his bike at the end of Lance's driveway, he approached the house, which loomed like a sleeping giant among the whispering pines.

There were no lights on, but the front door was open a crack. Eric thought about knocking, but something told him to just go inside.

"Hello," he called, as he shut the door behind him. Eric wiped his feet on the rug in the foyer, out of habit. He felt on the wall in the foyer for a light switch.

"Hello," he called again, as light filled the space. "Jenny? Lance? It's Eric."

There was no answer.

Worrying a bit, Eric made his way down the hallway, past the kitchen and the pantry. A light was on in the room at the end of the hall; he could see it under the door. He knocked twice on the door, then pushed it open.

It was a dim room with a low ceiling. Curled-up architecture plans were spread across a huge desk. There was a jar full of metal pencils and protractors, and books of all shapes and subjects were piled on top.

And in the corner, in an enormous cherry cabinet, were three long boards.

He walked over to them. Each board was yellowed and full of scratches and dents. One was painted with the design of a badger. Another, an eagle. And the third, a snarling wolf.

Eric reached out and touched one of them. He tried to imagine the swells it must have seen, the sharp lake rocks it had scraped against.

Framed photographs lined the walls. Some were shots of Lance, in various points across the world: standing in a rice paddy; spelunking in a dark cave wearing a miner's hat; standing in a crowd of men in front of a street café.

And in one photograph, three men stood together, shirtless, posing next to their boards, on a sandy beach. They had long hair and scraggly beards that reminded Eric of Jesus. A pier stretched behind them in the distance.

The man holding the badger board was his father. He didn't look more than twenty years old.

Eric closed his eyes. He remembered the touch of his father's hand in his as they walked down Bearclaw Street toward the lake years ago; how protected it made him feel, like he was wearing superhero armor.

The tears welled up in his eyes. And before he knew what was happening, the anger crashed right behind it, like a fierce twelve-footer against the coral.

Eric grabbed the photo of The Three Kings and smashed it on the floor. Bits of glass scattered and embedded themselves in the carpet.

He took the badger board from the cabinet and crashed it on top of the desk, as hard as he could. A sound like an engine backfiring echoed through the room. The board split. Pencils and papers and protractors leapt into the air and clattered everywhere.

I hate you. I hate you for what you did to me.

He overturned the chair. He kicked shelves full of knickknacks and shattered them against the wall. He tore at his hair. He beat his fists against his face until he could no longer feel the bruises.

"Eric. Oh, God."

He turned to the doorway and Jenny stood there, an expression of shock and bewilderment on her face.

"I—"

Eric swayed back and forth, his knees buckling. Jenny caught him just as he collapsed. He hung onto her tightly, sobs wracking his body.

"I'm sorry," he choked. "I didn't mean—"

She whispered to him that it would be okay, that she was sorry too, that everything would be okay.

"I didn't think he loved me. I didn't think he loved me."

"Of course he did," Jenny said. "How could he not?"

They stood there another long moment, tears clouding his eyes and burning his cheeks. "Come on down the hall," Jenny said. "Come sit for a while. I'll make us some tea."

"I wish he was here," Eric whispered.

"I know you do," Jenny said. "Come on to the kitchen and we'll talk about it."

She put an arm around him and together they left Lance's study.

Jenny turned on the light in the kitchen and tuned the radio to a classical music station. "Sit down," she said. "Would you like some cinnamon cookies?"

Eric nodded and sat down at the table. There was a sealed, plain white envelope on top of the straw placemat. He wiped the tears from his eyes, then took a deep breath. It felt safe in the room. Comfortable.

Jenny brought him the cookie jar. "I have jasmine tea or peppermint," she said, standing over him. "Whichever you'd like."

"Jasmine sounds great. I've never had it before."

"I promise you'll like it," she said. She was about to turn back to the counter when Eric saw that her eyes were red-rimmed. He realized she'd been crying, too.

"Are you okay? What's wrong?"

"It's been—" Jenny said. Her voice quivered. She could barely get any words out.

Eric knew then that she needed his help. It was a strange, new feeling for him—to have something to actually offer someone else—and he held it carefully.

"Would you like to sit down?"

"No," Jenny replied. "You've been through too much. I couldn't."

Eric smiled. "It's okay. I'm here now. Why don't you tell me what happened?"

She sat down at the table. Her hands shook as she took a deep breath.

"I feel like I've lost everything," she began. "Not just Lance. Someone else trusted me and—now he's gone. Gone for good. And it's all my fault."

The pain was sharp and clear in her voice, like a January wave smashing across his surfboard. Eric figured it was best that he didn't ask her about specifics.

"I know we don't know each other that well," he said. "Not yet. But I know what it's like to have someone split."

He reached over and took her hand. It was a gesture that simultaneously surprised him and felt perfectly right.

261

"Sometimes when I wake up in the morning, I have this gut feeling that the waves are gonna be incredible," he said. "I slam my egg sandwich and zip up my wetsuit and grab my board and I dash down to the lake. But then I get there and it's completely flat. No action. Nothing."

Jenny nodded. She brushed a few strands of hair away from her face.

"I feel like someone just took the only thing that mattered to me away from me, and I'm never gonna get it back. But one lesson Lance taught me is that there are waves crashing on beaches all over the world. Every shore gets its turn, like the hands on a clock turning round and round. I just have to be patient. Have faith. And be grateful when the choice waves come."

"Easier said than done," Jenny said. "But I'll try my best."

"It's not so gnarly if you have a friend alongside you," Eric replied. "Maybe that's why we ended up together."

"I think there's even more to it than that."

"How do you mean?"

"Your mom told me what happened. I mean, when she lost the baby."

Eric's first reaction was anger, but then he realized that it was time for him to try something new, like finding a more secure stance on his board. He took a deep breath and forced himself to look at her.

"That was really tough," he said. "I felt like it was my fault."

Jenny smiled at him with a look of reassurance and comfort that wielded enormous power, like He-Man's sword. "Well, I'm pregnant myself," she said. "I just found out yesterday."

"Wow," Eric said. "Congratulations. You look extra pretty for a pregnant lady. I mean, if you don't mind me saying so. My mom gained like sixty pounds last year."

Jenny laughed. "What I'm thinking is, maybe this baby can help you move past what you went through," she said. "I feel guilty about a lot of things in my life, just like you. Stuff I never talked to anyone about. But you and I, we can both do great things in this world. We can break the curse of this town by taking extra good care of this new life."

Eric considered this. "Maybe I could babysit sometimes," he said. "I can be a really positive influence on young people."

"I'm going to need all the help I can get," Jenny admitted, and wiped away the last of her tears with a gentle smile.

* * *

Long after midnight, waves still lapped at the rocky shore near Jenny's home. The crimson moon sank low in the darkness, as if weighted by a heavy burden. Slowly, the deep red drained from the perfectly full circle as cold tendrils of fog wrapped around it, turning it white again.

There was a sudden hush. Then, from Blackhawk Island, the music from an ancient carnival organ filtered through the heavy gloom. It was the last few bars of an ancient tune that suggested that the show was over for the evening; indeed, for many years to come.

About the Author

Christopher Stanton is a creative writer and artist from Columbus, OH who lives and works in Los Angeles. His short stories have been published in numerous literary magazines and he has shown art in dozens of exhibitions. This is his first novel.

You can find out more about him at christopher-stanton.com.

Made in the USA
Las Vegas, NV
17 November 2024